OF EARTH AND AIR

CAMEO RENAE

OF EARTH AND AIR

3

HEIR OF BLOOD AND FIRE

CAMEO RENAE

MORE BY CAMEO RENAE

In My Dreams
In My Reality
-
HIDDEN WINGS SERIES
Hidden Wings
Broken Wings
Tethered Wings
Gilded Wings
Wings of Vengeance
-
MIDWAY NOVELS
Guarding Eden
Saving Thomas
Dominating Dom
-
AFTER LIGHT SAGA
ARV-3
Sanctum
Intransigent
Hostile
Retribution
-
Misteria

NORTHFALL
MO
Forest of Murk
Dead Man
AQUARIS
BAELF
Blue Lake
Havendale
To Aquaria
SARTHA
HALE
Whisper Woods
The Bogs
Southport
Peddlers Pass
ARGENT SEA

TALBRINTH
To Incendia
CRIMSON COVE
SANGERIAN SEA
CARPATHIA
ant Port
of the blood

This book is dedicated to all those who
have the strength to stand up for what is right.

CHAPTER ONE

My mind was a whirlwind of agony and chaos as I propelled through the water toward Aquaris. My heart was thrumming loudly in my ears, my pulse racing. The dim sea, harsh and stifling, was threatening to devour me whole. Everything was a blur—a midnight watery funnel aimed toward whatever fate had in store for me.

War? Death? Failure? Redemption? It could be any one of those. Or all of them.

According to Kylan, when Trystan learned of my father's abduction, Trystan ordered his cadre to immediately rescue him. But this was what Roehl had been waiting for. He was betting on retaliation, but probably never anticipated Trystan would arrive before I did. Now he'd garnered the ideal situation. The upper hand, using them both as bait to draw me out, knowing I wouldn't hesitate to save them.

My heart was wrenching, aching to the point of shattering. Trystan, who from day one, had been watching out for me. Who first showed up in Sartha, and again in Morbeth after my capture, to offer an exchange—half of his kingdom's riches… for me. *Me.* A human, Incendian, and vampire mutt.

Trystan, who showed up in Incendia with his cadre in a funnel of air to save me. Trystan, who offered me his blood, something sacred amongst purebloods, so I could heal faster and become stronger. Trystan, who was now engaged. Yet, he still showed up and held out his hand to me, offering me safety, security, and a chance to run away with him, forsaking his father, his kingdom, and his crown.

I had turned him down, and had hurt him deeply, even after all he'd done for me. The impact of my decision would be permanently engraved in my mind. Because I was scared and felt like I wasn't worthy of someone like him. The *pureblood* Prince of Carpathia.

His father demanded his son to marry a pureblood, so he arranged a marriage with the Princess of Northfall. Northfall was a powerful and flourishing country, and I could understand why Trystan's father was creating such a diplomatic move. It would strengthen not only Northfall, but Carpathia as well.

But that wasn't what Trystan wanted. Trystan had made it clear from day one who he truly wanted. But I hadn't been able to bring myself to accept him, believing I was doing the honorable thing for him and his kingdom.

But I was wrong.

Trystan was his own man. Yes, he was the Prince of Carpathia, but he shouldn't have been required to wed someone he didn't love.

I'd heard stories that most royals had arranged marriages. It was accepted for them to marry cousins or other distant relatives to establish stronger political alliances and strengthen their families, but those days had diminished. Now they married for strength, riches, alliances, and to help prevent war or feuding as well.

The amulet warmed against my chest. The amulet that had once belonged to Trystan's mother but had somehow found its way to me. I wasn't certain what kind of magic it possessed, except for what Trystan had told me. It acted as a beacon, allowing his father to always find her, and I secretly hoped its warmth meant Trystan was nearby.

I didn't know Trystan's mother. But having an item like this, that had been owned by royalty, was priceless.

Inside, my stomach knotted, and my heart throbbed knowing Trystan and my father were in the devil's hands. By taking them, Roehl knew he had the upper hand. He knew my weakness, that I cared for those I loved over myself. He or his men had slaughtered everyone on board my father's ship, my mother included. He was ruthless, a cold-blooded murderer.

Roehl knew making me suffer wasn't enough to break me. It was hurting those I loved that would do it. I had already felt some of his wrath in Morbeth. With those cold, lifeless cell walls around me, with the manacles clamped around my wrists and ankles that made my skin raw and infected. I'd been starved, battered, bruised, and broken. He had barely kept me alive in the bowels of Morbeth's gloomy cell for too long.

He also knew that Trystan had claimed me and there was a connection between us. And being the vile demon he was, he would make Trystan suffer for it.

I was confident that Trystan's father, when he found out, wouldn't allow such a treacherous act to pass without consequence. Roehl had kidnapped the Prince of Carpathia, his only son and heir, and I knew they had a formidable army.

Hope. Mine was dangling on a delicate and fragile thread, but it was the only thing I had left to hold on to.

I was frightened and moving with no plan. Because the truth was… there was no suitable plan worth going up against Roehl. Not with the kind of power he possessed. Especially with his army, dark mages, and the alliance he'd made with Incendia's false queen.

He had the two men I loved most in this gods forsaken world. I would have to go to Roehl and try to strike a bargain with him, but knowing the wicked snake he was, I would have to pay a heavy price. A price I wasn't sure I could pay. I had no doubt he would use his power to break me, but with my newly awakened gifts, there had to be a way to stop him. Leora had said my powers were stronger than Roehl's. I just had to believe that. I had to believe my powers could overcome his dark magic and come to me when I needed them most.

I wanted to march straight up to him and thrust every ounce of power I had at him. But I knew that would be a foolish and hazardous move. My power was still raw and wild and untapped, and I knew Roehl could easily overpower me. But what I was afraid of most was that he would kill them both. And I wasn't sure I could withstand the pain of losing either one of them, let alone both of them.

Yes, I wanted to walk in and burn them all to hell, but I knew Roehl was ready, waiting for me to do something reckless. I had to be patient and focused. Even if it meant surrendering and going in with my arms in the air and letting him take me, knowing full well I'd be thrown back in a cell, starved and tortured.

But I would do it again.

For them.

My head ached as Kai relentlessly tried to contact me through our element bond, begging me to tell him where I was going and why. But I couldn't tell him. Kai had no association with Roehl or Morbeth. He would be coming because of me alone. Trystan's cadre had been ambushed and Trystan apprehended. They hadn't stood a chance. I wasn't going to jeopardize their lives or draw them into a battle I knew we couldn't win.

I knew I would eventually need the help of my friends, but not this time. I had to try to free Trystan and my father on my own. I had to believe that Leora, or any other relative or ancestor on the other side, would somehow find a means to help me.

Because right now, I could use any freaking help I could get.

A faint light flickered above me, letting me know I was reaching the surface and would shortly be breaching the waters near Aquaris.

I'd spent many summers in Aquaris with my grandparents and was told of how it came to be. Legends say there was a man who appeared in Aquaris. He was handsome and tall and as powerful as he was wise. It was said that he had once lived under the sea.

This man made many friends and allies and swiftly rose to power. He was eventually appointed ruler and gave his land a name. He chose the name Aquaris, after his former home … Aquaria. A mythical kingdom that survived under the sea, occupied with immortals who could manipulate water with their magic.

No one genuinely believed the legend, except my grandfather, who had met the King of Aquaria himself. I hadn't even believed in such a wild tale until I had witnessed Aquaria for myself and met the people who lived there.

And now, Aquaris was where my father and Trystan had been captured. Would Roehl be waiting on the shoreline? I had no doubt he had a way of finding out where I was. His dark mages could perform a simple tracking spell, and it was possible for me to be taken as soon as I emerged.

Slowing my pace, I headed toward a section near the shore that had a steep rock face. If they knew where I was, I'd make them work to get me.

As soon as I broke the water's surface, I inhaled the cool, crisp air. Above, the twinkling stars and moon cast a faint glow on my surroundings. The water was placid, and there was only a slight breeze, so I swam to the bank and scaled the rocks.

My boots, the ones Trystan had given me, didn't slip. It was like they were made for any condition, and it was another thing I was grateful for.

The amulet around my neck was growing warmer and when I looked down, the azure stone warmed against my chest and was glowing bright. Was Trystan nearby? Is that what it was telling me? I quickly tucked it into my tunic, hoping it wouldn't act as a beacon and call them to me.

Focus.

That's what I wanted to do, but my nerves were frayed, not knowing what was going to happen. It was that fear of the known and unknown. Of not knowing if there were mages here who could use their power against me. But also knowing I was soon going to be back in Roehl's clutches, and that thought alone was suffocating.

I knew things weren't going to end well. Not with Roehl in charge. He believed he was still the puppet master, pulling the strings, but I was going to fight with everything inside of me until Trystan and my father were free.

Exhaling, my mind kept replaying the prophecy of the Seer in Aquaria. *"Death lingers around you, heir of blood and fire,"* she'd said. *"And because of this, your blood prince will die.*

The prince with whom you share a bond."

Quietly, I scaled the rocks and peeked over at the sandy shore adjacent to me, and lo-and-behold, spotted six shadowy figures scouring the shore. *Roehl's men.*

The amulet was growing warmer and glowing even brighter, so I placed my hand over it, hoping to conceal it.

My clothes were soaked, and the air was cold, so I sat down and settled my back against some rocks and concentrated, just like Kai had taught me. Concentrated on my water power, on my wet clothes and hair. A few beads of water separated from my tunic and slowly drifted in front of me, like crystals glittering in the moonlight.

Goddess above. I was really doing it.

Focusing on my entire body, I pressed my power a bit further.

To my sheer delight, thousands of water droplets began pulling from my clothes and hair, hovering all around me, suspended with magic. *My* magic. I couldn't help but smile, knowing Kai would be proud. If I survived this, I'd eventually tell him, maybe even show him.

I sat in awe, watching the little beads of water glisten and glow floating all around me. Smiling, despite the fact that Roehl's men were on the other side of the rocks, scouring the shore to find me, ready to take me as soon as I was found.

I'd done it! My clothes and hair were dry, and that was a massive accomplishment for me. I'd performed something new with my water powers without help from anyone else. And that gave me a little more confidence that I'd make it out of this.

Movement from behind made me lose my concentration, and the thousands of glittering water droplets crashed down to the rocks and sea water below. The magic was over, and the tormenting darkness, and what awaited within, coiled around me.

Sounds of someone climbing the rocks made my heart hammer. I was about to call my flame, but I couldn't move or speak. Every muscle in my body had locked, and I was frozen. An icy trepidation coiled itself around me, and when I looked, a mysterious, hooded figure materialized to the side of me.

Roehl.

I struggled to scream, but my voice had been muted. The only sounds around us were those of the waves slapping against the rocks below.

The figure appeared three feet away, features shrouded within the dark shadows of their cowl. Whoever it was raised a finger and shushed me, which was entirely irrelevant. Whatever they had done made me mute and incapable of using any of my power.

The darkened figure stepped forward and, with a twist of their hand, we were suddenly shrouded in blackness. The rocks, the water, the moon and even the stars... dissolved into a thick, harrowing mist.

What the hell?

I was swiftly picked up and thrown over a shoulder. This person was strong, their power still coursing through my blood and bones, rendering me defenseless.

Gods be damned. I had to find a way to keep these bastards from doing this to me. There had to be a way to protect myself.

In seconds, the darkness surrounding us dissipated, and we were no longer near the shore. We were indoors in a small room. I struggled to get free, but I was still incapacitated.

The room looked like it could have been in a tavern. It had a single bed, a small table with one chair, and a door to what I assumed was an exit. That was it. There were no frills here. It looked like a place where they would drag a drunk person and throw their ass on the bed to sleep it off.

The hooded figure walked over to the bed and gently laid me on it. I was still unable to speak or move, but with another wave of their hand, I was free.

I made a move to stand, but the world around me began to spin. I quickly sat up on the edge of the mattress and doubled over, dry heaving.

I wasn't sure who this person was. Whoever they were, they were broad and towering over me. And they had powerful magic, so I didn't stand a chance of running.

"Who are you?" I breathed, feeling my power pulsing again beneath my skin. I would fight and would turn this bastard and this shitty room to ash if I had to.

The figure didn't speak, but slowly raised his arms, pulling back his hood to reveal his face.

I stopped breathing.

That face. I'd seen it before. Seen it in Melaina's magical bowl of water.

A handsome face with intense golden eyes. Eyes that looked like my father's. Like mine. He had broad shoulders and sharp features with mahogany hair that fell just above his shoulders.

"Hello, Calla. It's nice to finally meet you," Nicolae spoke, his voice low and melodic. He had an accent, but it wasn't strong. It was different from any I had heard before.

I shook my head, a tear escaping my eye. My heart was constricting, being in the same room with this man. I'd never thought this day would come. Never thought I'd meet Nicolae Corvus, especially at a time like this.

"H—how did you find me?" I could barely get the words out.

All my life, I thought he was dead, and at this very moment, it was as if I were staring at a ghost. So many emotions were running through me, I couldn't process exactly what I was feeling.

A dashing smile rose on Nicolae's lips. "It took some time, but I heard tales of a girl who defied Roehl, escaped Morbeth's prison, and boarded a vessel to Incendia." His smile suddenly turned solemn. "I have magical friends in high places, one in particular, who broke through my wards to tell me Roehl had sent out a death decree on your family because you were from my bloodline. I'm so sorry. Had I known I had kin, I would not have been so reckless."

"I know you didn't know you had any family," I said softly. "And I also know what happened wasn't your fault."

His head tilted to the side. "And how did you come by this information?"

I grinned and shook my head. "I met Princess Leora in the In Between, the day after the Shadow Fest."

Nicolae blinked, brow crumpled. "You met my mother?"

"I did. And she is stunningly beautiful. She told me the story about her and Romulus, and how his father came and destroyed Incendia. She also told me about you, how much she loved you, and that you were innocent. Then, she unlocked my power."

He gave a sad grin and sighed. "The woman who raised me was her handmaiden. Growing up, she told me wondrous stories of my mother and her magic. Maybe one day I'll also get to meet her."

"Well, it took the Shadow Fest, a witch, and being on the precipice of death, for me to see her. But I also got to see my mother, and that helped me cope with her death. Knowing they are still around, watching over us."

Nicolae cracked a smile. "Yes, I can imagine so."

I was glad Nicolae had sought me out. I wasn't sure if he would ever want to meet us or get involved in our lives after being absent for so long. But he'd found me. And I could tell he was just as overcome with emotion as I was.

"How did you find me?" I asked.

"A simple tracking spell," he answered casually.

"I knew it," I sighed. "That's how the men on the beach must have known where I was."

He must have seen the worried look on my face, because he responded, "Don't worry, no one can find you here. This entire room is heavily warded."

I relaxed a bit, but still, I had so many questions. So many things running through my mind that I wanted to ask him. I also knew I didn't have time for that. Not right now. Not while the lives of Trystan and my father balanced on my arrival.

Nicolae held out his hand to me and I noticed the tattoo on his palm. It was similar to mine, but not as bold. In the center of his tattoo was fire—Incendia's mark. I'd seen and felt Nicolae's magic. He was powerful. Maybe even more powerful than Roehl.

Even Melaina mentioned how great his power was just from witnessing it in her magical scrying bowl. She'd called him a handsome witch. Leora had said the royal women of Incendia had greater power than the men. So, if that were true, could I possess such a power?

I slowly held out my hand to him and when he took it, my palm instantly heated. The veins in my arms began glowing a golden color, and when I looked over, so were Nicolae's. Power buzzed through my veins, and when he finally let go, both of our tattoos were glowing.

"We are connected now," he said.

"But Roehl," I breathed. "He knew of the partial blood bond I had with Trystan, so he masked it. Will he be able to do the same with ours?"

"He can't break our bond. A family bond is the strongest. You share my blood, so he won't be able to tell there is a connection between us. Besides, he can't break a bond he has no knowledge of. He has no idea where I am, or that we've even met. There is a reason why people call me Shadow." He said, tilting his head to the side.

Shadow, how fitting, s ince it's w hat I h ad named my horse.

"However," Nicolae continued, "he could break the bond you have with the water elemental."

He was referring to Kai. "How do you know I share a connection with a water elemental?"

A sly grin rose on the corners of his mouth. "I know more than most, and not because I want to. It's part of my gift." He held up his hand, the glow of his tattoo dimming. "There is much to discuss, and we are running on borrowed time."

My gut knotted, and a coldness swept over me. "I have to leave. Roehl has captured my father and now has Prince Trystan of Carpathia because he tried to save him."

"I know," he replied, the furrow in his brow deepening.

He seemed to already know everything and that gave me hope that we could make it out of this alive.

"I'm so sorry, Calla. I know I wasn't there for you when you needed me before. But I will try to be here for you from now on."

I suddenly felt comforted. A comfort I hadn't felt since I'd left Aquaria.

It wasn't his fault he didn't come to our aid sooner. He didn't even know he'd had a son. And that made my heart ache with sadness. All those years were stolen from him. From my father. From me.

"I don't know what I'm going to do," I exhaled. "Roehl has already witnessed my power, and because I defied him and fled Morbeth, I'm afraid of what he'll do. He said if I don't come to him, both Trystan and my father will die."

Nicolae raked a callused hand through his thick dark hair. "Then, you have to go to him."

Those were not the words I was expecting to hear. I thought he'd say… *I'll go with you, and we'll end Roehl together.* But it didn't even seem like he was going to come with me. I guess I shouldn't have been surprised. He had never been there for us before. We were practically strangers.

"It's not what you think," he sighed, before walking over to a circular table that held a bottle of amber liquid and a small glass, then poured himself a drink. I stayed silent, watching as he tipped his head back and dumped the drink down his throat. Then I waited until he sat on the solitary wooden chair at the table. "I've already connected us. I will always know where you are and when you are in real danger. Roehl needs to believe that I am nowhere near Aquaris. He needs to believe that you hate me. Despise me. For all that has happened to you and your parents."

I nodded, sadly. I could do that because it wasn't long ago that I harbored those very feelings for Nicolae. Until Leora told me the truth.

"How did you become so powerful?" I questioned.

He laughed. "I am not more powerful than you."

"That can't be true. I can't do the things you can," I admitted. "I can't disappear, or travel through darkness, or glamour anything." If I could, that would be a huge advantage.

Nicolae glanced at me with an almost haughty smirk. "You are a female heir to the Incendian throne. You are much more powerful than I am." He sucked in a deep breath and let it out slowly, looking at me as if I were a helpless child. "All you need is the proper guidance."

Guidance. It was the reason I had traveled across the Sangerian Sea to get to Incendia. I was looking for someone to help me. But all I found was a queen who was in bed with my enemy.

Nicolae walked over and stood directly in front of me. "You are the only person walking on this planet with tattoos like these." He took my hands in his and raised them, turning them over so we could both see them clearly. "You've been branded by the Fire Goddess herself. You have the power of all the elements in the palms of your hands. Once you believe in your power, and that you are a worthy vessel of it, your powers will grow in strength."

Easier said than done. My powers had felt like they'd been limited. Like they were tethered to my palms. Maybe it was because I still felt like I wasn't truly deserving of them. I mean, I was an eighteen-year-old girl, living a simple life with my parents, and then *bam*! I had been bitten by a vampire, forced to leave my home to escape a wicked prince hunting me, found out my mother was killed, and my father was on the run. I was captured, tortured, and then found out I was heir to not only the Incendian throne, but Morbeth's as well.

And the powers. Great powers I knew nothing about or how to use were suddenly unlocked. It was an immense pressure. I mean, I just learned how to draw water from my wet clothes and hair and thought that was the greatest magic ever.

But like Kai had once mentioned, that was a trick an Aquarian child learned at a young age. The difference was, they had teachers and were born with these gifts. My powers were literally dropped into my hands with no instruction.

I could only assume that if Nicolae and I had powers… my father had some too.

CHAPTER TWO

"Do you have a plan?" I asked, hopeful Nicolae would have one, because I sure as hell didn't.

Nicolae nodded. "In order to save your father's life, and the life of the Carpathian Prince, you will have to go to Roehl alone. But he will not let them go easily. He will demand something from you." Nicolae came and stood in front of me, his golden eyes boring into mine. "Are you willing to pay whatever price he asks?"

"Yes," I answered truthfully. And I meant those words with my whole heart. I would do whatever Roehl asked if he would set my father and Trystan free.

A sad grin rose on his lips. "You are noble and brave and have a strength beyond your years. I am proud you are my kin, Calla." He took hold of both my hands. "I will be watching, and when the time is right, I will come when Roehl least expects it. But you will have to endure until then."

I nodded. "I've survived Roehl once before, without any power. I can do it again."

Nicolae let go of my hands and placed his palms on my shoulders. "He is waiting in an old, abandoned home on the shore, just up north. I can take you close, but I can't go with you."

I nodded. "Even if you aren't with me, knowing we are connected and that you'll know where I am, already gives me strength."

Nicolae took a step closer, wrapping his arms around me. It was a hug that was tight and filled with years of emotion. It must have been the bond, because I could feel how sorry he was. I could sense his sadness and how he wished things had turned out differently. How he wished he'd known my father and I had existed, because things would have been different. Much different. And his heart ached because of it.

He pressed his lips to the top of my head, and I felt a tingle. A sense of peace slowly traveling down the rest of my body. Then he stepped back and wiped away a tear that had trickled down his own cheek.

I wasn't sure what was in store for me, but I was glad I had another very powerful ally. My grandfather. A prince of Incendia and also of Morbeth. An outcast, just like me. But together, I felt we could be a force to be reckoned with.

"Drink this," Nicolae said, handing me a plain silver flask. "It's blood. It will strengthen you for what is ahead."

What did lie ahead of me? What evil plan was Roehl waiting to throw at me?

Knowing it was him, I could only expect the worst.

I quickly poured the coppery liquid down my throat and shut my eyes, letting the blood course its way through my body. When I was done, Nicolae asked, "Are you ready?"

I looked into those golden eyes that held so many tales of their own. Eyes that had probably seen and witnessed much more than they should have.

No, I wasn't ready, but I had to be.

"I am," I replied.

Nicolae took hold of my hand and in a blink, we were enveloped within his glamoured darkness. It coiled around us, ready to transport us to wherever he directed it.

I felt his hand squeeze mine, and then he wrapped me in one more embrace. "I will be near, but I cannot come until the time is right."

"I understand."

Nicolae kept his arms around me, so I closed my eyes, gathering up every ounce of strength I had, thinking about everything that could go right … or wrong.

In a few short moments, Nicolae released my hand.

"Be strong, Calla," he said, hugging me tighter, as if he were trying to impart his strength into me.

I sucked in a deep breath, and when we detached, I stepped out of his veiled darkness and onto the dark shoreline of Aquaris, alone. Nicolae was still there, only glamoured, and I wondered if he could still see me. Just in case, I gave a slight nod, then turned around and began walking down the sandy beach.

Nicolae had said the home was just up north, and I knew it would only be a matter of time before they knew I was here. Roehl wouldn't be alone. He would have his mages with him, ready to subdue me and my power.

In my mind, I couldn't help but hear the Seer's words. *"The blood prince will die by the hand of the one with the red-rimmed eyes."*

There had to be a way to change a Seer's prophecy, a way to alter it. Because I would not let Trystan die. The only reason he was captured was because he tried to save my father. *My* father, who he'd never met and didn't have any connection with.

Trystan. Whose beautiful azure eyes had been in my dreams and continually melted me, who had taken care of my needs after I drank from his sacred blood—the blood of a pureblood. He made me feel things that I had never experienced. Wonderful, mind-blowing things that even now, I couldn't get out of my mind.

I craved more of him. Everything about him made me weak in the knees, and his scent … it was like a drug. A wonderful, sensual drug.

A wave of frigid air slammed into me, jolting me from my thoughts. I gasped, my knees buckling. Dropping to the sandy ground, my body was frozen again. I was subdued, trying to stay calm, as tendrils of dark wisps of evil wrapped around me, squeezing, choking.

Ahead of me, three shadowy figures slithered into view. *Roehl's mages.* I knew it the moment I felt their power. Their power felt wrong. Violating.

I smiled to myself, knowing how furious they must have been after we'd locked them in Morbeth's dungeon after the white witches and Markus came to rescue me and Spring.

Behind the mages, a dozen more figures raced toward me with swords and shields in hands. Shields bearing Morbeth's insignia.

Fear tried to strangle me, so I sucked in a deep breath, not allowing it to take hold of me. I had to be strong. I had to endure, knowing my powers were subdued, and I was helpless to do anything at the moment.

Nicolae was still out there, and he had connected us. I hoped he was right. That Roehl wouldn't be able to find and break that connection between us. Because it was the hope in that very connection that would keep me alive and fighting.

Roehl's guards were on me quickly while the mages stayed back, their dark magic holding me tight.

One of the men grabbed my arms and yanked me up. My legs wobbled, but I stayed on my feet. Another pulled my arms behind my back, tying a rope around them, then he pushed me forward, making me stumble. I tripped and hit the ground face first, but the sand broke my fall, ending up in my mouth. Spewing out the granules, they pulled me back to my feet.

"Our mages are more powerful than she is," one of the guards scoffed. "Look at her. She's nothing but a helpless girl."

"Are you sure this is the right girl?" another laughed.

One day, if I survived this, I would learn how to protect myself from dark magic and every asshole that tried to bully me.

"This is the best Incendia can offer?" another voice jeered. "I thought they were all-powerful." He twiddled his fingers in front of his face, teasing.

"I heard they are all-powerful in the bedroom," another said. "Why do you think our prince keeps going back for more?"

The guards erupted in laughter.

"Get going." One of them kicked my leg, making me wince, but I kept the pain to myself.

"This one looks young," another added. "Probably needs someone mature to teach her."

"Oh, I could teach her a thing or two."

"Get her up. The prince wants her." A raspy voice ordered.

Another guard grabbed me by the hair and yanked me up. I cringed in pain as my neck was wrenched back. But I stood and fought through it.

I looked at all the faces of these bastards and would remember them. They had no idea what I was capable of. And I made a silent promise that they would eventually pay.

Right now, I was here for my father and Trystan, and I had to get to them, to save them.

Another guard placed a rope around my neck and tugged me forward.

"Remember what the prince said. Bring her back in one piece or we'll be in pieces," a younger guard spoke. The rope burned against my skin as they pulled me forward.

"Get moving, girl. Roehl wants his pet back."

It took everything inside of me not to speak. To tell these bastards that they were all going to burn in my fiery rage. Or be drowned by water. Whatever was most convenient at the time.

I would make it through this. I would get my revenge.

I focused my thoughts on Trystan and my father, what they were going through, and what they had already endured. It helped to mute my mind to the disgusting and degrading banter between the guards.

The mages stayed about twenty yards behind, no doubt working hard to keep my power locked up tight.

My neck burning from the rope, and arms aching from being clamped tightly behind my back, I was reaching my first tipping point. Horror roiled in my veins knowing this was just the beginning. I still hadn't seen the devil.

Just ahead, about a quarter mile away, I spotted a solitary house. The only structure on this shoreline for miles. Roehl was there. I knew he was. I could almost feel his dark and vile power surrounding the area.

My heart was racing, head throbbing, and my powers were still bound. Not even a whisper of it. I tried to call it, but my calls went unanswered.

I thought back to when I was in Morbeth's dungeon, when these same mages quelled my power. But I was able to get them back. Leora had told me my magic was greater than any dark magic. That they hadn't really taken my power away. They had glamoured it, like she had for most of my life, causing me to believe it was gone.

But this time, I knew better. I'd broken through their glamour once before, and I knew I could do it again. I just had to wait until the time was right.

Roehl would know if my power was back, so I had to keep up the charade. To play the victim until it was time to strike and make them feel my fire.

I focused on the water and the moonlight reflecting off the waves. Being one of the first elements to come to me, the water soothed my nerves, calming me, helping to refocus on why I was here, and quieting the fear trying to overcome me.

It reminded me of a much simpler time in Sartha, when I would sit out on my porch and watch the moonlight glimmer across the Argent Sea. I used to think a lot about my future, and never had I dreamed it would lead to all of this.

This life. This new life was incredibly far from the one I had previously imagined. So distant from the simplistic life I had fantasized about. With this present course, I couldn't count how many times I was threatened since the night of my eighteenth birthday. How many times I'd barely escaped death.

And yet, here I was again, in another life-threatening situation, not certain if I would survive this next encounter with Roehl.

The bastard. I could feel him even now. I could feel his power emanating around the area. He had taken measures and made sure I wasn't a threat.

As we reached the home and entered the weathered, paint flecked wooden fence that wrapped around the perimeter, I felt Roehl's dark magic tighten around me, squeezing until I could scarcely breathe.

My left palm started burning, pain radiated up my arm, and then … I gasped, feeling an icy hollowness. Like something inside had been stolen. Then, I knew what he had done. He had severed my connection to Kai.

The rope was taken from around my neck, and two guards—one on either side of me—grasped both of my arms, leading me to the front steps. As we neared the porch, the door swung open, and the devil appeared.

Roehl's raven hair was drawn behind the nape of his neck. He was wearing a black suit and matching cape. Those obsidian eyes rimmed with crimson narrowed, leering, while a sneer curved on his malicious lips. I could see it in his eyes, the look of triumph. He'd finally recaptured me. He'd won.

"Where is my father?" I choked the words out, staring at him with every bit of contempt I possessed. I would do whatever it took to free Trystan and my father, but I wasn't about to lie down, belly up, and abandon myself. Hell no. I would fight, with whatever breath I had left in me.

"Ah, the prodigal daughter returns." He let out a dark, growly laugh, his pupils dilated.

"Not on purpose." I spewed the words and watched his lip curl and incisors lengthen.

The darkness coiled tighter around me, compressing the air from my lungs. I collapsed to my knees but fought to get myself back up to my feet.

I wouldn't show him weakness. Not if I could help it.

Roehl slowly ambled down the porch stairs and stood in front of me, arms crisscrossed over his chest. I couldn't see the resemblance between him and Nicolae. Half-brothers, but nothing alike.

Nicolae, with his golden eyes, took after Leora. Roehl took after... the devil who spawned him. Which was his mother, because King Romulus wasn't this bad.

"Where is my father?" I demanded again, my power still smothered by the dark magic that was suffocating this entire property.

Roehl held out his hands to his sides. "As you can see, he's not here. But I'll take you to him."

He gave a terse nod and out from the darkness stepped three men—Wanderers, who looked similar to Erro. They were tall and fair with pointed features, silvery hair, and alabaster eyes.

Gods, he was going to take me away. Probably some place distant, where Nicolae couldn't find me. I prayed our bond wasn't broken, because if it hadn't been, he could still track my location. I was banking on it, because my hope was gradually slipping away.

I didn't want to mention Trystan's name, especially after what the Seer had spoken. I knew how vindictive Roehl was. He knew Trystan had claimed me first and that he held my heart, and he would never let that go. He wanted me all the more for it. I couldn't think about any of that right now. Not until I saw them both and knew they were safe.

Roehl's dark mages stepped forward. Their black cloaks looked too large on their thin frames. Long cowls draped down, obscuring their haggard, withered faces. I could feel their souls were just as black and wicked as their magic.

Roehl stepped forward and placed his hands on my shoulders. I shuddered from his defiling touch. Everything about him was revolting. I tried to back away, but the two guards that accompanied me were right behind me, making sure I had nowhere to go.

I scowled, but he grinned at me like I was a cute little puppy and slowly leaned in close, his darkened gaze burning through mine.

"Did you truly think you could run away from me without consequence?" He spoke slowly, nostrils flared, and the muscles in his jaw twitched, sending a chill down my spine. Suddenly, his arms wrapped around my sides, and from behind, the ropes were removed, and familiar cold cuffs snapped tightly around my wrists. "You will pay for defying me, pet. For running from me, after all I did for you."

Fucking bastard. Did he honestly think he did me a favor? He murdered my mother, had held me prisoner and tortured me, captured my father and Trystan, and now this.

It took everything inside of me to bite my tongue. I didn't say a word because I knew he was baiting me. Waiting for me to say something so he could demonstrate to his guards and everybody else around him how powerful he was.

But I wasn't going to play his game. I wasn't going to speak right now, so he could beat the hell out of me. No. I would wait until the time was right.

Gods, I detested him with every thread of my being. I never thought I could hate someone so deeply that it radiated in my blood and bones. Whenever I was close to him, it was as if he had a blade and was hacking away at the good left inside of me. At my happiness. At my life. My future.

This bastard had taken everything from me. What else did he want?

I knew for a fact, I would never be his. *Never.* Even if he tortured me until the brink of death.

The guards and mages encircled us while the Wanderers stood on the outside of us, creating a triangle with their arms outstretched. In moments, we were enveloped in darkness and wind that carried us toward the sky and away from Aquaris.

CHAPTER THREE

The wind whipped violently around us, throwing the guards off balance. They were knocking into each other as the three Wanderers whisked us into oblivion. But Roehl held me steady with his cold and uninvited hands.

I closed my eyes and steadied myself, and in moments the wind died. As the surrounding darkness dissolved, I glanced around and found we were surrounded by snow and mountains. The air was thin and frigid, and we were nowhere near Aquaris. The balmy sea breeze was gone.

We must have been somewhere within the Morose Mountains—the massive range that ran straight through the center of Talbrinth.

Morose. The perfect definition of what I was feeling. Sullen and ill-tempered.

But, despite the circumstances, knowing the worst had yet to come, I was anxious to finally see my father and Trystan.

I hadn't seen my father since before my eighteenth birthday, before he and my mother left on their merchant ship to Traders Port. I wondered if he knew my mother was dead. If he'd witnessed the slaughter of everyone on his ship. Or if he escaped while it was happening.

I was most anxious to see Trystan and wondered if I would be given a chance to apologize. I needed him to know how I truly felt and beg for forgiveness, even if it was too late for us. Even if he would never be mine.

The guards dispersed and slowly moved down a rocky trail without instruction.

"Move," Roehl ordered, gesturing for me to follow. I was surprised he didn't use more vulgar words. But I knew they would come, sooner or later. I could see it in his eyes and the tenseness of his jaw and in his posture.

He was waiting to unleash his wrath on me, just another form of torture. I knew he was holding it in. He was just too calm, like a predator circling, waiting for the right moment to pounce.

The ground beneath my feet was rocky and uneven, and snow crunched under my boots as we walked. I was tired and weak. Multiple times I tripped and nearly fell, but Roehl made sure I stayed on my feet. Made sure his prize made it to wherever we were going, so he could carry out his twisted, wicked plan.

He and his mages stayed right behind me, their dark power along with Roehl's spelled cuffs, still smothering mine.

I thought back to earlier in Aquaria when I was attending a

ball held in my name and treated like royalty. I was surrounded by friends, and we were laughing without any care, for just a moment.

Yet, here I was, somewhere in the remote, frigid mountains, trudging with the devil and his advocates. They despised me, not only because I was an heir to the throne of Morbeth but also feared me because I was an heir of Incendia, possessing great power.

This entire mess started because of envy. Roehl didn't want anyone to take his throne. I knew Nicolae never had any intention of ruling Morbeth, but when Roehl found out about his father's bastard son, he hunted him down because he *thought* he was a threat.

That single act proved how misguided and twisted his mind was. His jealousy caused him to want to kill a half-brother he never knew. And because of it, his brother, Rurik, was killed.

Roehl wanted Nicolae. To skin him alive for killing his brother in self-defense. But now, he also wanted me. I was a member of the family, heir and an Incendian royal with great power ... and I'd rejected him, broke the curse he placed on his father, and ran away.

Which was probably why he was out here, in the middle of nowhere. His ill and evil intentions caused him to be the King of Nothing.

Being the asshole he was, there was no way he was going to let me go without destroying me. He loved to display his power.

Especially to those who defied him. I just had to stay strong. Had to endure whatever was coming, all while praying that Nicolae would find me.

We traversed the rocky, snow-covered trail, and finally came to a large peak. On its side was a small opening that led into a dark tunnel. It reminded me of the opening to the mountain in Incendia that led to the Fire Goddess. Except this time, there were no friends with me.

Where the hell was Flint? Wasn't he supposed to come to my rescue? Isn't that why Helia gave him to me as a gift?

Worthless bird. The last time I'd seen him was in Incendia, right before Kai took us underwater. That was hundreds of miles away.

I wondered if he was still alive or if I'd ever get to see him again. He was probably flying around with Nyx, gods who knew where, causing all kinds of trouble. The thought made me crack a smile, thankfully out of Roehl's line of sight. If he caught me smiling, the bastard would lose it.

The guards moved into a single formation and began disappearing into the dark crevice that led into the mountain. I glanced up into the sky, one more time and said a prayer. A prayer to the gods and goddesses that they would help me.

"Move," Roehl growled, shoving me forward.

The opening must have been glamoured because I couldn't see anything beyond it but darkness. As soon as I stepped beyond the threshold it opened up into a large corridor, brightly lit with torches. The walls and floor of the corridor were not what you'd find in the middle of a mountain. This place must have been carved out by magic. The ground, no longer dirt, was made of smooth cobblestone.

"What is this place?" I asked no one in particular.

"My secret kingdom," Roehl answered from behind. "Somewhere deep in the Morose Mountains."

I knew it. I stayed quiet and kept my pace with the guard in front of me. We twisted and turned down the corridor before we came to a large area—a balcony of sorts, that opened up into an enormous tavern below.

My eyes took in the unbelievable sight.

A town—no, not a town, an entire city was built inside the mountain. How he had managed to do that, I had no idea.

There were men and women and even children strolling the city below. In the distance were homes and even a small palace in the background. But it was cold and colorless, the buildings and walkways made of gray stone. There was no sky. No sun or moon or stars to gaze at. It was … another prison.

"Welcome to my kingdom," Roehl said, stepping up beside me.

"Who are these people?" There were many races and colors of people, but none of them looked happy. They looked pitiful and … like puppets. Roehl's puppets.

"They are here of their own will, if that's what you're wondering," Roehl replied with a scowl. "They are outcasts. Vampires, witches, and men whose gifts and abilities were looked down upon. The unwanted, who weren't given a chance to use their unique gifts and thrive in the real world."

Outcasts and undesired. These were the perfect people for Roehl to rule over.

There's a reason why someone is an outcast or unwanted. Why society deems them that way. Were they evil, lying, thieves or murderers? Were they using their magic for their own gain?

These were the only people I could imagine wanting to live inside of a colorless, viewless mountain. Ruled by an arrogant, narcissistic bastard. Or maybe these people were poor destitute souls that had no help and nowhere to go. Maybe they didn't realize how wicked Roehl was. The bastard was cunning and could be very charming.

I wanted to question him, but now wasn't the time to piss him off.

"Where's my father?" I asked instead.

Roehl turned to me with a wicked glint in his eyes. "Your father is here, and you'll be reunited soon."

Two of the guards turned back and chuckled, like they thought what he said was funny. I glared at them, wishing I could do something to show them my power was still there. But right now, in Roehl's territory, which was heavily warded with dark magic, with my hands cuffed behind my back, I couldn't even feel a spark or twinge of heat roiling under my skin. The only things I could feel was the agonizing concern for Trystan and my father, and my hatred for Roehl, growing by the second.

They led me down a long stone staircase that exited into a modest marketplace, bustling with people. Small stands were set up at the outer perimeters, filled with wares. I could smell herbs, saw candles, wooden carvings, jewelry, pottery, and grimoires.

There was a man butchering a pig right at his stand, intestines and limbs of the animal were hanging behind him on small hooks attached to the roof above.

A group had gathered to watch, but the sight made my stomach turn.

As we descended, the crowd's attention turned to us. Their eyes wide and faces lifted to see their prince.

As we hit the bottom of the steps, I felt as if I'd stepped into a nightmare.

The marketplace fell silent, most of the citizens glaring at me like I had killed someone close to them. Like I was the evil traitor. And then, the entire area erupted with cheers and people clapping. The crowd was welcoming Roehl like he was some champion hunter, returning with his prize. And Roehl, the bastard prince, standing tall and soaking it all in.

I felt bare and vulnerable, my magic suppressed, hands fastened behind my back.

The guards continued to move us through the crowd that had gathered.

As I passed one woman her dark scabrous lips curled back to reveal a full row of razors sharp teeth as she hissed at me. Dark, angry eyes sliced through me like daggers. "You'll get what's coming to you."

The crowd began yelling, calling me traitor, and a slew of other obscenities. And Roehl did nothing. He was reveling in this moment. Reveling in the fact that his people bought into and believed his vicious lies.

What made my heart ache was that I had never seen these people before. Never met them or even spoke to them. Yet they were condemning me. They hated me and they didn't even know me.

I tried to calm my nerves, to block out the horrible things they were saying. Lies. All lies.

From the corner of my eye, I spotted something flying toward me. Before I could move or duck, it slammed into the side of my head.

I staggered back, bumping into Roehl, my vision blurred. Shooting pain and warm liquid began dripping down the side of my face and neck. I blinked a few times, then spotted what had hit me. On the ground was a rock, about five inches around, with jagged edges.

Growls and hisses erupted, and fear slammed into me like a brick. Vampires were amongst the crowd. Vampires who were hungry and scented my blood.

Roehl quickly gave a command, and I was suddenly hemmed in by guards who drew their swords to protect me.

Liquid continued to trail down my face when I heard Roehl's voice. I couldn't make out what he was saying over the raucous crowd, but I knew he was trying to get his people under control, but they weren't listening.

Painful screams erupted out of monsters trying to get to me but were met with guards swinging double-edged swords.

Roehl's kingdom was starting to fall. His people dying by the hands of his own guards.

A deafening, horrifying roar rattled the stone kingdom. Rocks fell and cracked on the ground, and suddenly the crowd hushed.

Roehl's voice boomed through the entire marketplace. "Whoever touches her will meet my wrath!" He turned to me, his eyes completely black. He bent down and picked up the stone that had hit me. "Who threw this stone?" He held it up in the air.

There was silence, before eyes started to turn toward a big, burly man with a long scraggly beard and stern eyes. He looked gruff, like a big old bear. I'd never seen this man in my life, and he'd thrown a freaking stone at my head. What an asshole.

Roehl growled, standing a few feet away from me, but in a split second, was across the marketplace, his hand gripped tightly around the man's neck, lifting him off the ground. The man sputtered, trying to speak, but Roehl twisted his fingers, snapping the man's neck. He then dropped his lifeless body to the ground.

"If you beasts want something to feed on, here it is," he said.

I turned to where Roehl was standing a moment ago, but he was gone.

Six or seven bodies dropped to the ground, feeding off of the man.

"I am the only one who can touch her," Roehl ordered. "Unless you have a death wish, you will obey."

That's why he did it. That's why Roehl murdered the man who threw the rock at my head. It wasn't for me. He did it because his people were getting out of hand, and he was losing control of them. He was losing the upper hand, and that pissed him off. He broke that man's neck to show them who was in charge. Who was King of Assholes.

I had yet to see the demon's wrath, but it was slowly unfolding, and I knew it would only be a matter of time before it was taken out on me. He wouldn't let what I'd done go lightly. I'd wounded his pride and embarrassed him.

One of the guards grabbed my hand and slipped a damp navy handkerchief into my hand. When I looked at him, he had no smile, but gave a single nod. I didn't know why he'd done it because my hands were clamped behind my back and there was no way for me to use it. But I was thankful, nonetheless.

The guard was around six feet tall and muscular with tanned skin and short black hair. But his eyes. Those deep brown eyes weren't like the others. They held a softness like I'd seen in Brone and Markus.

He was kind. The only one to extend any form of help to me, and he stayed right next to me as we were pushed forward. As we neared a corner of the marketplace, the crowd cleared the area, revealing a scene behind them.

It felt as if the ground beneath me would open up and swallow me whole.

My heart shattered into a million pieces as my eyes caught two men, beaten and bleeding, arms strung up over their heads.

They were shirtless, which revealed dark purplish bruises all over their bodies.

I wailed running forward toward them, but one of the guards threw out his leg, tripping me. With my hands still fastened behind my back, I fell forward, face first against the stone ground. My face stung with pain and my vision blurred. A wave of nausea overcame me, but I sucked it up and held it in.

"She tripped. It was an accident," the guard said loudly, making those around him chuckle.

The guard who had given me the handkerchief, who still wore a straight face, bent down and picked me up.

I felt no pain, because every ounce of my pain was contained in my chest.

"Calla!" my father called, his voice hoarse.

"Father," I sobbed, tears blurring his face.

It was the first time I'd seen him in months. He looked nothing like the man who had raised me—a man filled with so much life and joy, a man who would give the shirt off his back to anyone in need, who would feed the hungry and donate to the poor.

No, he looked like a shell of the man he used to be. He'd lost so much weight, becoming almost emaciated. His eyes enclosed with dark circles, his hair matted, his trousers and body covered with dirt and filth.

I stepped forward and to my surprise, the guards let me go.

Running to my father, I pressed my head onto his chest. His warm lips pressed against the top of my head. "Why are you here?" he asked, his voice weakened. I wondered when he'd last had food or drink.

I leaned back, looking into his bloodshot eyes. "Mother is gone," I sobbed.

He nodded, tears leaving trails down his pale, dirty face. "I know, darling. I'm so sorry."

I shook my head, my heart shattering. "It wasn't your fault."

"Are you hurt?" His eyes observed the blood on my face.

"I'm fine," I replied in my strongest voice.

My father closed his eyes and shook his head. He looked defeated, like the life had been drained out of his soul.

"I love you, Calla," he whispered, his chest heaving with deep sobs. "I love you so much."

"I love you, too."

I glanced over to Trystan, his beautiful eyes carefully watching me and my father.

"Calla," he smiled, his eyes also tired.

I faced him, eyes burning with new tears. "Trystan. I'm so sorry. You shouldn't be here. You shouldn't have come."

His eyes closed, and a smile rose on his beautiful lips. "I had to. He's your father."

My heart shattered over and over again. But I had to tell him. Had to let him know.

I took a step away from my father and focused solely on Trystan.

"I'm sorry for what I said to you. I was wrong, and I was scared. But I want you to know that if given another chance, I would take your hand and run away with you."

Those azure eyes brightened, and a beautiful smile bloomed on his lips.

"My hands are tied up at the moment. How about another time?" He laughed, then coughed and blood dripped down the side of his mouth.

"What did they do to you?" I breathed, my body trembling.

He slowly raised his head. "Nothing I can't handle."

I pushed toward Trystan, but my body froze in place. I couldn't move, not an inch, and turned to see Roehl heading toward us. His eyes were darkened, and teeth curled over long incisors.

"Trystan," I wailed, my entire being in agony, my tears unending.

"Don't cry, Calla. We'll get through this," he said with a sad smile.

He was the bravest person I knew. He didn't show one ounce of fear. Just concern. For me.

I could feel Roehl come up behind me, but I was incapacitated. I fought to release my power, but it wasn't answering. *Why the hell wasn't it answering?*

"I told you she was mine," Roehl growled, his eyes affixed on Trystan.

He pressed his front against my back and from behind, wrapped his arms around my waist. Pressing his nose into my hair, he breathed in deeply. I closed my eyes, disgusted by the way I felt when he was so close. The bastard. He was only doing this to taunt Trystan.

Then, without notice, Roehl sunk his teeth into my shoulder.

"No," I screamed, trying to fight him off, but his grip and magic were too tight.

Trystan's eyes turned black, incisors lengthened. He fought against the chains binding him, shoving himself forward, but the chains didn't give, glowing bright red with Roehl's magic.

"I'll kill you," Trystan growled, the muscles in his chest and arms taught. "I'll kill you and my face will be the last you'll ever see."

Trystan was still fighting against the restraints, his wrists were already raw and bleeding. I couldn't watch him hurt himself anymore.

"It's okay," I whispered to him, knowing he could hear me. A new set of tears streaming down my face. With Trystan's darkened eyes on mine, I mouthed four words. "I'm yours, Trystan. Forever."

Trystan stopped fighting and closed his eyes, but his jaw was tense. A tear escaped, trailing down the side of his face. He let out another pained cry and pushed hard against the chains binding him. The wall holding him back started to crack but held. The manacles glowing bright red.

There was nothing he could do. Nothing any of us could do right now.

Roehl finally released my shoulder and licked the wound he'd caused. He'd marked me, releasing the partial blood bond which would allow him to connect with me. To find me if I should ever flee.

Roehl turned me around, his eyes now filled with obsidian, the edges thick with crimson

"My pet," Roehl snarled with a raged glare in his eyes. "You escaped me once, locked up my mages, turned my head guard against me, and healed my father." His fingers wrapped around my cheeks, squeezing tight, his face inches from mine, an evil grin spreading across his lips. "No one knows of this place. No matter how loud you scream, it's so heavily warded that you will never be found."

The devil had finally come out to play. But I wasn't afraid of him. I was here for two things only. Trystan and my father.

I stood firm, staring into his obsidian eyes rimmed in crimson. "What do you want?"

"You knew there would be consequences for your disobedience."

He let go of my face and grabbed my arms, pulling me away from my father and Trystan. When we were about ten yards away, he turned me around to face them, his arms wrapped tightly around me again from behind.

"Take them down," Roehl ordered.
Four guards went up to my father and Trystan and lowered their arms. They both dropped to their knees, severely weakened. My father's limbs were visibly trembling.

With another nod of Roehl's head, another guard walked up behind them, carrying a long whip.

"Stop!" I demanded. "I will do whatever you want. Please, let them go."

"No," he replied. "I gave you a chance to be my queen, and you threw it away."

Roehl raised his hand, and the guard pulled back the whip. Helpless to do anything, helpless to save him, I watched the wicked man swing hard. The whip came down with a snap, lashing my father in the back. My father cried out in pain, his body arched as the whip tore into his flesh.

"Stop it! You're killing him!" I screamed. My heart. My heart was breaking—cracking in two—making me double over with agony. But the guard continued …

One.

Two.

Three.

Four more grueling lashes until he finally stopped, and my father's body slumped forward, the open gashes across his back oozing blood.

I cried out, pain ripped through my chest.

Then, he moved to Trystan.

"Please," I wailed. "Please. They are innocent. They have done nothing to you."

Trystan's eyes found mine, wracking my chest with pain. But a thin smile raised on his lips—a smile that let me know he would be okay.

How could he smile at me? How could anyone be okay in the midst of being tortured?

I groaned in agony, wishing, praying their suffering would end. But I couldn't look away from him, from those beautiful eyes that were fastened to mine.

The guard swung the whip down hard, and it cracked against Trystan's back. I felt it in my chest.

He went rigid, his teeth clenched, as it tore through his flesh.

I tried to be strong for him, but my heart was shattering, tears falling in torrents down my face.

After four more brutal lashes, Trystan's back was torn open, skin hanging from the wounds. I could see pain etched in his bloodshot eyes. But he held it in, trying not to show weakness.

"That's enough," I demanded.

My heart couldn't bear to watch them being tortured because of me.

Roehl raised his hand again, and two guards—each carrying a heavy wooden block—placed one in front of my father and the other in front of Trystan, pushing their heads down onto the blocks. *Chopping blocks.*

My body was shaking, my heart and pulse racing. This couldn't be happening. There had to be a way to free them. If only my gods damned power would wake.

I twisted back to Roehl. "I will do anything. Anything you ask. Just set them free."

"No, Calla," Trystan bellowed from behind.

A wicked grin rose on Roehl's lips. He liked this game. He liked the torment he was putting us through.

"I'll make you a deal then," he finally said.

Roehl released his grip on me and moved between Trystan and my father. Smiling, he held out his hand to the side, and a guard strode to him, handing him a large, double-edged sword.

This couldn't be happening. I would rather die, right now, then to see either of them murdered in cold blood by Roehl.

"Please. Tell me what you want. Anything," I sobbed.

I called to my power, over and over again.

But I felt nothing. Fucking nothing.

Roehl dragged the tip of his sword against the stone ground as he made his way to my father. "Here is my deal, pet," he spoke slowly, clearly. "I will let one of them live. But *you* will have to choose. You, Calla, will play god for the day, and will get to choose which one of these men in your life lives or dies."

Shaking my head, I dropped to my knees, my emotions churning like a violent storm. I looked to my father who had given me life. A selfless man who worked hard to provide for me and my mother and had given us everything we had ever needed or wanted.

My eyes found Trystan. This beautiful man, who had come into my life and risked everything for me. He came to Sartha to claim me, in an attempt to save me from Roehl. And from that moment on, he showed me, time and time again, how far he would go to protect me. Even now, when I looked at his beautiful face covered with bruises and blood, my heart grew even more for him. He'd proven that he would risk his own life to save *my* father. A man he had never met.

I loved them both. And there was no way in hell I could choose one over the other.

"Kill me instead," I begged. "I'm the one who left you."

My world was spiraling out of control. I couldn't lose them.

Roehl shrugged his shoulders and sighed. "I can't kill you, pet. I have plans for you." He smirked, twirling the sword in his hand. "If you don't make a choice soon, then I will have to make it for you."

He was giving me the same ultimatum with Spring. By my choice or his.

I continued shaking my head, heart anguishing, tears streaming down my face. This fucking asshole was going to kill one of the men I loved.

Where was the justice? He'd already murdered my mother. And where in the gods damned *hell* was my magic?

It was still stifled. Suppressed by the demon and his mages.

My entire body was shaking. There was no way I could ever choose. There was no life that was greater than the other. There was only one who deserved to die. And that was Roehl.

Then the words of the Seer haunted me again. *"The blood prince will die by the hand of the one with the red-rimmed eyes."*

He was going to kill Trystan. But Trystan was my future … I'd come to realize that now. And even if it was too late for us, we were still connected, and I would do anything to save him.

Roehl glanced at my father and then at Trystan. My heart stopped, breath seized when he took a few steps toward Trystan.

"I think the Prince of Carpathia is the greater threat here. Without him, you will have no bond or heartstrings left. If he is dead, maybe you will grow to love me.

Besides, your father is old and weak and barely alive. He has no power that I have witnessed, and he can't save his own life, let alone yours. He already let your mother die."

Tears were rolling down my father's cheeks. My cheeks.

"Please, don't," I begged, dropping to my knees, on the rocky ground.

Roehl paused, his midnight eyes glaring at me. He pulled Trystan's head back and pressed the sword to his throat.

"Give me one good reason why I shouldn't slit his throat right now."

I looked into Trystan's eyes. Those beautiful azure eyes that had captured me the moment I spotted him across the pool at Brynna's house. Those eyes that matched the stone warming against my heart, that had seized me, heart and soul. And replied…

"Because I am in love with him."

CHAPTER FOUR

The look in Trystan's eyes and in his expression was indescribable. Without a word, his teary eyes had spoken a thousand words, directly to my heart. He'd forgiven me. And he loved me too. Unconditionally.

I felt somehow freed speaking those words, because Trystan finally knew what I really felt about him. And so did my father.

A deep and guttural growl erupted from deep within Roehl's chest. I witnessed the rage grow in his eyes and tighten on his face. He couldn't stand that I had chosen Trystan over him. That I loved Trystan and would never love him.

Trystan was my first love. My hero. My dark knight that traveled from a land far away to save me. From the moment we met, we had connected, and that connection went far beyond what either of us could try to explain or rationalize. It just… was.

Trystan had known it from the beginning, but it had taken some time for me to catch up. I was still young and immature. I'd never been in a relationship and didn't trust easily.

But he never gave up. He never backed down, even going against what his cadre and his own father said or thought. Putting himself in danger for me and those I loved.

Now … here we were, and the look in Trystan's eyes. The look of pure happiness and satisfaction, despite the pain and the situation we were in, was worth it. Even if Roehl killed me right now, I would die happy.

I glanced at my father, and he smiled at me. It was a smile I understood. A smile that also spoke to my soul. A smile that told me that he loved me and was happy I had finally found someone worthy of my love, who he seemed to approve of.

Roehl ordered the guards to put Trystan and my father side by side. His sword was long enough to behead them both with one blow.

"Wait," I begged, wailing. "Don't do this, Roehl. You are going against the treaty. They are royals."

"Who would stop me?" he said. "You've turned my father against me, severing me from ever being King of Morbeth."

"You put a spell on your father and turned him against you," I said carefully.

This couldn't be happening. How could the gods be so cruel to let him go around murdering innocent people and getting away with it? He used his magic to make his *own* father sick so he could play king. Where was retribution? Where was the gods damned karma?

Roehl raised his sword and glared at me. "Choose one now, or they will both die."

My entire soul was travailing. There was no way I could choose.

"I can't," I sobbed.

Roehl smirked. The asshole smirked. "Then their blood will be on your hands."

He had no heart inside his chest, nothing but a black, rotted pit.

I stood to my feet and rushed forward, but before I reached Roehl, the guards yanked me back.

My father looked at me, a peaceful smile on his face. "I love you, daughter. Always and forever."

"No," I wailed, with tears pouring down my face.

I watched helplessly, my heart and mind anguishing as Roehl swung the blade down.

Everything from that moment had become muffled, playing out in slow motion.

My father twisted his body, kicking Trystan off of his block. Trystan flew to the side, rolling to safety. But Roehl's sword still came down, slicing through my father's neck and chest.

My father cried out and fell to the ground, his eyes wide as he gasped for air. On his back, I screamed, seeing his chest had been flayed open, exposing dark flesh and bone. But it was the wound on his neck, a fatal blow to an artery, that had me fighting the guards to get to him. "One less vampire prince to contend with," Roehl said casually.

I was going to kill him.

But then it hit me. My father was Romulus' and Nicolae's heir. He was a blood prince, and we had a very strong connection. It wasn't Trystan the Seer spoke of. It was my father.

"Father," I wailed, tears streaming down my face as I pushed and pushed until the guards finally let me go.

Racing to my father's side, I fell on my knees beside him. My nostrils stung as I scented the coppery liquid pouring like a waterfall from the sliced arteries in his neck. I knew I should put pressure on it, but my hands were tied behind my back. My father was dying.

"No, no, no," I cried. "Don't die. Please."

My father looked at me with tears in his eyes. "It's okay, Calla," he breathed, forcing a smile. He was struggling to speak, coughing up blood. "Your mother—and I — will be together — again. We will–be watching—over you."

"Don't talk," I grieved, dropping my forehead to his chest that was soaked in blood.

My father placed a weak hand on the side of my face.

"I love you—so much, Calla. I've always been—proud of you."

"I love you too," I wailed. "So much."

His breath was ragged, his eyes glassy. Blood gurgled in his throat as he raised a finger and pointed to my chest. "You are stronger, Calla. Just believe."

His arms suddenly went limp, and his head dropped back. His eyes were looking upward, but they were no longer seeing.

My father was gone. *He was gone.*

I let out an agonizing cry. The pain in my chest radiated through my entire body. I couldn't take any more. The pain was too much to bear.

I heard Trystan struggling and looked over to see Roehl pouring a vial of liquid down his throat. Roehl was going to kill him next.

"Trystan," I screamed, trying to get to him.

With terror and fear wrapping around me, I closed my eyes and called to my power. I didn't ask for it to come. I demanded it.

I am fire. I am water. I am earth. I am air. And I am worthy.

I call upon the power inside me, and I demand you be released.

I suddenly felt a tingling, from the top of my head to the souls of my feet. I knew my power was fighting whatever hold was subduing it. I felt it slowly ignite in my core, and travel through my veins, writhing under my skin and scratching at my palms.

I called to the air, and even though we were inside the mountain, a strong gust of wind swept through my hair and all around me. I pushed it toward Roehl, and it slammed into him, sending him flying away from Trystan.

Air. It was Trystan's power too, and it didn't go unnoticed.

Trystan smiled, giving me a nod, and it made my heart swell.

Next, I called to my fire and felt it burning in my hands, still fastened behind my back. Concentrating on my breath and my power, my entire body soon engulfed in flame.

I'd broken through Roehl's and the mage's bindings! My fire magic *was* more powerful, just as Leora had said. As Helia, the

Fire Goddess had said.

"No," Roehl snarled, his angry glare slicing through me.

The cuffs that bound my wrists fell away, but Roehl turned to me with a wicked smile, revealing the empty vial in his hand.

"This is not over, pet," he seethed. "It's far from over. After this, there will be an even greater price for you to pay. Even better than death. Because your prince … the one you claim to love with your entire being—" He laughed an evil laugh that reverberated through my soul. "Your prince will forget you, and he will *never* love you back."

Rage encompassed me in flame. I raised my arms and thrust my power at Roehl. He threw his arms up, barely managing to quell my fire with his magic.

It rattled him. I saw it in those embittered eyes, that hint of fear.

I threw my flame, again and again, but he continued to block it.

"I will come for you, Calla," he vowed. "And next time, you won't survive."

Snapping his fingers, a Wanderer appeared at his side. With eyes raked with disdain, Roehl and the Wanderer suddenly vanished.

"You coward!" I shouted at the top of my lungs.

I ran to Trystan, who was now unconscious. Miraculously, every guard had disappeared, and so had all of Roehl's mages. Wicked pricks. All of them.

I turned to my father and watched a man suddenly appear from thin air.

"Erro," I gasped.

Erro bowed his head and smiled. "Don't worry, Calla. I will take your father from here. I'll take his body someplace safe," he said, taking a knee at my father's side. His alabaster eyes flickered up to meet mine. "Go. Quickly. In case he returns."

I placed my hand over my heart. "Thank you, Erro. I owe you."

I knew he was risking his life, and the lives of his family. Knowing the repercussions, he still helped me, regardless of Roehl's threats.

Erro smiled, bowing his head once more, then touched my father's arm. As soon as he did, they dissolved into a wisp of air.

I turned around and faced the crowd. Their wide eyes filled with what I could only describe as fear. They were terrified of me. And they should have been.

I called to the earth, and the ground shook beneath us. Like waves, it rose and fell beneath the citizens of Morose Mountain. They screamed in terror, running for shelter, back towards the buildings.

A loud caw echoed through the marketplace. From the entrance above flew a black crow with fiery eyes that blazed like torches. Flint. My prodigal pet had finally arrived.

Flint dove, transforming into the firebird I had first met. He flew between me and the citizens of Morose Mountain, setting a huge blaze behind them, blocking them from returning to where I was.

As he flew around, I held out my arm, and he landed on it. The two of us were engulfed in flame.

"Where have you been?" I scolded. Flint cawed and tilted his head.

At the top of the stairs, another figure emerged.

"Calla!" Nicolae bellowed. He paused a moment, taking in the sight of me and Flint, burning brightly.

"Trystan needs help," I yelled.

"Where's Roehl?"

"Gone. The coward left."

As Nicolae reached me, I quelled my power and took him to Trystan. "Roehl gave him a potion. I don't know what it was."

Nicolae kneeled down and ran a hand across Trystan's chest. "He's alive," he said. "But we need to get him out of here."

Nicolae's golden eyes scanned the area, then he paused, staring fixedly on a pool of blood. "Where's your father?"

Tears welled and burned my eyes. I shook my head, only managing to say two words. "He's gone."

Nicolae closed his eyes and exhaled. "I'm so sorry, Calla." He then placed one hand on Trystan's shoulder and grabbed my hand with the other. A surge of energy burst through me, and instantly we were shrouded in darkness.

This time I welcomed it. But there was something different about this darkness. I felt unsteady, almost as if we were flying.

When the darkness finally dissipated, we were standing inside of a building. It was large and open and had modern furnishings.

Flint cawed and spread his fiery wings.

"Thank you for coming," I said, petting his head. He nuzzled against my palm, then shook his feathers, morphing back into the black crow.

"You have a firebird?" Nicolae asked, a brow rising.

"I do." I smiled, looking at Flint, who had come to me when I needed him most. I guess we were connected, just like Helia had said.

"Where's Nyx?" I asked the bird, knowing he understood me.

I wondered if she was nearby, or if she had flown back to Carpathia.

Flint cocked his head to the side and then began dancing on my arm. He wouldn't stop, so I carried him over to the door and swung it open. Raising my arm, he took off into the sky. He was such a strange bird, but I appreciated him.

"In all my years, I've never seen anything like it," Nicolae said. I turned back to watch him walk inside of a room and lay Trystan on a large bed.

"He was a gift from Helia, the Goddess of Fire. I didn't want him at first because he seemed like he'd be a pain in the ass, but he provides me with wings, and he also has fire magic, so I can't complain."

Nicolae laughed. "He has a strong connection to you."

I nodded and took a step out the door, onto a patio.

We were on a bluff, overlooking the sea. The sky was blue, and the sun was already over the horizon. The landscape looked like it was designed by fairies. It was magical.

There was a small, cobbled path that led down to the sea and on either side of it were trees and flowers in every color. But as far as my eye could see, there were no other homes. No other people.

"Where is this place?" I asked.

"We are on a secluded island off of Carpathia. No one knows, but I happen to own this land. It is one of the places I've built over my many years. A safe house, as you will."

I felt a sting on my shoulder and gasped. I touched the area where Roehl had marked me. His bite had created a partial bond between us. A bond that would let him know where I was.

"Roehl marked me," I said.

Nicolae walked casually to a cabinet and opened it up, taking out a glass and a bottle filled with amber liquid. "Don't worry, Calla. As soon as I touched you, the bond between you and Roehl was broken."

I shook my head. "How did you know?"

He turned back to me with a glimmer in his eye. "Roehl is not the only gifted one in the family."

My head was still spinning, my heart still breaking. I knew once the adrenaline wore off, I would be in a world of pain and agony.

"How did you find me? Roehl said that place was heavily warded."

"It was our connection, and the blood we share. I told you it cannot easily be traced or broken."

"He killed my father," I breathed. I was still in shock over his death. I didn't want to accept it. I couldn't. It all happened too fast, and I didn't even have a chance to say a proper goodbye.

Nicolae set his drink down and walked over to me, wrapping his arms around me in a tight embrace. As soon as he did, a well of emotion sprung up inside of me. Tears and sobs ripped from my chest.

"I'm so sorry, child. I'm sorry I didn't get the chance to meet my son. And I'm sorry I wasn't there to save him."

"You would have loved him. He was the best man I've ever known. He gave his life to save Trystan. He …" the words stopped in my throat and the tears were never ending.

My father was the most selfless man. A man who loved me so much, he gave his life for me … for my happiness.

Nicolae stroked my hair, holding me tight, just like my father used to. "He sounds like he grew into a wonderful man. Will you tell me about him one day? I'd like to hear more."

I nodded, because words were too difficult to speak.

My heart was crushed, battered and broken beyond words. I had lost both of my parents within the span of months. I'd just gotten the chance to see my father since I left Sartha. He'd been running for his life, avoiding Roehl. And when I had the chance to finally see him, Roehl ruthlessly murdered him.

I closed my eyes and envisioned my father meeting my mother in the In Between. I saw him running toward her, through the tunnel of light, both of them with tears of joy in their eyes. When they reached each other, they embraced and cried, laughed and kissed.

I envisioned them hand-in-hand, smiling at each other, as a bright light encompassed them, and they crossed over into the next realm. I believed they were together again. They were happy. And they were still in love.

That vision gave me the strength to move on. I knew it was possible because I had visited my mother in the In Between.

"You will see both of them again. One day." Nicolae sucked

in a deep breath and exhaled, waiting patiently until I had no more tears left to cry.

I was glad he was here to offer me support, and I knew if anyone could help me defeat Roehl, it would be him. He knew about Incendia's powers. He knew how to use them, and he was very powerful himself.

"Erro took my father's body somewhere."

Nicolae took a step back and looked at me. "Your father is safe. Erro is preserving his body."

"Why would he do that?"

"Because Erro is a very good friend of mine." His golden eyes glimmered. "The Wanderers had no choice, Calla. Roehl threatened them."

"I know," I sighed. "Erro told me why they had to obey him. He threatened to kill their families. I know it's not their fault. I just miss my parents so much."

"Once this is all over, if we are still alive, we will bury your parents together."

I glanced up into his eyes, my heart mending just a bit more. "Thank you."

At least I had Nicolae. He would never be able to fill the gaping, oozing void left from the death of my parents, but he was still family. And I wasn't completely alone.

I walked over to the bedroom and peeked in. Trystan was lying there, so still. I watched his chest rise and fall, thankful he was still alive.

"Roehl forced a vial of liquid down his throat before he fled. Can you tell what it was or what it has done?"

Nicolae walked into the room and sat next to Trystan. He placed his hand directly in the middle of his chest and closed his eyes. When he opened them, he shook his head.

"I'm sorry. I don't know what he gave him. But there is nothing wrong with his breathing or his heart. He seems to be in good health. I guess we'll just have to wait and see."

"He said that he would forget me and would never love me."

The crease between Nicolae's brow deepened and he let out a deep sigh.

"He probably used the Lethe potion."

"Lethe potion? What is that?" My already aching chest began to ache a little more.

"It is a potion that causes the one who drinks it to forget their past. Roehl has used this many times before. He's learned to target specific memories and wipe them away."

I felt my heart shatter again. "So, when he wakes, he won't remember me?"

Nicolae's eyes saddened. "I don't know. We will have to see."

A sudden knock at the door caused my insides to jump.

Nicolae gave me a broad smile. "You have guests."

I had guests? I turned around and when Nicolae opened the door, my heart swelled, and tears fell from my eyes.

CHAPTER FIVE

Sabine stepped in with a scowl on her face, head slightly tilted to the side, hands planted firmly on her hips. "Why the hell did you leave without telling us? We are supposed to be a team, Calla," she barked. Behind her was Thalia, Markus, and Kai.

She then took in my face and chest and gasped, probably seeing the blood smeared on me. "Goddess. You're bleeding, Calla. Are you hurt?"

"No, it's not my blood." Tears burned my already swollen eyes. I shook my head, body trembling.

"She lost her father. Roehl murdered him," Nicolae replied.

"Goddess above," Sabine breathed. She threw her arms around me. "I'm so sorry, Calla."

"I'm sorry," I sobbed. "I had to leave quickly. It's Roehl we are dealing with. I couldn't let him hurt any of you."

Sabine pulled away, her eyes narrowed on me. "Oh, but you would go in without help and let him hurt *you*?"

I couldn't answer. Because no matter what answer I gave, they wouldn't understand.

She let out a breath and threw her arms around me again. Then, I felt others around me. Thalia came first, then Markus and Kai joined in.

"I'm sorry for your loss." Markus gently patted my back.

Thalia repeated what he said, stroking my hair.

"I'm sorry, Sea Star. But you should have answered me. You are not alone," Kai added.

Hearing my friends, knowing they were surrounding me, made me weep even more.

When I was able to speak, I asked, "How did you all know to come here?"

It was Nicolae who replied. "When I connected us, I also connected with Kai. I told him what was happening, and to have him meet you here. I figured he must have been a true friend for you to connect with him."

I nodded and looked at Kai. "He is." Kai gave a dashing smile.

"How is Kylan?" I asked, knowing he had been on the brink of death, an arrow through his chest, when I'd left him in Aquaria.

"Kylan is well and healing. The arrow missed all vital parts. He'll be up and slaying bad guys in no time."

"That's good." I was relieved to know he was healing.

Sabine grabbed my hand and squeezed. "Where is Trystan?"

I wiped my eyes and pointed to the bedroom.

They all moved to the doorway and peeked inside.

"Gods, he took a beating," Markus said. "How did you manage to get away?"

I shrugged my shoulders. "My power came to me when I needed it most. But Roehl and his mages disappeared before I could do anything." I looked at Trystan, at his battered body. "Roehl gave Trystan a potion before he left."

"What kind?" Thalia asked.

Nicolae's voice came from behind. "From what Calla told me, I believe it was the Lethe potion."

"Lethe. That's not good," Markus replied with a deep sigh. "Roehl uses the Lethe potion combined with his magic. With that, he can erase a person's specific memories, or even alter them." Markus must have known, being Morbeth's Captain of the Guard.

Sabine's eyes widened as she finally noticed Nicolae. I stepped back, introducing him to my friends. "I'd like you all to meet my grandfather. Nicolae Corvus."

"Goddess above," Thalia exhaled, throwing a hand over her chest. "I have heard tales of you in Incendia. The child of Princess Leora who most thought was dead. But there were tales that you had escaped Morbeth's wrath. I never thought in a million years I would ever meet you." She swallowed hard. "You are a legend to our people."

Nicolae's brow raised as he glanced at me, and I smiled.

"I can totally tell he is related," Sabine said, walking over to him. "You both have the exact same color eyes." She held out her hand to Nicolae. "It's so nice to meet you. I am Sabine, Calla's friend."

"One of my best friends," I added, and she gave me a broad

smile. "She and Markus saved me in Morbeth."

Nicolae took her hand and lifted it, pressing his lips to the back of her fingers, and I swear I heard Sabine gasp.

"It's a pleasure to meet you, Sabine," he said gently. "Thank you for saving my granddaughter."

"You don't look like you could be a grandfather," Sabine laughed, making Nicolae grin.

She was right. Nicolae looked like he was in his mid-thirties.

I aimed a finger at Markus. "That is Markus, Morbeth's Captain of the Guard. He is a hero, and my protector."

If I didn't know any better, I thought I saw Markus blush. Nicolae walked over to him and held out his hand. "Markus, it is an honor," he said, bowing his head. "Thank you for protecting my granddaughter. I owe you my life."

I was taken aback by Nicolae's response.

Markus slapped a fist to his chest and bowed his head. "It is my pleasure. I serve your father and your granddaughter, and now, I am also in your service."

Nicolae placed a hand on Markus's shoulder. "You don't need to serve me. All I ask is that you continue to help me protect Calla."

"I will." Markus again bowed his head in agreement.

I don't know why, but that entire conversation made me emotional. Even Thalia and Sabine's eyes looked glossy.

Trystan moaned, so we all went to his room. I watched his eyes slowly flutter open.

"Trystan," I breathed, pushing past the others and making my way to him. I sat next to him on the bed and grabbed hold of his hand.

When his eyes met mine, he slowly pulled his hand away. Confusion riddled in his eyes. "Where am I?"

"You're safe," Nicolae said, stepping to my side. "You're a guest in my house."

"Who are you?" was Trystan's next question, his eyes looking between me and Nicolae.

"Trystan," I said softly, but there was no recollection in his eyes. He was looking at me like I was a complete stranger.

"How do you know my name?" he asked, studying my face.

"You claimed her, Trystan," Kai said, also stepping further into the room.

"Kai?" Trystan obviously remembered his friend. "Why are you here?"

"We're here to check on your ass," Kai snickered. "Roehl tried to kill you, but Calla saved your life."

"Roehl? Why would Roehl want to kill me? And who is Calla?"

"I am," I said softly. Trystan's azure eyes landed back on me. "Roehl only kidnapped you because he was jealous. He was jealous that you had claimed me, and that I had chosen you over him."

This time Markus spoke. "Roehl sent out a decree to capture anyone in Nicolae's bloodline. He was going to execute them because they were a threat to his throne. When you heard of this, you went to Sartha to claim Calla. You went there to save her."

"What?" Trystan sat up, raking his fingers through his hair. "Why would I do that?"

"Because you said you felt a connection between us." I was hoping that something would spark in him. But the more questions he asked, and answers he was given, the more confused he seemed to be.

Trystan shook his head, looking directly into my eyes. "I don't know you. And I don't feel a connection with you. I am engaged to be married. I have to leave."

It took everything inside of me not to walk out of the room. But I couldn't. Trystan had proved his love and loyalty to me. It was my turn to do the same and try to build back all the memories Roehl had stolen.

"You can't leave," Nicolae said, stepping in front of Trystan. "Roehl gave you a powerful potion that stripped away all memory of Calla and what you both went through. He wanted you to forget her. To forget what you both had together. You are not safe out there alone. He will come after you."

"Why would he do that?"

"Because you love her," Sabine finally said. "You claimed her and then sent your cadre to protect her. And when she was captured, you went into Morbeth and tried to bargain half of your kingdom's wealth for Calla's freedom. You even went to Incendia, in a freaking tornado, to save her."

"You're lying. I would never do anything like that, for any female."

For any female? Wow. That hurt.

"You did for her. And she's not just any female," Kai said.

Nicolae stepped in front of me, looking directly at Trystan. "You are under a spell, Trystan. Roehl used the Lethe potion on you. You were his prisoner, captured because you went to save Calla's father. He used you both as bait to lure Calla to him. And he wanted you to forget."

"Why? Why would he go through all that trouble?"

"Because Calla is a great threat to him. She is heir to both the Morbeth and Incendian throne."

Trystan's face was one of utter confusion. "Who are you?" Trystan asked Nicolae.

"I am her grandfather. Her father died while saving your life."

Trystan dropped his head into his hands and let out a heavy breath. "I don't remember anything." He slowly raised his head, his beautiful eyes meeting mine. "Especially you. I have no memory of you."

My heart crumbled to pieces. Trystan had told me the reason why he claimed me was because he felt a connection between us ... from a portrait of me. Maybe, with time, he would be able to feel that again.

"I need to get back to my kingdom," Trystan said, attempting to stand. But his legs were weak, making him drop back down onto the bed.

He glanced at his dirty bare chest and the already fading wounds and bruises. Assessing them, he grew quiet. I wondered what he must have been thinking. Did he remember how he got those bruises? Or was that wiped from his memory too?

"Come, Calla," Kai said, holding his hand out to me.

I took it and he pulled me up to my feet.

"Our connection has been broken," he murmured, looking down at our connected hands.

I nodded. "Roehl broke it when he marked me."

"Why don't you claim her Kai," Trystan said, startling me. "It seems like you two are close."

Kai let go of my hand and walked up to Trystan, his face serious, as were his luminous blue eyes. "Believe me, Trystan. I would have already claimed her if I could." His head twisted back to look at me and there was a sadness swirling within them. Then, he turned back to Trystan. "But her heart belongs to you. I don't know why, but she loves your freaking ass." Kai shook his head. "She's never looked at me the way she looks at you. And as much as I'd not like to admit it, you two *do* have something special. When you are together, everyone around can feel that connection. And I wish, for Calla's sake, I could slap those freaking memories back into that thick skull of yours."

Trystan shook his head. "Maybe I don't want those memories back. Maybe it's better this way. Especially if I am to be married soon."

"Do you love her?" Kai asked. "Do you truly love Princess Ivy of Northfall?"

Trystan paused, his eyes distant. "It's not about love. It's about joining two kingdoms for a greater cause. And in time, I believe we could grow to love each other."

I couldn't even look at Trystan. Hearing those words come

from his lips… it was tearing me into pieces, crushing every part of me. Just a few days ago, he was willing to run away with me.

Maybe this was Karma.

Maybe I was suffering because I broke his heart and rejected his proposal—to be together despite what everyone else thought.

Heat surged through me.

"Calla, I think you need to take a breather and cool down a bit," Kai said, his eyes narrowed.

I glanced down to see my body engulfed in flames and turned to see Trystan wide-eyed, gaping at me.

Shit. That's all I needed … was for Trystan to see me like this, a freak of nature.

He was staring at me with a look I couldn't read, and I couldn't tell if he was horrified or confused. If his memory was wiped clean, he wouldn't know I could wield fire.

Nicolae casually walked over and placed a hand on my shoulder. His touch was cool and instantly quenched my fire and the insurmountable pain in my chest. I was thankful he was here, not only for the help he had already given, but for the extra support I would need in the forthcoming days.

"Come, Calla," Nicolae said, taking hold of my hand and leading me out of the room.

Markus, Sabine, and Thalia followed us into a dining room that had a long table and chairs. After we all sat down, everyone remained silent. But there was a thickness in the air. A heaviness filled with so many questions and worries.

I could hear Kai and Trystan in the other room, but their conversation was muffled.

"Everything will be alright," Sabine said. "There is no way Trystan cannot feel anything when he is around you."

I just smiled at her, hoping she was right, knowing he might not ever feel that way again. Right now, the Trystan I knew was gone, and I wasn't sure if he would ever return. And that alone would be a pain I would carry to my grave.

CHAPTER SIX

"Others have arrived," Nicolae announced, getting up from his seat and casually walking to the door.

I looked at my friends, and they all looked just as baffled as I was. There wasn't a knock, or any other noise to signal us that anyone was here, other than Kai and Trystan talking in the other room. But when Nicolae swung open the door, I immediately saw a familiar, intimidating face and dashed off my seat.

"Brone!" I hollered, running toward him. A broad smile rose on his lips.

Stepping inside, he opened his arms and caught me as I ran to him, swinging me around in a circle. He then set me down and looked me over.

"You're still alive. That's pretty impressive."

I shrugged, so happy to see him again. "I try."

Brone laughed and stepped aside, revealing Feng and Andrés standing side-by-side behind him. They both bowed and gave me warm smiles.

"It's good to see you again, Calla," Feng said. "Is Trystan here?"

"He is." I turned around to see Trystan and Kai standing behind us.

Brone tipped his head to both of them. "Trystan, it's good to see you alive, but you look like shit," Brone said in his deep, gruff voice.

"I feel like shit," Trystan responded. "It's good to see your asses alive as well." Trystan looked at each of his cadre and then at me. "You all know her?" He asked his cadre, directing his finger at me.

Brone let out a barking laugh, but Trystan's face was stone, complete seriousness, and it made me feel uncomfortable. This was a side of him I had never seen.

"Of course, we know her," Andrés replied, stepping in beside me, his face also riddled with questions.

"How? How do you know her?" Trystan asked again, his eyes staring fixedly on his cadre.

"This is a joke, right?" Brone's deep voice questioned, glancing sideways at me. I shook my head.

"Do I look like I'm joking?" The tone of Trystan's voice made me shudder.

Brone let out a loud huff. "Gods, you're in a foul mood. When was the last time you fed?"

I looked at each of his men—his most trusted core. His cadre. "Roehl gave him the Lethe potion. He doesn't remember me."

Their eyes went wide, and brows knitted with shock.

Brone wrapped a muscular arm around my shoulder, his eyes on Trystan as he pointed his large finger at me. "Are you telling me you don't remember her? This girl who you'd never met but traveled across the continent to claim and then sent us to protect? This girl who kept your mind and heart occupied ever since you held her portrait. Not to mention, the endless nights you stayed awake, searching for answers to help save her and her family? To top all of that, you willingly gave her your blood, so she could heal."

"What?" Nicolae snapped, wrenching his gaze toward me. The look in his narrowed eyes reminded me of my father. The side that was protective of me.

"Nothing happened," I said, holding up my hands. "I had used my power to fight Roehl in Incendia and was very weak. I hadn't fed in days, so Trystan gave me some of his blood so I could heal faster. After that, I fell asleep."

It was mostly true. I'd only left out the part that his blood had made me horny as hell and had me practically clawing and throwing myself at him. And then he did— goddess above—he did the most incredible things to me using those fingers, mouth, tongue, teeth to pleasure me. Warmth bloomed inside my core and across my cheeks just thinking about it.

Trystan's brow crumpled, as if he were trying to pull these memories from the recesses of his mind. But those eyes still remained void of any recollection.

"You seriously don't remember her at all?" Andrés asked, his brow crumpling.

Trystan's bewildered gaze moved to me, studying me with piercing scrutiny and shook his head. Again, my heart shattered, the pieces scattering across the floor.

"Does this mean she's up for grabs?" Andrés came up beside me linking his arm in mine and gave me a wink. "Hey, Calla."

"Hey, Andrés." I returned a sad smile. "The answer to your question is no."

I knew he was playing, and I was thankful Trystan's cadre was on my side. If anyone could convince Trystan, it would be these men, plus Kylan. They knew him best. Knew his secrets. What made him tick and what ticked him off.

Feng walked past and pivoted to face us, his eyes narrowed to slits, glaring at Brone and Andrés.

"No jokes right now. Leave Calla alone. She's had enough bullshit to last a lifetime."

Feng then strode to Trystan and assessed his wounds. He pulled a small flask out from a pouch hanging at his side and handed it to him. Trystan unscrewed the cap and downed the contents. We stood still and witnessed the rest of his bruises fade and wounds mend. To be honest, it was one of the few things I liked about being part vampire. We did get injured, but once blood entered our system—healing us inside and out—the superficial wounds mending instantly.

Kai cleared his throat. "Kylan should be arriving soon. He was in Aquaria under my physician's care."

"Is Kylan injured?" Trystan looked genuinely concerned, and Feng was the one who replied.

"You ordered us to follow you to Aquaris to save Calla's father, who was captured by Roehl. We were ambushed and surrounded by hundreds of his men. Kylan was struck with an arrow in his chest but managed to get away, but Roehl's mages targeted you. When they subdued your power and cuffed your wrists with magic, we had no choice but to back down and regroup."

Kai then added, "According to Kylan, he found an Aquarian who brought him directly to Aquaria so he could tell Calla what had happened. When she learned that you and her father were captured, she left—*in the middle of a ball my kingdom was throwing in her honor*—to save you." Kai turned his icy blue eyes to me. "She ignored me," he muttered, a brow slanting in heavy disapproval, "even though I called to her over and over through our bond. But she made me promise to take care of her friends."

"I'm sorry," I exhaled. "I couldn't bear putting any of you in danger."

Kai offered me a devilish grin, then turned to Trystan. "Calla may not have admitted it out loud, but everyone—hell, even a blind man could see that she loves you just as much as you love her."

Trystan shook his head and raked his fingers through his onyx hair. "How can I love someone I know nothing about? I have no memory of her, nor do I have any feelings." He then took a step toward me, his azure eyes much brighter since he'd consumed the blood Feng had given him. "They are telling me these stories of us, but I look at you and I see a stranger."

He squeezed his eyes shut, the muscles in his jaw tensed. "Maybe it's better this way," he said. "I am engaged to be married soon. My father and my kingdom are depending on me."

"I understand." My heart was tearing in two, but I feigned a smile.

As much as I tried to hold in my emotions, a damned tear somehow escaped my eye and rolled down my cheek.

"Yes, it's probably for the best," Markus added. Sabine inhaled sharply and slapped his arm. Hard.

"What?" Markus yelped, rubbing his battered limb.

"It's not for the best!" she blurted, tears flooding her eyes. "You don't know anything about love, Markus." Sabine whirled around and stormed out of the room.

Markus glanced over to Thalia, blinking with wide doe eyes. Thalia shrugged, but I knew why Sabine was so emotional. She knew the connection Trystan and I had. She loved him and had been rooting for us all along.

The room fell quiet until Kai charged forward and grabbed hold of my hand.

"This is bullshit. Come with me, Calla." Kai's eyes were like cold chips of ice, his face rigid with anger. He yanked me outside, away from all the others, leading me down the pathway that led to the sea. Away from all the vampire ears in Nicolae's house.

When we reached the shore, he sat me down on a rock and paced back and forth.

"I don't know how a freaking potion could completely erase the memory of one person. There has to be a way to get it back."

His eyes connected with mine, deeply concerned.

Kai was a good friend. A loyal and true friend. One I was glad to have on my side.

"What if he never gets it back?" I breathed.

I hated to think Trystan would forget me forever. I couldn't even think about it, because doing so would push my already fragile emotions over the edge. I was barely holding back another wave of tears.

"Then, maybe I might have a shot?" Kai paused a minute, taking in my befuddled expression, then started laughing. "In all seriousness, there has to be a part of Trystan that feels you two are connected. Especially after hearing the testimony from all of us and his men." Kai paced a while more, looking out over the sea. He suddenly turned back to me, a glimmer in those luminous blue eyes. "If we can't bring back his memory, then maybe we have to make him fall back in love with you."

That sounded crazy, because he seemed pretty sure about his marriage to Princess Ivy of Northfall. But I'd hear Kai out. I was just interested in … "How?"

A sly grin rose on his handsome face. "We make him jealous."

"Jealous?" Trystan didn't seem like the type that would be jealous. Protective, yes. "I'm not sure Trystan would get jealous."

"He doesn't. Not with any other girl. But with you… he most definitely can be. I've known him since we were infants. And I watched him up there, while he was looking at you.

He was battling within his own mind. Trystan won't admit it, but I would bet my life that he does feel some kind of connection when he looks at you. What you both shared wasn't some fling. It was real. Real enough for him to seek you out and do whatever he could to try to save you and your family. We just have to draw that back out of him. He is a stubborn bastard. But he is also very loyal. He would give his life to defend those he loves."

I nodded, knowing everything he said was true. Trystan was honorable and loyal.

But now that he'd forgotten me, I felt the hole in my chest grow even darker, colder.

"I wouldn't know how to act or what to do," I said honestly. Just the thought of trying to make him jealous was making me uncomfortable.

Kai walked up to me and took a knee, holding up his hand, revealing his tattoo. "If we're going to do this, we need to re-establish our connection."

I placed my palm against his and immediately felt our elements connect. Kai smiled and laced his fingers in mine, the veins in our arms glowing blue.

"Just follow my lead, Sea Star. On my part, it will be easy. But just know, this is for the greater good." I tilted my head to the side, wondering if Kai had ulterior motives. "If you want Trystan back, you'll have to trust me."

I sighed and looked out over the sea, watching the waves ebb and flow.

Trystan risked his life to save my father, and in turn, my father saved his life. I would do whatever it took to make him remember me.

Kai stood up and unlinked our fingers. "I'll need to talk to Nicolae. We need Trystan and his cadre if we have any chance of defeating Roehl. We need to make an agreement with him, to stick with us until Roehl is dead."

"Why would he stay and help me when he doesn't even remember me? We have no connection now, and like he said, he has a father and kingdom counting on him. He's also mentioned his fiancé repeatedly and that he will be married in a few months. It's annoying he didn't forget that."

Kai sighed loudly. "Yes, and he needs to avoid that relationship at all costs. Believe me, Calla. Trystan does *not* want to marry that Northfall bitch. There is no man I know who would take her hand, even with her wealth and status. Her parents have been trying to dump her off for years, but no prince in his right mind would take her. Roehl included. Which speaks volumes to her character.

"I truly believe that deep down, Trystan despises her and is only saying those things because he doesn't remember you and thinks he has no other choice. Like I said, leave the details to me. You just need to trust me. Take my lead and follow along. Okay?"

"Okay." I let out an exasperated breath. This was going to be uncomfortable.

"Good." He slapped his hands together with a sinister grin on his lips.

I narrowed my eyes, glaring at him. "You are a little too excited for this."

Kai grabbed my wrist and tugged me up from the rock. "Be worried, Sea Star," he chuckled. "Remember, just be yourself and let me do the rest." He let out another snickering laugh, then led me back up the pathway toward the house.

I just hoped that Kai didn't piss him off instead of making him jealous. I was putting my hope in him.

Goddess, please help me through this.

CHAPTER SEVEN

Back inside Nicolae's home, it felt a little cramped and claustrophobic. Not that it was small, by any means, but because the tension inside was ramped up. There were too many royals and warriors in one small space and so much pent-up testosterone.

Nicolae called for discussions with Kai, Markus, Trystan, and his cadre, probably discussing what was going to happen next with Roehl. I didn't mind that I wasn't in on it. I knew they would eventually let me know, but they had done this for countless years, and I had zero experience. I knew Nicolae was also looking out for my best interest. He didn't want me worrying about things I didn't have to. And I was grateful for that.

While they talked, Sabine, Thalia and I went outside and explored the small island, and I was happy to be alone with my girls again. We walked toward the back of the house and made our way to the opposite side of the island. I wanted to explore this small paradise that belonged to my grandfather.

"This entire island is Nicolae's?" Sabine questioned, giving the land a three-hundred-and-sixty-degree scan.

"Yes, he said it was."

I looked at the sea on one side and on the other, a huge mass of land. Nicolae said his island was off the coast of Carpathia. Trystan's country.

"Look! There's a trail that leads down to a small beach," Thalia noted, already heading in that direction. "Let's go swimming!"

"We don't have anything to swim in, or towels to dry off," Sabine noted.

I wiggled my fingers in front of her. "We don't need towels. I learned a new trick."

Sabine's brow furrowed. "You aren't going to use fire on us, are you?"

I shrugged, making her eyes widen, then burst out in laughter. "Of course not. I can pull the water out from your clothes and hair, leaving you completely dry."

She elbowed me in the side. "Did Kai teach you that trick?"

"As a matter of fact, he did."

Sabine linked her arm in mine. "Well, I can't wait to see it. Let's go swimming."

We both ran after Thalia, who was halfway down the trail. She had grown up on an island surrounded by water but seeing her so giddy made me happy. She had been so stiff and serious when we first met her. A guard of the island. Now, she was like a typical girl, carefree and just wanting to have some fun.

Reaching the small beach, we were in awe. It was not larger than a hundred yards, but the shore was covered in velvety white sand. On either side were beautiful shade trees and rocks to sit on. There were birds singing, and a gentle breeze blowing. The sun was bright and glittering across the crystal-clear water which was a light turquoise. So clear, you could see the sandy bottom.

Thalia began stripping down to her undergarments.

"Hey, there are men on this island," Sabine spluttered. Thalia turned with a devilish gleam in her eyes and shrugged. "You can go right ahead and swim in those heavy clothes, but I'm not. Besides, the men are busy trying to save the world from Roehl." Thalia flipped her golden hair over her shoulder and raced toward the water. She dove in, headfirst, and when she surfaced, turned to us with a bright and glittering smile on her face.

"Goddess, this feels amazing. Are you two coming in or not?"

Sabine gave me a sinister side-eyed glance, then began jogging toward the water, stripping off her clothes and tossing them on the sand along the way. When she was down to her undergarments, she dove in and let out a bellowing hoot as she surfaced. "Calla, what are you waiting for? Get your ass in here now!"

Shaking my head and laughing, I peeled off my clothes, placing them in a neat pile on the shore. Giving a war cry, I took off sprinting toward them.

It had been a long time since I'd not had to worry about death or Roehl or anything other than being eighteen. I needed this. Needed to remember that I was still allowed to have some fun. I know my parents would agree. I deserved moments of happiness. We all did.

I dove into the water, and gods, it felt refreshing. The cool water caressed my heated body and this time, I would enjoy it. floating on my back, I soaked up the heat of the sun while Sabine and Thalia swam around me, chatting about what they'd eaten for breakfast.

"What are you going to do about Trystan?" Sabine finally said to me, probably not wanting me to feel left out. But I didn't care. The banter between them kept my mind occupied and not stressing on things I couldn't fix.

I knew she was bothered by the situation, and because we were finally away from the guys in the house, she could finally speak freely.

"I don't know," I sighed, my chest starting to ache again. "He doesn't remember me at all, or anything that happened between us." I watched a cloud above transform from a dragon into a cute little bunny.

"Is there any spell that can counter it?" Thalia questioned.

"None that I know of."

"Kai was right," Sabine added. "It is bullshit, and it pisses me off because it's so obvious you two were meant to be together."

I sank under the water and came back up to see her melancholy expression.

"I know. I wish there was a magical spell to undo it. But if there is, no one knows it."

"How are you holding up?" Sabine definitely wasn't holding back on the questions.

"I'm fine."

Her brows arched, head tilted, arms crossed over her chest. "Calla, let's be real. You act like you're fine, but I know your heart is crushed. Trystan isn't just some guy. He's your soul mate. I mean … he felt a connection to you from a portrait—*a gods damned portrait*—of you and your parents. He has to feel something when he's looking at you. And if he doesn't, then I'm sorry, but he's dead."

"He's a vampire," Thalia noted. "So technically, he *is* dead."

Sabine's eyes rolled skyward.

"Hey now," I interjected. "When bitten, you do die, but then come back to life as an immortal. Unless you're born one, like Trystan."

Sabine laughed, tipping her head back into the water. "Girl, sometimes I forget you're part vampire."

"So do I," I sighed. "Except for when I'm hungry." I opened my mouth and let my incisors lengthen.

I swam toward them and both Sabine and Thalia screamed, swimming away from me.

Sabine suddenly stopped and faced me, splashing water at my face, making me squeal. The three of us laughed and splashed and were having a great time when Thalia suddenly stopped, her eyes wide with fear, her finger aiming out toward the sea.

"What the hell is that?" she screeched.

I turned to see three large dorsal fins heading straight for us.

Sharks. I hated sharks.

They had probably heard our splashing around and were coming for lunch.

Sabine and Thalia screamed and made a beeline for the shore, but there was no way they'd make it out in time. We were about fifty yards away and those sharks were coming fast.

Dark clouds began rolling in, covering the sun. I should have been concerned but had no time to waste. I had to deal with the immediate danger first. No shark was going to eat my friends.

Focusing, my water power kept me steady as I thrust my hands out in front of me, and a line of water shot out, following my movement. I smiled, feeling that this power was strong and wouldn't fail me. Concentrating, with my arms stretched out in front of me, the water around the sharks began to swirl, faster and faster, causing a spiraling vortex around them. I felt the power coursing through my veins, emanating out of my palms.

But this power felt much different from the fire. This power wasn't harsh and heated. It was cool and soothing.

Slowly raising my arms, the whirlpool of water followed my movement, rising into the sky. It continued to swirl, faster and faster, creating a waterspout. Within the spout were three massive sharks, each looked around fifteen feet long with razor-sharp teeth.

Thalia and Sabine were still swimming and splashing toward the shore.

Directing my attention to the dark blue water, at least a mile out, I slowly brought my arms back, then thrust them forward. Then, like a cannon being fired, the waterspout and sharks blasted out toward the sea, crashing into the dark water, causing a massive explosion. The sharks were no longer a threat.

Dropping my arms to the side, I gloated a bit. My power felt strong. Felt natural. And I didn't feel tired at all.

Suddenly, loud cheers erupted from behind me and when I turned, I saw Sabine and Thalia crawling onto the shore. But behind them, standing on the shore, were the men.

Kai, Markus, Nicolae, Brone and Andrés were on the beach, but Trystan and Feng were up on a ledge looking down.

As I swam toward them, I noticed Sabine and Thalia were on shore safely and already dressing. Sabine was explaining to Markus what had happened, and Thalia was heading toward Kai. But Kai didn't notice her and ran straight for me, standing at the water's edge. The waves washed over his bare feet.

His smile was bright, and his eyes were almost the same color as the sea.

"You never cease to amaze me," he marveled. "I'm very impressed."

I smiled widely. "You saw my shark tornado?"

"I did. It was pretty freaking amazing." Kai held his hand out to me and when I exited the water, his eyes widened, scanning my body from head to toe.

Andrés gave a whistle, and I suddenly felt naked, remembering I only had on my undergarments.

"Watch yourselves. That's my granddaughter," Nicolae warned.

I smiled at Nicolae, and he winked back. "The sky darkened. Is there trouble?"

"No," Kai answered. "We heard screams and because there are vampires, Nicolae had to summon clouds to block the sun. None of us realized the power he possesses. He seems just as strong as Roehl."

"The only difference is, Roehl uses forbidden, dark magic."

"Yeah, no one likes a cheater," he smirked. He removed his shirt and handed it to me, and I couldn't help but admire his abs. Just for a moment.

"Thanks, but I don't need it," I said, turning down his offer. "My clothes are right there." I pointed to my neatly folded pile of clothes not more than ten yards away. I hated the feeling of dry clothes on a wet body, so I raised my hands and called the water from my body and hair.

Water droplets formed and hovered around me, glimmering like thousands of crystal beads.

"Shit, Calla," Andrés blurted, fanning himself. "I think I need to take a dip in the cool sea."

With a flick of my wrist, I sent the water droplets toward him. They hit him like pellets, drenching his hair and face. Andrés gasped, wiping the water from his face.

Brone slapped a thick hand on his back and let out a boisterous laugh. "Feeling better, brother?"

"Calla," Andrés coughed. "That was not cool."

I shrugged and grinned at him. "You said you needed to cool off, so I helped."

Everyone started laughing, and when I looked up at the ledge above, I even saw Trystan smiling. But as soon as his eyes connected with mine, the smile vanished.

Gods, this sucked, and it was annoying as hell.

I quickly dressed, and something caught my eye. Another figure came walking down the trail toward the beach, and I knew exactly who it was. When he saw me, he began jogging toward me, and when he reached me, wrapped me in a hug.

I hugged him back. "Kylan! Gods, it's so good to see you." I stepped back and assessed him. "You look like you've completely healed."

"I'm alive because of the Aquarians." His gaze turned to Kai who was standing behind me. He placed a fist to his heart and bowed his head. "Thank you, Kai."

Kai smiled and gave him a nod. "I'm glad we were able to help. Calla was the one who demanded help. My healer just happened to be nearby and heard her yelling, begging for someone to help you."

Kylan turned back to me with a furrowed brow and a sad smile. "Thank you, Calla. I'm so happy to see you alive. And I cannot thank you enough for going to Aquaris and saving Trystan. You are one of the bravest people I know." He placed a fist over his heart and bowed his head to me.

Tears burned my eyes. "My father was the one who saved Trystan. But I wasn't able to stop Roehl from pouring a gods damned potion down his throat."

Kylan placed a gentle hand on my shoulder, and I glanced up to see Trystan watching us closely. I wondered if he could hear what we were saying. Who was I kidding? He was a pureblood vampire. He could hear every word. And the wind was in his favor.

"They told me what happened, but don't lose hope, Calla," Kylan said. "It will take some time. The Lethe potion ruins lives. And from what Trystan told me, it not only erased his memory of you, but I think Roehl also wanted him to hate you."

"He told you that?"

Kylan nodded. "Roehl is a bastard who has turned many friends against each other using that potion and combining it with his dark magic."

My heart was throbbing again. "Did he say he hates me?"

I wasn't sure if I wanted to know the answer. His cold indifference was already a yes.

"No. He didn't say that. He just said his mind is telling him that you are his enemy."

What the hell?

"Look, we are all here to help Trystan remember. We all know what happened between the two of you, and we all know the connection you had. It may take some time, but I believe we can get him to see."

I nodded, wishing I hadn't pulled the water off my skin so they couldn't see the tears falling down my face. "Thanks, Kylan."

I missed Trystan so much. The way he could melt me with a look. And always seemed to find me, even when I was floating on a pirate ship in the middle of the Sangerian Sea.

The Trystan on the ledge was someone I didn't recognize. His eyes were hollow. That damned potion had not only taken his memory, but it was also making him hate me.

Kylan bowed to me and Kai before making his way back up to where Trystan and Feng were standing.

Trystan's eyes were fixed on me, but when Kai came up to my side and took my hand in his, he turned and walked away.

Turning to Kai, I glared at him. In turn, he winked back, shooting me a dashing smile.

"Don't worry, Sea Star. It's all part of the plan."

I sighed, deep and pitiful. "It better be."

CHAPTER EIGHT

Over the next few days, we laid low.

Every time I looked over at Trystan, he was staring at me with a look I didn't understand. It was as if he was trying to weigh what everyone had said inside his mind, but he was having trouble.

Kai hadn't made a move or said anything since the beach, and for that I was thankful. I wasn't sure if I could handle the stress of him trying to make Trystan jealous. I wasn't even sure if it would work, or if it would make him hate me even more.

That night we all sat around the dinner table, and I made sure Sabine and Thalia were on either side of me. Markus was next to Sabine, and Kai next to Thalia. They were all talking and laughing, and I was in the middle feeling awkward and uncomfortable. Uncomfortable because Trystan and his men were sitting directly across from us.

Nicolae sat at the head of the table, watching everyone closely. And it was Brone who finally started a conversation with me.

"Calla, do you remember the first time we met?"

I smiled at him, thinking back to the cave. "That was a meeting I will never forget. The first time I saw you I was terrified. But you surprised me, Brone. You are a gentle giant."

Andrés began to pet the top of Brone's head. "Yes, very gentle."

With a swift move, a move I could barely see, Brone had Andrés' hand twisted behind his back.

"Don't ever pet me again," Brone growled.

Andrés moaned, his eyes clenched in pain. "No petting. You're not gentle. You're a beast."

Brone let go of his hand, then glanced over to me, giving me a wink that made me giggle. "You got that right. And it's best you remember it," he said, roaring into Andrés's face.

"Calla, remember our dance at the Shadow Fest?" Kylan added.

I choked on the water I'd just sipped. "Oh gods, yes. Actually, it was with you in Lord Huxley's body. I didn't want to dance with you."

"You did have a look of utter disgust on your face," Kylan said, laughing. "I don't blame you. I would have been disgusted if I had to dance with Lord Huxley too." Kylan took a sip of the crimson liquid in his glass. "I wonder what happened to the old man."

"He's dead," I replied, trying not to remember the gruesome way his death took place. "When Roehl found out that Brynna was gone, he blamed Lord Huxley. Roehl fed on him, then ripped out his throat, right in front of me."

"Goddess," Sabine gasped, taking hold of my hand. "Is that the same time he took Spring?"

I nodded, not wanting to relive that horrible memory.

"Who is Spring?" Thalia asked.

Sabine squeezed my fingers and answered for me. "She is a young girl. A maid. She and her mother were given charge to care for Calla," Sabine said. "When Brynna disappeared, Roehl also took Spring, thinking she might have helped Brynna escape. Then, the bastard told Calla to feed on her as punishment for not telling him who took Brynna."

Kylan's eyes widened, because none of them had heard this before. "What happened?"

Kylan knew I was a newly turned vampire, and he'd seen me give in to the bloodlust.

I swallowed hard and looked at him. I could feel Trystan's eyes boring, scrutinizing me too. "I had to feed on her, because if I didn't, he would have—he would have killed her."

Markus leaned forward, placing his elbows on the table. "I was there. I witnessed the entire event. Every man in that room could feel Calla's pain. I could see how badly she wanted the girl to live. She wouldn't let Roehl touch the girl, so she agreed to feed off of her." Markus shook his head and let out a loud breath. "We all thought the girl was going to die, but in the middle of the feeding, Calla stopped and saved that girl's life.

96

"I know that every man in that room stood in awe. She not only stood up to Roehl, but she proved how mentally strong she was. She was a new vampire, who overcame the bloodlust and unlatched during the middle of feeding, which was something no other man in that room could have done, including me."

Everyone stayed quiet. This was the first time Trystan and his men had heard this story and by the looks on their faces, they were in shock. Even Nicolae's eyes widened, but he also stayed silent.

"If you are Morbeth's Captain of the Guard, why are you here?" Trystan asked Markus.

"I am here to protect her, as ordered by King Romulus. But even if he hadn't ordered it, I would have come of my own free will." Markus looked at me and smiled. "Calla is special. She is kind, brave, selfless, and recklessly offers her life to save others." Markus leaned forward and gave me a glaring stare. "Don't you *ever* leave without telling me where you are going. You could have died, and I wasn't there to protect you."

I hated that everyone felt like they had to protect me but was thankful they would.

"Yes, I could have died, but Roehl wants you dead just as much as me. I couldn't risk that."

"You are not my protector, Calla," Markus snapped, slapping his fist on the table.

I looked dead into his eyes, tears now streaming down my face. "No, I am not. And I'm sorry for leaving the way I did. But I am still my own person. I won't watch Roehl murder anyone who is trying to protect me. Especially my friends. Especially those I love." I stood, about to walk away, but stopped with hot tears pooling in my eyes. I then turned my attention to Trystan. "Roehl wanted me. He captured you and my father as bait to lure me to him, because he knew you were the one thing I couldn't resist.

"I went to Aquaris to do whatever it took to keep you safe. Why? Because you saw me before I even knew you. You claimed me when you thought you had no other choice. You came into Morbeth to bargain for my freedom, even when you knew Roehl would never give it. And even though your father arranged your marriage, you came to me and held out your hand and told me to run away with you. That's why I went alone. Because it was my turn to give back to you. And I was willing to do whatever it took to save you, even if it was with my life."

Trystan didn't say a word and the expression on his face, embedded in his beautiful azure eyes, was unreadable. But before I saw anything that would break my heart even more than it already was, I turned and walked away.

I heard a chair pull back across the wooden floor and turned to see Kai standing.

I held up my hand and smiled at him. "I'd like to be alone."

He nodded and sat back down while I headed outside.

I couldn't breathe in the house. The tension was too heavy, and my emotions were haywire. It felt like every time I had a conversation, I ended up crying.

The night breeze was soft and cool and felt wonderful against my heated skin. I sucked it in and exhaled, taking the pathway down to the shoreline in front of the house.

The moonlight was dim but glinted like thousands of crystals across the top of the water. The sound of the water crashing against the rocky shoreline reminded me of my home.

I closed my eyes and thought back to that simpler time, not too long ago. I missed my porch and my chair and my books, and the little bird that would come and visit me. I also missed my horse Shadow.

But most of all, I missed my parents. I missed their faces, their smiles, their voices, and their warm hugs. My stomach clenched and chest ached as I let out a deep and sorrowful wail. I fell to my knees, onto that sandy shore, and everything… all the pain and death and worry and stress and hate and love started pouring out of me. I travailed over all that had transpired since my eighteenth birthday, because at this moment, there was nothing else I could do.

Was I destined to live a life without happiness, constantly running for my life? Would Roehl always be one step ahead of me, or would I ever defeat him?

Right now, I was living a cursed life. But there was so much more. I was greater than this. I wasn't going to let the darkness overwhelm me. I was fire. I was light. And I would change my course because I had no other choice but to do so. Because the darkness was quickly closing in on me, making it hard to breathe. And even harder to live.

I pulled myself up onto a stone and gazed into the eggplant-colored sky. About a hundred yards up, two black birds soared. I immediately knew one of them was Flint, and the other was Nyx. Flint had brought her here, to Trystan.

Or maybe Nyx already knew he was here because they also shared a special connection.

I held out my arm as they descended, and Flint swooped down and landed on my left wrist.

"Hey, you," I said, running a hand down his silky feathers. He ruffled them, then looked directly at me and cawed. He was growing on me and always seemed to come when I needed him.

Nyx landed on a rock nearby, but I held out my right arm and as if she could read my mind, she flew over and landed on my other wrist.

"What have you two been doing? Causing trouble out there?" I sniffled.

Flint cawed loudly and tilted his little head to the side and those fiery eyes fixed on me, seemed sad.

"I know. Don't mind me. I'm an emotional wreck right now."

He hopped up my arm and nestled his head against my cheek, as if he was trying to comfort me.

"I'll be fine," I breathed. "I just needed a good cry."

Tears were threatening to fill my eyes again. But I wouldn't allow them to. I'd cried enough for a lifetime, and I didn't have the strength to do it anymore.

I heard a sound and turned toward the path, watching a figure amble down the trail toward me. By the silhouette alone, I knew it was Trystan.

Kylan and Markus were also outside, but stayed near the house, probably making sure nothing happened between us.

As Trystan came closer, his eyes caught on Nyx, who was sitting on my wrist.

"Go to him," I whispered to her, raising my arm. Nyx flew toward Trystan, landing on his shoulder.

He paused as he reached the bottom of the pathway about twenty feet away from me, those azure eyes studying me and Flint. "How do you know Nyx?"

I smiled sadly, hating that he didn't remember. But I would gladly relive every moment with him in my memory if I had to.

"When you claimed me, we shared a partial bond and whenever I slept, we would meet. During one of those sessions, I met Nyx for the first time. At the time, I was hidden in a cave with your cadre when you showed me, through Nyx's eyes, that Roehl and his men were coming for us."

Trystan raked his fingers through his thick raven hair, his eyes went distant, gazing out at the dark sea.

"Everyone is telling me we are connected, but my mind has no memory of you. Not even a trace. I look at you and see a complete stranger. A stranger I have no feelings for." He paused, shaking his head, his eyes wincing. "There are these voices in my head constantly telling me that you are my enemy, and I cannot trust you. Whenever you are near, they grow louder and stronger."

The ache in my chest grew.

From the beginning, Trystan said he felt a connection between us. Was there really nothing now? Was Roehl really that powerful that he could sever the bond between us?

I sent Flint into flight and Nyx flew after him. But they stayed close, circling overhead in the darkened sky.

I stood to face Trystan and … *gods*. The way the moonlight glinted off the panes of his face made my heart thrum louder. So loud, I knew with his acute hearing, he heard it too.

I took a few steps toward him but not too close. Just close enough that we could see each other clearly.

A gentle breeze wrapped around us, carrying his scent—that perfect blend of everything I loved. I closed my eyes and breathed it, savoring the wonderful way it made me feel. The way his closeness made me feel.

Opening my eyes, Trystan was searching my face, and I wished he could find some trace of familiarity. Even a glint would be better than nothing.

Gods, how I wanted him to snap out of it and pull me into his arms. To hold me and kiss me like he had in Aquaria and say this was some horrible nightmare.

Looking into those penetrating eyes that held so many questions, I was swept up in a wave of emotion. Tears of remorse flowed down my face.

"I'm so sorry, Trystan. I'm sorry you were caught up in the middle of this mess, when you had nothing to do with it. You don't deserve this.

"I wish Roehl had given me the potion instead, because my heart gets shredded to pieces every time you look at me like I'm a total stranger. Like you despise me. Like we've never touched or kissed or shared a partial blood bond.

"I wish I could take away this gaping, oozing hole in my heart because I *know* we belong together, Trystan. Yes, it took me a while to accept it. I wish I could turn back time and be given another chance, because now, I see it's too late.

"Maybe it's what I deserve, because I never thought I was good enough for you. You are a pureblood Prince of Carpathia. You are trustworthy, kind, and an honorable man. A man I've grown to love wholeheartedly. And yet, here I am …" I couldn't even finish the words, my tears unrelenting. I still wasn't sure where I fit into his world. Or even if I fit in at all. But I had to know…

"When you look at me now, do you feel… *anything?*"

Trystan's eyes strayed to the sea, his gaze unreadable, jaw tightened, and hands fisted at his side.

Then, those glimmering azure eyes turned and met mine.

"My mind is telling me to hate you, but my heart won't allow it." He then tucked his hands in his pockets and walked away.

Tears fell in currents down my already drenched face as I watched him leave. I didn't expect those words, and they left me reeling.

His beautiful heart. That compassionate, unyielding, and unwavering heart… felt something. It meant there might be hope for us after all.

Even if it was a sliver, it was something.

That night I couldn't sleep. My mind was a whirlwind, distracted by those words Trystan had spoken down at the shore.

I was glad he had come, and I was able to pour out my heart to him. At least he now knew how I felt. And I had gotten a glimpse into his mind.

There was a war waging inside of him, Trystan's ardent heart was still in there, fighting like it always had. *For me. For us.*

I'd bet Roehl had never expected for this to happen. For everyone to rally around us. But he truly never anticipated the power of love—a tried-and-true love—or the power of a heart as fierce and passionate as Trystan's. Because he never experienced it himself.

In the end, we would see which was stronger—Trystan's heart or Roehl's spell.

I had already placed my bet.

CHAPTER NINE

The next morning, I woke to loud voices outside my room. Sabine and Thalia shared a room with me, and when I glanced over, I noticed their beds and the room was empty.

I groaned, my body ached, my stomach rumbled with hunger. I had taken a few sips of blood before I'd left the table last night, but that wasn't enough. Especially after the shark tornado feat yesterday. Ultimately, I felt fine, but everything that happened yesterday was weighing heavily on me. And I knew that blood—ruby wine, as the Aquarian's called it—was the only remedy.

My mind instantly went back to Aquaria, and the powerful, delicious taste of Trystan's blood and how it made me feel. All those euphoric and sensual feelings that vibrated through my core and entire body. I moaned, just thinking about it.

"Umm, are you going to wake up anytime soon? Or are you just going to lie in bed and moan like you're having the best damn sex dream ever?" Sabine giggled.

"Sabine," I gasped. "There are men in this house with super hearing." She shrugged and I laughed, tossing my pillow at her. "Go away. I don't want to get out of bed yet."

"Mm-hm. You were dreaming. And I'll bet my breakfast I know who it was about."

"I was moaning because I didn't want to get out of this warm and comfortable bed."

"Yeah. Sure you were," she snarled, crossing her arms over her chest. "Anyway, Nicolae wanted me to come and get you." She gave a dramatic bow. "You are wanted at the dining table, Princess Calla," she said with a heavy accent.

"Why?"

She shrugged. "I guess they have some important news to discuss. I also don't know what it's about, so don't ask me." She winked and turned but paused after a step. "Don't forget to brush your hair and teeth before you come."

As I entered the dining area, everyone was already seated with serious faces. Goddess, were all of them early risers?

"Good morning, Sea Star," Kai chimed, offering me a broad smile.

I gave him a grin and a slight bow of my head. "Good morning, highness."

His smile immediately fell, and I swear I heard a growl exit his lips, which made me giggle.

"You got me," he murmured through our newly established bond.

"Serves you right."

"I said Sea Star. There is nothing royal about that."

"Well, Sea Star is our thing. It's not everyone else's,"

"It's a nickname. Unless you would rather I call you Princess?"

"Nope."

"Are you two talking through that bond again?" Thalia asked, pointing between me and Kai.

Kai raised his brow, glancing at her. "How did you know?"

"Because you're both looking at each other like you're having a conversation, but your mouths aren't moving."

"We are," Kai said. "I reconnected our elements last night. With the heat turned up, I like to keep the communication between us open." He gave me a narrowed glare. "Even if she chooses to ignore me."

"Ignoring you was for your own good," I defended, taking a seat. "And by the way... is there some kind of switch to turn it off? Because I could barely think over your constant yelling."

Kai shot me an exasperated look. "There is, but I won't tell you."

I narrowed my eyes and growled, which made him chuckle.

"What do you mean you connected your elements?" Kylan asked, sitting on the other side of Trystan. "How is that possible?"

"Because Calla and I are both water elementals, I can connect our elements. It allows us to communicate through that connection. Like telepathy, only we can hear each other clearly."

"I've never heard of that being done before," Brone said with his baritone voice.

Kai took a bite of a juicy red apple, making my mouth water. He glanced up and saw me gawking and a broad smile rose on his lips.

"I know you want it."

I glared at him. *"Tease."*

Kai chuckled but explained. "It's not something that is taught. An elder Aquarian showed my father how to connect his element with my mother. And my father showed me."

"Calla can wield all four elements," Sabine noted, sitting beside me. "Does that mean she can connect to anyone with an elemental gift?"

"I suppose she could," Kai said, with a shrug, sinking his teeth into another piece of apple. "The only ones I know who have connected their elements are my parents, and of course… me and Calla. I wasn't even sure it would work."

"It can be done, as long as they share the same element," Nicolae said out of the blue, sipping from a large, golden goblet. "I have also connected to Calla because we share the fire element.And because she shares my blood, through her, I also connected to Kai. Which was how I was able to contact him to come here."

"How does one make this connection?" Kylan asked again.

I knew he was asking these questions because Trystan was an air elemental. As was I.

I glanced at Trystan, sitting directly in front of me. He looked stiff and uncomfortable. But what else could any of us expect? This entire situation was a nightmare, and I couldn't imagine the things bombarding his mind.

Kai held up his palms and placed them together. "You place your palms together and, in your mind, open up a connection between the two of you. It's simple, really." He then picked up his apple and took another bite.

Trystan's eyes slid to mine, making my entire body tingle with heat. Even though he couldn't feel anything, I sure as hell did. His presence made me feel like there wasn't enough air in the room. And the heat… it was almost stifling.

I wondered if it would be possible to connect my air element with Trystan's. However, right now, that was probably the furthest thing from his mind.

Sabine slid a glass of crimson liquid in front of me with a crooked grin.

"Thank you," I mouthed to her.

I took a sip, and the blood instantly made my tongue tingle and incisors lengthen. I willed them back up, as I didn't want any of them to think I was weak. But I knew I had to feed. And right now, I didn't care what anyone thought.

Placing the glass to my lips, I gulped down the blood, letting it flow straight down my throat. When I was done, I gently placed the cup down on the table and dabbed my lips with my napkin, then closed my eyes, letting the blood run its course.

I felt the power of the crimson liquid surging through my veins, healing me from the inside out. It was always a euphoric rush. But would *never* compare to what I felt when I drank Trystan's blood.

Trystan's blood was powerful and indescribable. His exquisite taste was the most heavenly thing to ever touch my tongue. It was mind-blowing, but also made me horny as hell—for him, and him alone. But Trystan made sure to thoroughly take care of that burning need. The taste of it still lingered in my mouth, like a phantom drug. I craved it, even now.

A drip of liquid ran down the side of my lip, so I licked it away. Opening my eyes, Trystan's unreadable gaze was fixed on my mouth, then they slid up to mine.

His eyes weren't as cold or skeptical as they had been these past few days. Right now, there was a hint of emotion in them, but I still couldn't read which one it was. Like he was debating whether he liked me or not.

Feeling a little self-conscious, I turned my attention to Nicolae. "You called for me?"

Nicole had been mostly quiet since we'd arrived here, but we did have a lot of guests and he had been very busy trying to find a way to save us from Roehl's wrath.

One day we'd get a chance to sit and discuss all the years we missed together. I could only imagine the grand tales he had to tell, and honestly, I was looking forward to hearing every one of them … *if* fate allowed us to live through whatever dark days were coming. Because we all knew they were coming.

Roehl wasn't going to stop until he'd won. Until me and Nicolae were dead. Especially now that he was exiled from Morbeth and had nothing left but a hole-in-the-wall kingdom in Morose Mountain.

The only reason he'd fled was because he knew he had no other choice. He knew my power was greater than his, so we would have to anticipate the measures he would take to defeat us. Roehl was a narcissist, who had to be in charge. He had to be the most powerful, biggest asshole. And if he wasn't, he'd do whatever it took to take down those threatening his ego. Including murder.

In Morose Mountain, he'd felt my power. He'd seen that even through his spelled cuffs and the power of his three dark mages, I broke free. And that made him furious. He wouldn't stop now until I was dead. He'd said it himself. We just had to be prepared for an attack at any given moment.

Nicolae gave me a comforting smile from where he sat. I saw so much of my father in him. They both had a smile that could light up a room and made you feel warm and welcomed. A smile that always brought comfort. He leaned forward on his elbows, tenting his fingers.

"The reason why I wanted you here, Calla, is to let you know that the King of Carpathia is demanding his son and cadre return home at once."

My heart dropped and my stomach began to knot, knowing Trystan and I would be separated again. I was afraid this would happen, because I knew if we were apart while his memory was gone, I could easily fall out of his life forever.

"Will we be staying here?" I asked.

The look in Nicolae's eyes told me that he wasn't sure what we were going to do. But before he answered me, Trystan responded.

"I am hoping that you all will join us," he said, then turned his attention to Nicolae. "If you agree, of course. I have given you my word, to help you defeat Roehl, and until that time, I invite you all to come to Carpathia. You will be safe there for the time being, and we will accommodate you until we can uphold our end of the bargain."

Goddess above. Was he actually inviting us to go to Carpathia with him? All of us, including me?

My stomach was doing flips and twists, and my heart was racing, but I tried to keep my expression as normal as possible.

I glanced at Kylan, and he smiled at me. Brone, Andrés, and Feng also wore broad smiles, like they were happy Trystan had made such a bold decision.

Markus, on the other hand, wasn't smiling. In fact, he looked like he'd eaten something sour.

I turned back to Nicolae, trying to remain calm. "Will we be going?"

He gave me a knowing smile. "I guess we should. I would like to meet the King of Carpathia. I think it's time I introduce myself to him."

Goddess above. This was really happening. My heart flip-flopped inside my chest.

I was finally going to see Trystan's kingdom in person, and not in a dream. But I was also anxious. Anxious because I was also going to see Brynna. It would be the first time since I'd seen her in

Morbeth, although she was spelled then, so she probably wouldn't even remember.

I hoped she would forgive me. I knew the death of her parents hit her hard, and even though it wasn't my fault, they did die because they were on my father's merchant vessel and connected to us.

Sabine grabbed my hand under the table and squeezed. When I turned to her, she had the goofiest, widest smile I'd seen on her yet. Even Thalia was beaming and seemed happy about visiting Carpathia.

"When will we be leaving?" I questioned.

"Tonight," Trystan replied. "We leave when the sun sets."

Was I ready to visit Carpathia?

Gods no. And I sure as hell wasn't ready to meet Trystan's father.

The man had arranged a gods damned marriage for his son because of me. He also said Trystan was making reckless choices unfit for a Prince of Carpathia … *because of me.*

Just thinking about it, turned my excited nerves into nerves of anxiety and filled my mind with visions of all the worst-case-scenarios.

Were Trystan and I destined to be star-crossed lovers? Were we destined to fail?

Or was the universe testing our grit to see if we were worthy of each other?

CHAPTER TEN

As I headed back toward the bedroom, I felt a gentle tap on my shoulder. Turning, Trystan was standing directly behind me, but took a few steps backward.

"Could I have a moment of your time," he asked. Those beautiful azure eyes were still void of any feelings or recollection of me, and I wondered if it was difficult for him to even touch me, knowing he had evil voices in his head telling him to hate me.

"Sure." I smiled and nodded, then without another word he turned and walked out the door.

Okay.

Of course, I followed, but he didn't stop to wait for me, just trudged on down the pathway in the front of the house, toward the sea. Gods, I couldn't help but admire him from behind. How could one person be so perfect? Even his ass was attractive, perfectly proportioned and shaped, fitting p erfectly i n those lucky trousers.

As we made our way down the cobbled path, I heard familiar caws from above. Flint and Nyx were soaring in the blue sky overhead. How the hell those two knew when we'd be outside was a mystery to me.

Trystan waited on the rocky shore. His eyes focused on the distant sea as I took a seat on my favorite rock. I heard a noise above me and looked up to see … not Flint, but Nyx swooping down toward us. Trystan held out his arm to her, but she didn't fly to him. Instead, she came straight for me, landing on my shoulder.

"Oh!" I exclaimed. I wondered if it had upset Trystan.

I side-eyed the bird, and she cocked her head to the side, her black beady eyes staring into mine. "What are you doing, Nyx?" I chimed, running a finger down her silky feathers.

She squawked and began pecking at my chest, at the pendant, which had been covered by my tunic. I pulled it out and held it in my fingers.

"I told you this is mine. You can't have it."

Trystan's eyes widened as he looked at the pendant.

Of course, he didn't remember I'd had it. Because his memory had been wiped clean of me and everything that had transpired between us.

"I know this was your mother's," I said softly, my eyes on the beautiful gem. "I know it was lost, but my best friend Brynna found it in an old antique shop in Sartha—where I'm from—and gave it to me on my eighteenth birthday." I unfastened the clasp, slipping the necklace from around my neck. "When we were in Aquaria, you told me the story behind this, and when I tried to return it to you, you told me to keep it.

But now that circumstances have changed, you can have it back." I held out the amulet to him, wondering if he was going to take it from me.

But he didn't move. Instead, his eyes clenched shut and his head shook, like he was trying to rid himself of a memory or…

"The voices in my head are telling me to take it from you and give it to my fiancé. That you have no right to such a precious family heirloom. Especially one this priceless that belonged to my mother."

Ouch. That freaking hurt like hell. I'd never had words cut me so deeply.

His eyes opened, brow furrowed. "I hear these voices, but… I'm conflicted. How can you be so evil? My cadre trusts you. And even Nyx flew to you instead of me." His eyes softened on his pet. "She has never gone to anyone except me. Not my parents. Not even my men."

I glanced at Nyx and gently pet her head and she leaned into my hand, begging for more. "She's probably being nice to me, trying to make up for the time she showed me the scene of my mother's death." I glanced up to see Trystan watching us closely. "I thought you were the one who showed me, but you didn't even know it happened. I later found out that Nyx did it herself, through the partial bond we shared. She showed me what she thought I needed to see. And I appreciate what she did, because I would have wondered what happened." I rubbed my cheek against Nyx's soft feathers. "You did it because you thought it was the right thing to do, didn't you girl?" Nyx cawed, dancing on my shoulder. She gently nipped at my cheek before taking off. I assumed it was a friendly peck, because it didn't hurt.

"I'm sorry about your parents," Trystan said, but his eyes were focused back on the glittering sea.

"Thank you," I breathed, trying to fight away the vision and sadness attempting to

overwhelm me. "I know they are together again, and that they are happy. I was blessed to see my mother in the In Between during the Shadow Fest. She told me that she is watching over me. As is my great-grandmother, Leora, the Princess of Incendia."

There was a pause before Trystan's all-consuming gaze found me.

"You are an heir of Incendia." It wasn't a question.

"I am." Tucking the amulet into my pocket, I held out my palms and showed him the tattoos.

"How did you meet Kai?" His question took me aback, and I hoped he didn't think what Kai and I had was more than friendship.

"After I escaped from Morbeth's prison, Markus, Sabine, and I boarded a pirate ship and sailed across the Sangerian Sea, heading for Incendia. During the trip we were attacked by a Sangerian sea serpent, but I killed it using my water power. During the battle, I fell into the sea. I thought I was going to die, but Kai saved me."

"You have a close connection." It was another statement.

"Yes," I exhaled. "But it's strictly based on friendship ... on my part. Kai teases that he'd like to be more than friends, but he knows my heart belongs to … someone else."

Trystan's eyes slammed shut, his smile turned grim as he placed his palms on either side of his head. "These voices are driving me mad. I can barely think, especially when I'm around you." He glanced up at me. "I find that as long as I listen to them, they subside for a short while. Until I'm close to you again." His eyes shut and brows knitted together as he groaned like he was in pain.

I wanted to run to him, but I couldn't. I hated that fact. I was helpless to do anything to try to help him.

The gods-damned voices must have been wreaking havoc on his mind, especially with our current conversation.

Watching him, I almost broke down. My insides were grieving over what he was going through. Knowing this curse came from Roehl, it had to be hell. I wasn't even sure I would have been able to cope with my memory being erased of Trystan, on top of the constant voices telling me he was evil and my enemy.

But he was handling it like the Trystan I'd grown to love. He was stronger than I could have ever imagined. Even though the demons inside were unrelenting, he still gave ear to that still small voice, whispering the truth.

I stood from the rock and cautiously strolled up to him, taking the amulet from my pocket. Grabbing hold of his hand, I placed the amulet in his palm.

"Take it," I said, closing his fingers over it. "I hope this buys you some peace."

As much as I didn't want to, I turned and walked away from him, hoping the distance would also give him a reprieve from the wicked, lying voices.

As I made my way back up to the house, a loud caw from above made me stop and glance skyward. It was Flint, soaring about twenty-five yards above me. "We're going to Carpathia tonight," I yelled to him. "Take Nyx and go. I'll meet you there."

As if he understood, Flint cawed and took off in the direction of Carpathia, with Nyx right behind him.

Twisting my head back, Trystan's eyes were on me, so I shrugged. "He's smarter than he looks," I said, then headed back toward the house.

Markus and Kylan just happened to be right inside of the door, where the sunlight didn't hit.

"Hey guys," I said, walking past them.

Markus followed after me. "Calla, are you sure you're up for going to Carpathia? We are likely to run into the princess." He was talking about Ivy.

I paused before turning to face him. "I'll be fine. Yes, I had a meltdown in Aquaria over their engagement, but I'm over it now. My best friend is in Carpathia, and it's finally time to be reunited with her, no matter what she thinks of me."

Kylan stood next to Brone. "Believe me, Princess Ivy *will* be there. That wench wants to make sure her talons are sunk deep into Trystan. But you don't have to worry, Calla. You have all of us. And my take on the Princess of Northfall? She can kiss my ass. She's a chocolate covered roach who has a detestable reputation. And if you and she just so happened to get into a fight, I'd bet money to see you put her on her ass." Kylan gave me a smirk.

For him to think so poorly of another, I couldn't even imagine the kind of person she was. Was she really that horrible?

"I assume she has a gift since she is a pureblood?" I wanted to know who she was and what we would be dealing with.

"She is not an elemental, but is gifted with magic, like Roehl. But she is not nearly as powerful as him, or as you are." Kylan shot me another devilish grin.

That was good to know. As soon as I had the chance, I needed to ask Nicolae how to shield myself from anyone trying to subdue my powers. Because I was *not* going to let that happen in the future. I would not be put in a position where I was helpless again.

"Does Carpathia have a secluded place where I can train?" I asked Kylan. I wanted to be ready, especially now that all of my powers were unlocked. I'd gotten a taste of my earth and air gifts, and I wanted more. I wanted to see how far I could push them.

"We do. We have a private training facility in the mountains, not too far from the castle. It is specifically used for the cadre and the training of top guards."

"Perfect." Maybe being in Carpathia wouldn't be so bad after all.

Feng called to Kylan, so he bowed his head and stepped away, toward the dining table where the rest of them were seated.

Markus stood in front of me, muscular arms crossed over his chest, giving me a pointed look.

"Markus, I know it's not the ideal situation, but I promise you, I'll be fine. Besides, I could still use a little sharpening. I never want to grow dull."

His eyes suddenly softened. "You could never grow dull, fire princess. I'm just worried about what will happen to your heart when you see them together."

I was surprised Markus was even having this conversation with me. I knew he was here to protect me. But my heart? That was a new level for him.

"Thanks for caring, but I can handle it. Heartache is part of growing up, right?"

"Right," he said. "Just prepare it for the worst." He gave me a slight bow and walked toward Trystan's cadre.

"You have a great group of warriors protecting you," Nicolae said, leaning back on a chair in the living area, reading a worn book. "I will be with you in Carpathia, and as your kin, I will also ensure your safety."

"Thank you," I said, then strode over and plopped down on a navy sofa next to him, sinking down into its soft cushion. I wanted to pick his mind a bit. Get to know this elusive man a little more.

"Can I ask you a question?"

"Sure." Nicolae placed his open book down on his lap and gave me his full attention.

I still couldn't believe he was my grandfather. He looked just as young as my father, and they shared a lot of the same features. Eyes, nose, smile.

"Where were you, all these years?"

He gave me a warm smile. "I have lived the life of a vagabond, traveling across the world, never staying in one place for more than a month's time." He closed his book and placed it on the stand next to him. "These eyes have seen many things, both wonderful and devastating. And all that time, I thought I was alone."

"What happened to the woman who raised you? Leora's handmaiden?"

His lips turned down, eyes saddened. "She has passed on from this world. She was a mortal, who taught me everything she knew about Incendia. She helped me through the most difficult years of my life. When I turned twenty-two, she became ill and passed on."

"I'm so sorry," I said softly.

Nicolae nodded. "I have fond memories of her and keep them in my heart."

"Have you never been with anyone other than the farmer's daughter?"

His eyes widened. "You know about her?"

"Leora told me about you and her when I was in the In-Between."

"Ah. That was during the Shadow Fest, right?"

"Yes," I nodded. "She told me a lot about you. At first, I didn't like you much. I thought you were a murderer who brought a curse upon our family. After my mother died, I hated you. But when Leora told me that you killed Roehl's brother because they were coming to kill you first… I felt horrible for making a wrong assumption."

"No," Nicolae breathed, placing a warm hand over mine. "They were justifiable feelings, and if I was put in your position, I would probably hate myself too." He folded his hands on his lap and leaned back. "When I first heard about you, I was in shock. I never knew I had a child, let alone a granddaughter. I didn't know what to think. All I knew, all I wanted to do from that moment on, was to find you." He leaned forward, his hands resting on his elbows, eyes welling with tears. "I am so sorry I wasn't there for you or your father. I wish I had known. I wish I could turn back time and be there for both of you." He quickly wiped away his tears. "But I am here now. And I will make sure you are safe… and happy."

"Thank you." My own eyes were brimming with tears.

Nicolae leaned back and crossed a leg over his knee. "Now tell me about your visit to Incendia."

For the next half hour, I told him about our adventure in Incendia and then about what Thalia had seen.

"The Queen is in bed with Roehl. She is evil and needs to go. You should be king. You are also a royal of Incendia."

"I am, but men do not rule in Incendia."

I gave him a pointed look. "Well, maybe it's time for a change. Maybe, once we defeat Roehl, we go back to Incendia together and we show them who the rightful heirs of the Incendian throne are."

Nicolae paused, then stood and held out a hand to me. "If we defeat Roehl, I will return with you to Incendia."

"You will?" I gasped. I wasn't expecting him to agree.

"It's time for me to return home," he said, his eyes solemn. "I've been running and hiding for too long. Besides, you will need help to dethrone that false queen."

"I do. And you have a deal," I said, standing and shaking his hand.

Nicolae pulled me into a hug. A hug from a grandfather to a granddaughter. A comforting hug filled with warmth and love. It was a hug that filled the void of years of being apart.

"Can I ask you one more thing?" I asked.

"Sure."

"Can you show me how to stop others from suppressing my power?"

Nicolae put his hands on my shoulders and "It's really just believing that your power is greater than any other … because it is. The gift the Fire Goddess imparted to you can burn through any spell."

I guess I already knew that. When I had called my power back in Morose Mountain, it took some time to come, but it *did* come. I was becoming more aware of that power inside me and was becoming more connected to it each time I used it.

CHAPTER ELEVEN

As soon as the sun dipped beneath the horizon, we all stood on the porch.

"How are we getting to Carpathia?" Sabine asked.

It was a good question, and I doubted we could all ride in a wind tornado or take the underwater route with eleven of us.

"We have a boat on the back side of the island," Kylan said.

Markus gave him a pointed look "I have been around the entire island. There is no boat."

"It's glamoured," Nicolae replied. "To keep spying eyes away from this island."

"It's time to go," Kylan said, taking the lead and heading behind the house.

Making our way down another long path that led to the sea, Sabine linked her arm in mine. "Doesn't this feel like we're going on some grand adventure? I've always wanted to visit Carpathia."

I smiled at her. "Who knows? Maybe you'll fall in love with the place and want to stay."

"We'll see," she said, then leaned over to my ear and whispered. "And maybe things work out with you-know-who, and you'll stay too."

I sighed and laid my head on her shoulder. "We'll see. I just have to keep hoping."

"Well, I have enough hope for the two of us," she said, loud enough for all the vampire ears to hear. "I'm free, because of you. And I never thought that would be possible. So, my hope is through the damn roof for you two. You were made for each other, Calla. Even though he is like a hundred years older than you." She leaned closer to me. "How old is he?"

"Sabine," I whispered, smacking her arm.

"Do you even know?"

"No. I don't."

"Well, it doesn't matter. Age is just a number. You two were made for each other."

I clenched my eyes shut, hearing a few of Trystan's cadre chuckle.

"It's true," Thalia added, speaking softly. Did they not realize that everyone in this group could hear them? "When he came to Incendia, riding in like a dark knight in that tornado, and then kissed you … it was like the world paused. And that kiss …" Thalia fanned herself. "I know everyone else who was there felt the raw emotion behind it."

"Oh, I did," Andrés blurted, raising his hand. "That was super-hot."

Brone smacked a thick hand on the back of Andrés head. "You didn't feel it, you horny bastard. Your dick did."

Andrés shrugged. "Same thing."

Trystan turned back and glared at them. And from that moment on, we walked in silence.

As we came upon the shore, Nicolae casually waved his hand and a boat appeared.

It was nothing like I expected. I was expecting a decent sailing vessel, but what we had was a small rowboat with a single sail that looked like it would barely fit the eleven of us.

"Are we all going to fit in that thing?" Thalia asked with a worried look.

Andrés nodded. "It will fit us. We had to bring the rowboat because we didn't have Trystan to give us wind to get here."

Trystan's cadre pushed the boat into the shallow water and then we all hopped in. I made sure to sit on the opposite side of Trystan, hoping the voices in his head wouldn't be too bad during the trip. But we were facing each other. And I wasn't sure if that was just as bad.

"There is no wind," Brone announced.

Kylan pulled up the sail. "Then it's a good thing we have Trystan on board."

But Trystan wasn't the only one who could summon air. I had done it at Morose Mountain and wondered if I could do it again.

Trying to remain inconspicuous, I turned my palms upward on my lap and closed my eyes.

Concentrating, I called to the air and soon felt a stiff wind sweep around us, tossing my hair.

"Trystan, the sail isn't fastened yet," Kylan grumbled.

"It's not me," Trystan replied casually.

Opening my eyes, I witnessed ten pairs of eyes staring at me.

"Calla, was that you?" Nicolae's smile burst with pride.

"I'm sorry. I just wanted to see if I was able to summon the wind."

"Well, you did it, Sea Star." Kai held up his hand, and I slapped it. "You will be unstoppable once you master your elements, and you have the perfect trainers, right here in this boat."

"Who?" Andrés asked.

Kai's smile widened. "I am the finest water elemental. Nicolae is an Incendian royal, so I'm sure he can show her a thing or two about fire. Thalia can teach her earth. And Trystan is a master with air."

"There are too many duties to attend to in Carpathia, which gives me little to no time for extracurricular activities," Trystan said, his voice so matter-of-fact.

"This isn't an extracurricular activity," Kai huffed. "And you agreed to help them defeat Roehl. Calla *can* defeat him, but her powers are new to her, and she needs our help. You just have to show her a few of your best tricks. I've already taught her how to throw water daggers and conjure a water sword."

Brone laughed. "A water sword? What can a water sword do?"

Kai's eyes narrowed while he stood and placed his hand out over the water. In a split second, a double-edged water sword formed in his hand. He then pointed at a large stone that was about three feet round and fifteen feet from the shore.

Kai aimed his sword, then thrust it at the boulder. It flew at lightning speed, hitting its mark and shattering the rock into dust.

Brone's brow raised. "I will never diss a water sword again."

Kai grinned and sat back down, sealing his title as water master.

"All right," Kylan said, taking his seat on the boat. He turned to Trystan. "Let's go."

Trystan's eyes met mine, and I swear, every time he looked at me, I felt like I couldn't take enough air into my lungs.

"Trystan, we need to go," Brone urged.

His huge body looked uncomfortable on the tiny boat seat. Markus sat opposite of him to keep the balance even.

Trystan shook his head, crossing his arms over his chest. "Since she needs practice, let her take us." He was referring to me.

"Wait. I don't know if I can hold the wind for any length of time. This is new to me. Like brand-new."

Nicolae reached over and grabbed hold of my hand, and I instantly felt a wave of peace surge through me, calming my frayed nerves.

"You were born for this, Calla," Nicolae spoke softly. "Air is a part of you, like fire and water and earth. It flows around you, in you, and gives you life. Now, steady yourself. Close your eyes and feel the air around you. Feel its charge. Its energy. Its power. Breathe it in and let it calm you. Air is your friend.

Ask for her help to guide us to Carpathia."

With my eyes closed, I sucked in a deep breath. I called to the air and asked it to come. Asked it to fill the sail and push us to Carpathia. And it responded.

At first, the air was gentle and calm, but as I concentrated more, it grew in strength, pushing us faster toward our destination.

"You're doing it, Calla." Sabine's voice remained soft and encouraging.

The others murmured amongst themselves, but I kept my eyes closed, concentrating. I had to show them I could do this. That I was worthy of this gift, and I would master it, even if I had to do without Trystan's help.

Nicolae kept holding my hand, and I found that as he did, it gave me strength.

The wind was firm and constant against my back, and before we knew it, Nicolae let go of my hand.

"You did good, Calla," he said.

Opening my eyes, I saw a small dock with a few boats tied to it. Feng and Kylan stood and as soon as we were close enough, they jumped out with ropes in their hands, pulling us tight and securing the boat.

Everyone climbed out, but Feng reached down and offered me his hand.

"Thank you."

"You're welcome," he said with a bow of his head. "You are truly a force to be reckoned with, and when the time comes, I will be on your side."

I wasn't sure what he meant by that, but I knew, coming from Feng, it was profound. Feng wasn't a man of many words, but I knew that in his mind, there was a lifetime of lessons and advice. And I was honored he would be on my side.

Markus and Kylan were up front talking and seemed to be hitting it off. I was happy that he was fitting in with Trystan's cadre. If anyone knew Roehl best, it was Markus, and I knew he could share some detailed insight on how he worked.

Markus's orders were to protect me at all costs. And I knew King Romulus wouldn't put a limit to that order.

Sabine ran over and linked one of her arms in mine, and Thalia did the same to my other arm.

"Girl, we finally made it," Sabine squealed.

As we reached the end of the dock, three luxurious, covered carriages pulled up, and at least a dozen guards on horseback, six in front and six in back, all wearing uniforms with Trystan's crest across their chest.

Sabine squeezed my arm and whispered, "Now this is a welcome party."

"No kidding. In Incendia, we would either have to walk or ride on horseback. This is next level royalty," Thalia giggled.

Trystan, Kylan, and Feng hopped in the first carriage, Brone, Andrés, Markus and Kai were in the second, and Nicolae was with me, Sabine and Thalia.

Two guards stood on either side of the stairs that led up to the carriage, assisting Sabine and Thalia inside.

Before I took my first step, the guard to my left slammed the carriage door shut and bolted it. Footmen at the other two carriages bolted their doors shut.

What the hell was happening?

There was a swooshing sound and when I turned around, Nicolae was wrapped in some kind of rope, pulsing with red. My heart nearly dropped out of my chest as I sensed the source of its power.

Roehl.

They bound Nicolae's wrists with spelled cuffs, and he was pushed to the ground.

"If you hurt her, I will kill you," Nicolae roared, fighting against the restraints. But they were strong, and that worried me. If Nicolae couldn't break from them, how would I?

The footman to my right grabbed my wrist and twisted it behind my back, a blade pressed to my throat.

"Come quietly with us, and you will live," he murmured in my ear. "Fight us, and your friends will die."

We were suddenly surrounded by dozens of men who were not part of Trystan's guard. They had been hidden in the trees, ready to attack. Three of them had swords pointed at the carriage Sabine and Thalia were inside.

Trystan's guards had dismounted their horses and were on the ground with swords drawn, fighting off the enemy. But they were outnumbered.

"I'll go," I said. "But promise me you won't hurt them."

I could hear Trystan, Kai, Markus, and the cadre banging on the carriages, desperately trying to get out. But the locks were glowing red. They'd also been spelled.

"One wrong move, and you'll all die," he said, binding my hands behind my back with a rope.

When he was done, the blade was back against my throat.

A sudden, angry rush of wind blasted around us, knocking us off balance. It picked up the first two carriages like they were feathers, carrying them about twenty yards into the air, then… the wind died, and they dropped, crashing into the ground, breaking open.

The men came rushing out, but it was Trystan who took me by surprise. His eyes had gone completely black and were cold, venomous. His face was hard as stone, jaw clenched, brows tightened.

"Don't move, and don't make a sound," the man behind me growled, pressing the blade deeper into my skin. Liquid dripped down my neck. It cut deeper but wasn't vital. Not yet.

Trystan's nose flared, his dark eyes snapped to me. To my neck. He'd caught the scent of my blood, his incisors lengthened. But so did every other vampire around me.

Shit.

"Get her out of here!" A voice hollered to the man holding me.

Horse's hooves came loud and fast, and in seconds, I was easily lifted onto a saddle. A large man wrapped his arms around me from behind, then clicked his tongue and we took off down a dark, dirt road.

I heard screaming from behind and knew a battle ensued.

My heart was hammering inside my chest. Tears burned in my eyes, feeling like I was worthless. I kept getting kidnapped by these assholes.

"Where are you taking me?" I asked the man behind me, but he didn't answer. "Where are we going?"

"That's none of your concern."

Far enough away that Sabine and Thalia were safe, I closed my eyes and called to the power inside, to protect me and kill this freaking bastard.

There was a loud whooshing sound in the air, and suddenly, the man's grip loosened from my waist, pulling the reins back and making the horse stop. His body fell from the horse and landed on the ground with a thud.

I glanced down at the lifeless body. Sticking out from the back of his head was the hilt of Trystan's ancient dagger. The runes glowing bright red.

My heart hammered as Trystan stepped out of the shadows, his eyes murderous. He slowly raised his hands, and a bolt of wind flew right past me. The sound of bone cracking filled the air, and a man standing right behind me, sword drawn and aimed at me, dropped to the ground.

Holy shit. Breathe, Calla. Breathe. Breathe. Breathe.

Back at the dock, I could hear the others still heavily engaged in battle.

Trystan's darkened eyes swirled with rage, aimed at a new set of men who were coming from ahead of me.

I called to my fire, which was my strongest gift, and felt it burn in my palms, instantly disintegrating the rope binding my hands.

I slid off the horse and ran toward Trystan, his midnight eyes moved to the blood still trickling down my neck. He closed his eyes and breathed in, brow furrowed, like he was fighting another one of his mind demons.

His onyx eyes opened and narrowed on me.

"Stay here," he commanded.

Trystan was like a blur, moving like the wind. Cracking bones and screams filled the thickened night air. One by one, the men dropped, their eyes void of life. All of their necks were broken, some had their throats ripped out, some had their hearts torn from their chests.

All except one.

Trystan gripped the man's throat tightly in his hand. The muscles in his arms and back bulged.

"Who sent you?" Trystan growled, blood dripping down the sides of his mouth. I should have been disgusted, but on him, the sight of it was driving me wild.

The man didn't answer, so Trystan squeezed his neck tighter, making him gasp for breath.

"Who sent you?" Trystan roared this time, baring his teeth.

The man smiled, then showed him something he had between his teeth. He bit down, and in seconds the man's eyes rolled back and foam bubbled from his mouth.

Trystan cursed and drove his hand through his chest, tearing out his heart, dropping the man to the ground.

With my focus on Trystan, I was distracted. Not seeing the body charging at me from the side, it suddenly slammed into me. We tumbled down a hill, through shrubbery and bramble before we slammed into a tree.

I couldn't catch my breath. The world around me was spinning.

A man was suddenly on top of me, fingers wrapped tightly around my neck, squeezing. Squeezing the life out of me.

I called to my power, wrapping my hands around my captor's wrists.

A burst of flame ignited in my palms, melting the skin from his arms. He rolled off of me, wailing as the fire grew, consuming his entire body.

A gust of wind brought Trystan right in front of me. He walked up to the burning man, and with a blink, tore his head from his shoulders and tossed it to the ground like he was discarding trash.

He turned back to me, his dark eyes met mine. I was mesmerized as he strode forward, stopping a few feet away from me.

"Are you hurt?" he asked, his eyes assessing me from head to toe.

I shook my head, trying to process what had happened.

Men on horses rode toward us, but they were Trystan's guards along with Feng and Andrés.

One guard jumped off his horse and dropped to his knees at Trystan's feet.

"I'm sorry, highness. The footmen were new recruits. They've been with us for the past month. I had no idea."

Trystan closed his eyes, hands fisted at his side. I could hear his ragged breath, saw his chest rise and fall, but he kept his composure. "Bring all the new footmen and staff, those who have joined within the past six months, directly to me."

"Yes, highness," the guard said, throwing a fist over his chest while bowing his head.

Feng and Andrés had just dismounted their horses and were heading toward us. Trystan gestured to them.

"Tend to her and get rid of the bodies. I'll meet you at the castle."

He walked away and didn't turn back, then mounted a black steed and rode away.

My mind was still reeling about what had just happened.

Trystan had saved me.

Despite the wicked voices in his head telling him I was the enemy and couldn't be trusted, despite the fact his memory was erased of all traces of me ... *he saved me.*

Trystan saved me. Again.

Feng held out his hand to me. "We need your help," he said, pulling me to my feet.

I nodded then rode back to the dock with him and the others, spotting Nicolae on the ground.

"Calla!" Sabine cried, running up and throwing her arms around me. "I never thought I'd see you again."

"You should know by now that my kidnappers usually can't handle me and give me back."

"You are so lucky." Sabine shook her head and pointed a finger. "I think they need your help."

Markus and Kylan were sitting next to Nicolae, trying to release the spelled binds and cuffs from him, but they were tight and not giving.

"Step back," I said, taking a knee at his side.

"I'm sorry, Calla," Nicolae breathed. "It was the first time I'd ever let my guard down. I should have—"

"You don't have to apologize," I interrupted. "None of us knew this was going to happen."

I raised my hands, palms upward. "I'm going to use fire to break the spell. It worked against Roehl's and the mage's magic in Morose Mountain."

Nicolae gave me a knowing smile and relaxed, while Markus and Kylan stepped back with the rest of the group, telling the guards to also step back.

I felt my gift writhing under my skin. Felt its power and heat growing inside my chest. I called it and watched it burn brightly in my palms, before consuming my entire body. Everything was brighter, clearer, when this happened. I felt… untouchable.

Reaching down, I placed my hands on the spelled cuffs.

I allowed the flame inside me grow, raging against the dark magic placed on the cuffs. It soon encompassed both me and Nicolae in a blaze of fire.

I pushed harder. Pushed against the evil living in that spell.

But the spell was stronger this time. Much stronger than what I'd felt on Morose Mountain.

I strained, pushing my gift to its limit. My power became an inferno, and I watched it slowly eat away at the curse, the cuffs let out a shrill scream as they disintegrated into whips of black.

With the dark magic dispelled, I released my hands. I was spent. My body weak and now trembling. I fell backward but Kylan and Feng ran over and caught me. Feng placed an arm under my knees and lifted me into his arms. Every muscle ached and trembled, and my head began to throb.

Kylan reached into a pouch and pulled out a flask, popped the lid, and placed the lip to my mouth. I gulped the liquid down, letting it work its magic, mending, healing me from the inside out.

"We'll have to ride on horseback to the castle," Feng said, holding me steady. "Are you strong enough?"

"She can ride with me," Nicolae said, standing at Feng's side. "I will never allow such a thing to happen to me again."

Feng nodded and handed me over to Nicolae. He carried me over and helped me mount our horse, then hopped on behind me.

Sabine was riding with Markus, and Thalia was with Kai. Brone and Kylan led our group, while Feng and Andrés rode behind us. There were three guards left of the dozen that arrived, and they took the rear.

I was weak, and the world was still spinning around me, but I was glad we were going to the castle where I could shower and get some needed rest. I finally relaxed, knowing that Nicolae had the reins. I knew he wouldn't let that happen again. Roehl was testing his power against us. We all knew the men were sent by him. And now, they were dead.

The cool breeze felt good against my heated skin. Relaxing against Nicolae, I studied the landscape as we rode. Carpathia was just as I had imagined. It was beautiful, even in the winter months.

A normal mortal wouldn't be able to see anything beyond the road but thick inky darkness, but I could see everything clearly with my heightened sight.

I caught faint scents of the meadow and moss and pine, but it was laced with something sweeter … but I couldn't place it.

From what I could see, Carpathia was filled with trees and rolling hills, and I couldn't wait to explore during the daytime.

Even the air smelled different here. It was refreshing.

"Look," Sabine said, pointing to a structure that was lit in the distance.

The Carpathian Castle—Trystan's castle. It was even grander than it had looked in my dream. It was Trystan's home. A place I had visited, through our partial bond. But this time, I wouldn't be invited to his room or his terrace. Especially if the Princess of Northfall was going to be there.

The thought of her sharing a bed with Trystan turned my stomach sour.

I hadn't met her yet, but I wasn't looking forward to it. Especially after what Kylan and even Kai had said about her. Even Sabine told me how terrible she was.

Maybe I could avoid meeting her altogether. And Trystan's father as well.

One could only hope.

CHAPTER TWELVE

We rode through a familiar black iron gate, and up a cobbled path toward the castle. Once we arrived, we were met with about fifty guards, all lined up and at the ready.

When his cadre dismounted their horses, the guards bowed to them. One of them walked up to Kylan and pulled him to the side, probably discussing the protection of the castle.

Letting my head fall back, I glanced upward at the massive structure and was in complete awe. The castle was even taller and grander than I'd imagined, and right above us flew a large flag. The flag of Carpathia's kingdom.

Every stone that went into building this castle was perfectly squared and placed precisely. The structure had at least four levels, with a long battlement on top, and on either side were tall towers.

Nicolae dismounted our horse and helped me down, but I was still a little woozy and wobbly in the knees.

All I wanted to do was get into a room and relax. I didn't care to meet or greet anyone right now, not in the condition I was in.

Nicolae kept a hand around my arm to keep me steady, and I was grateful for that. Grateful he was here with me.

Sabine and Thalia had just been in the middle of a bloody battle, but looked bright eyed and wide awake, giddy to finally be at the castle. It showed just how much they'd seen and were used to. Especially Sabine, who came from Morbeth. Thalia was a guard, so she'd have seen her fair share of battles.

"Follow me," Feng said, waving us toward the entrance. As the guards moved away, heavy doors opened, and my heart began to thrum.

We entered a massive open room with ornate rugs and tapestries and furnishings, more glorious than I had ever seen. Aquaria was a close second, but this … this was wealth and luxury.

The color scheme was red, black, and gold. Above us hung enormous chandeliers, with thousands of teardrop crystals, gently lighting the receiving area.

There were a few separate staircases that led to upper floors. One could easily get lost here.

"Carpathia is even grander than Morbeth," Sabine breathed, and I nodded in agreement.

Although Carpathia's castle was grand, there was a coldness to it. Cold because I knew I wasn't truly welcome here. I was only here because Trystan was fulfilling a promise to Nicolae.

Feng led us toward our guest rooms, which were up one of the staircases on the left side of the room. Making it to the second level, Feng stopped.

"Gentlemen, you will follow Brone," Feng said pointing to the left, "and girls, you will follow me." He pivoted to lead us down the right hallway.

I looked at Markus, Nicolae, and Kai and smiled at them. "We'll see you soon."

"Sleep well," Nicolae said. I nodded before they turned and headed down their wing.

As we followed Feng, Kylan bounded up the stairs and finally caught up to us.

"Calla, you are to come with me," he said. "You will be staying elsewhere."

"Wait, she's not staying with us?" Sabine questioned.

"She will be across the way," he pointed to a separate stairwell across the huge entry. "Trystan wants her closer to us, just in case."

I didn't know what to say. Sabine looked at me and shrugged. "You will probably rest better knowing his cadre is near." She walked up to me and wrapped her arms around my neck. "Be safe, Calla. And get some sleep. Don't worry about things that haven't happened yet. We'll deal with them as they come, together."

I wrapped my weak arms around her and squeezed. "Thank you."

Thalia came and hugged me too. "Be safe, cousin."

"I will. And you both behave yourselves."

"Behaving is overrated," Sabine said with a wink.

I laughed and watched them walk away with Feng.

"Are you okay with being in our wing?" Kylan asked.

I nodded. "Yeah, I'm okay, as long as you guys won't have wild and noisy parties that will keep me up all night."

Kylan smiled. "Only once in a while, and you'll be invited. I make a wicked bloody martini."

"Bloody martini?" I grinned. "I'll look forward to that."

We both headed back down the stairs and as we crossed through the great room to get to the opposite staircase, a guard hurried in. "Kylan, can you come with me? It's urgent. About the new recruits."

Kylan shot me a worried glare, but I smiled and shook my head. "Your duty calls. Go ahead. I'll be fine."

He pointed to the stairs. "When you reach the top, take a right and your door will be," he paused. "The fifth door on the left."

"Fifth door on the left?" I had to make sure. I didn't want to walk in on a naked Brone or Andrés.

"Yes, fifth. You have a suite, so there will be an adjoining washroom. I'm sorry, Calla. I'll come and check on you when I'm finished."

"Don't worry about me. I'll be fine."

I watched Kylan dash out with the guardsman before I made my way to the stairwell.

Being alone in this huge castle was unnerving. Especially when I was out in the open. I hurried toward the staircase and made my way up. I was almost to the top when I turned around and looked behind me. The room was empty, thank the goddess.

Turning back around, I slammed into a body.

Shrieking, I lost my balance and started to fall backward, but a strong hand gripped my waist and yanked me up, right into a firm chest.

I gazed up into the most beautiful, azure eyes.

"Trystan," I gasped, trying to push away from him, but he held me tight, his eyes searching my neck.

My heart was thrumming, pulse racing, and his scent was filling my lungs, making me dizzy.

"Why are you alone? Where is Kylan?" There was an angry tone to his voice.

He finally let me go and we both took one step away from each other.

I swallowed loudly. "He had to leave. Guard business," I said, thumbing down the stairs.

"Your neck is healed," he said, his eyes still fastened to the area.

I rubbed my fingers where the man had pressed his blade, but the skin was smooth, with no trace of it being cut. "I guess the blood worked its magic."

He nodded with no expression, but his eyes clenched. I knew the demons inside his mind were wreaking havoc. He turned and walked up the stairs.

"Kylan told me my room was the fifth door on the left, right?" I said, making my way up to the last step.

Trystan paused, glancing over his shoulder. "I'll take you to your room."

I stayed at least five feet behind him, not too close and not too far.

The hallway was large and open with ornate fabric lining the walls that were decorated with exquisite paintings and glowing gold sconces placed every few feet.

Trystan walked me past door three, four, and then five and kept going.

I paused in front of door five on the left. "Isn't this my room?"

"Not anymore," he said, continuing to move down the hall.

Okay. Where was he taking me?

We took a left down another hallway that was even larger and grander. But there were no doors on the left, and only two doors on the right.

The hallway was so large, in fact, there were tables with floral arrangements and a desk with chairs. Trystan stood in front of the first door on the right. "This will be your room while you are here."

I bowed my head. "Thank you so much for your hospitality."

He twisted the knob and swung open the door, gesturing for me to enter. As soon as I stepped inside, my breath halted, and eyes bulged.

"This is where I'm staying?" I exhaled, throwing a hand over my chest.

His brow crumpled. "Do you not find it accommodating enough?"

"Yes. Gods yes. It's just... I've never been in a room this... amazing."

This bedroom was larger than my entire cottage in Sartha. It wasn't a simple room for guests. No, this room was fit for a Queen, and made Morbeth and Incendia's rooms feel common.

I slowly spun around, taking it all in. Walking over to the far side of the room was a large archway with red gossamer curtains blowing gently in the breeze. Sliding between the curtains, I stepped outside onto a large veranda with a white marbled floor.

On either side of me were tall alabaster columns rising up toward the ceiling. But there were no dragons wrapped around these. These columns were bare.

Stepping further toward the railing outside, I peeked over. It was so odd, the overwhelming sense of déjà vu. That I had been here before, just not physically.

Before me was the same view, I'd witnessed when I'd met Trystan in my dreams—through our partial bond. Back then, I was standing on his veranda, much like this one. We were on a mountainside overlooking the greenest rolling hills flecked with lush oak and pine trees. Between them, was that familiar river that hurriedly flowed its course toward the boundless sea.

"You seem familiar with this place," Trystan said stepping out onto the veranda.

I turned toward him, his eyes seemed a little softer.

"I've been here before. Not physically, but I was here with you, on your veranda. You brought me here through our bond."

"My veranda?" His eyes narrowed. "How can you be sure it was mine?"

I faced him, resting my back against the balcony railing. "You have a fireplace, and next to it, a comfortable, black leather armchair where you like to sit and have a drink. And your veranda has alabaster columns like these, but yours are special. They have dragons carved around them."

Trystan's eyes widened, brow furrowed, lips tightened.

"I'll leave you now," he suddenly said. "I'm sure you can find your way around the room. If you need anything, go back down the hall and knock on any one of the first four doors on the left. One of my men will answer." He took a step backward, through the gossamer curtains, and into the bedroom.

My chest ached as he left, but I hurried after him.

"Trystan, wait," I breathed, keeping my distance.

He paused, only turning his head slightly. The demons were back, and he was trying to escape them. Yet, despite them, he kept finding his way back to me.

"I just wanted to say thank you. For saving my life tonight."

He paused again, his fingers running through his thick, unkempt hair. He nodded and then headed for the door, but just before he walked out, he paused, like he wanted to say something.

I waited in silence, but he moved again, walking out of the room and shutting the door behind him.

I stood there, staring at the space he was no longer in.

Confusion battered my mind. I wondered what was going on in his mind. What were the demons telling him this time?

But I could see he was still trying. Still fighting the curse that was demanding him to hate me. I was just afraid of the repercussions.

My heart ached as I spun around, taking in the room, wondering why he'd moved me to this more private area. Maybe it was to keep me hidden away from his father. Or maybe even his fiancé. If that was the deal, then I was all for it. With a room like this, I wouldn't mind being tucked away for the entire stay.

As I walked past the huge king-sized bed filled with fluffy pillows, draped in luxurious bedding, I couldn't wait to tuck myself in and get a good night's sleep. On the other side of the room was a sitting area. A plush couch and two armchairs with a table in the center that held the most beautiful floral arrangement of red roses.

Heading toward the washroom, my jaw hit the floor when I stepped in to find how massive it was. In the center of the washroom was a large tub, also made from marble, already filled with steaming water. It was so deep, there were three steps that led into it.

I walked over and dipped my fingers in the water, and it was the perfect temperature. What was baffling was that I hadn't seen a maid. So, who had filled the tub? Maybe they had done it before we'd arrived.

There were towels and bathing soaps and combs and even a black robe with Carpathia's insignia sewn onto the chest, neatly folded on a long marble counter.

After sniffing the soaps and picking my favorite—a sweet floral scent—I made my way over to the tub and stripped down. I stepped in, submerging my aching body under the water. Gods, it felt amazing. The steaming hot water gently caressed my weary being.

Closing my eyes, I sank under the water, placing an air bubble around my head. It was so peaceful under the water. No ambient noise. Just a calm serenity.

Tomorrow, I would ask someone to take me to Brynna. She was here, somewhere in this castle, and I couldn't wait to see my best friend. To wrap my arms around her and tell her that I loved her and that we would get through this wretched life together. At least, that's how I hoped it would go. For all I knew, she would push me away or punch me in the face. And I rightly deserved it. But I was really hoping for the former response.

After my bath, I pulled the water from my wet hair, letting the water beads drop back into the tub, then wrapped the soft, warm robe around me. On the nightstand, there was a wine bottle and a single wine glass. A small note was next to it on the table, along with a freshly picked red rose. I picked up the rose and breathed in its sweet scent. It immediately transported me back to the time Trystan had left me a similar rose, along with a note and the flask of blood on my bedside table back in Sartha. *That* note had changed my life forever.

This note had very similar writing and it made my heart warm. It had to have been from Trystan. It read:

Have a drink before bed.

You will feel better in the morning.

I popped the top and sniffed the contents. It smelled sweet and coppery and made my mouth water. After pouring myself a glass, I swirled the bright crimson liquid, carrying it with me to the veranda outside.

Barefoot, I padded across the frigid marble tile and leaned against the railing.

In the distance, the town filled with mortals was gently lit, most of its residents already in a deep slumber.

A cold, wintry breeze nipped at my skin, but I welcomed it. It was so peaceful in Carpathia. I still couldn't believe I was here. I just wished it was under different circumstances.

It wasn't long ago when Trystan had said, *"One of these days, when you arrive, I'll give you a formal tour."*

But that was a different time and things were much different now.

The breeze picked up, swirling around me, tousling my hair, and I swear I caught *his* scent. That perfect blend of earth and wind and spice. I inhaled it deeply, filling my lungs. No matter how many times it caught me, his scent still made me weak and warmed my insides. But this time, the scent made my heart ache.

Finishing my drink, I made my way back into the bedroom. Pushing half the pillows to the other side of the bed, I disrobed and climbed in.

Heaven.

That was the only way to describe it. I had never felt sheets this soft against my skin. And the bed … it felt like I was sleeping on air. Sinking deep into the soft mattress, my mind became numb. The blood was working, and the sound of the crackling fire lulled me into a deep sleep.

CHAPTER THIRTEEN

Morning came much too quickly, my sleep interrupted by someone knocking.

"Come in," I moaned.

"Are you decent?" A voice called from the other side of the door. It sounded like Kylan.

Glancing down at my bare breasts, I quickly scrambled out of bed, threw on the robe, and hopped back in, throwing the blankets over me.

"Come in," I hollered.

Kylan stepped into the room, fully dressed in his uniform.

"What time is it?" I yawned.

"Three in the morning."

"Why are you here at this ungodly hour?" I grumbled.

Kylan stood in front of the fireplace, which someone had stoked and added firewood too.

Gods. Whoever it was must have seen me naked. It was probably the maid, but still. I needed to ask for some sleeping gowns while I was here.

"You told me you wanted to train," he replied. "We can't be out when the sun rises, so we train early."

I moaned and threw my arm over my eyes. "Can't you train after the sun sets?"

"No. We are on watch at night," he said. "But, after a few hours of training, you can come back and sleep the day away if you wish."

"Fine," I sighed. "But I don't have any training clothes."

"You mean these?" He pointed to a stack of pants and tunics on the dresser that must have been brought in by the same person who'd stoked the fire.

My eyes widened. There were at least six sets.

"Was it Trystan?" I asked.

"Feng had your other clothes tailored from a seamstress in town—the ones you've been wearing that were gifted from Trystan. After a discussion about you last night, Feng talked to Trystan about getting you a few more training outfits. He approved … so we immediately sent a maid to the seamstress. They were brought in from the town a few hours ago."

I sat up, hugging the robe to my chest, overwhelmed with their kindness. "You guys were talking about me?"

Kylan nodded, then turned to warm his hands by the fire. "It's hell for him, you know. The voices, the loss of memory. Trystan wants to know the truth, but whenever we start to tell him about you, he gets these piercing headaches. And they seem to be getting worse."

My emotions brewed and dripped from my eyes. "I wish there was something I could do."

Kylan turned to me, his expression saddened. "For now, I think it's best if you keep your distance. He said the pain is much greater when he is around you. The voices, and even the anger. He's afraid they might make him do something to hurt you. Which is why none of us understands why he chose to keep you so close to him. But Trystan has confounded us more than a few times with his reasoning, especially when it comes to you." Kylan shrugged, giving me a slight grin. "He's stubborn that way."

My heart ached so badly for him. For the situation. And yet, I was helpless to do anything about it. "I don't understand his reasoning either, but I do know Trystan would never hurt me."

"No, he wouldn't. But you have to remember, he doesn't know who you are anymore, Calla. The real you. In his mind, you are a stranger to him. A stranger his mind is calling the enemy. That you are using him, lying to him, and your ultimate goal is to destroy him and his family."

I shook my head, knowing this was the furthest thing from the truth. "If that's what his mind is telling him, why did he invite me here?" I sobbed, tears trickling from my eyes.

"Because his heart is warring with his mind." Kylan glanced at me and gave me a sad smile. "So much so, that he even moved you here, to the room directly next to his."

"What?" I gasped. I knew the view looked too familiar, and

his scent in the air last night, it had to have been him. Maybe he was standing on his balcony, sipping a glass of his amber liquid.

"This room has been off limits for years and has only been used by one other."

"Who?" I asked, wondering if it was the Princess of Northfall.

"Trystan's mother," he replied.

"I don't understand."

"I'm not sure if I should be telling you this, but because Trystan is not in his right mind, I think you deserve to know." Kylan moved away from the door, coming closer to the bed, his arms crossed over his chest.

"Trystan's mother and father had an arranged marriage. She was the daughter of the King of Hale, and when they were married, they were blissfully happy. The queen was very adventurous and loved to travel and experience new lands.

"Because the king couldn't be with her all the time, he gave her a magical amulet. It was spelled with his blood, so no matter where she went, he would know where she was and would be able to easily find her if something should happen. It was her most treasured possession, and she never took it off.

"For hundreds of years, they remained happy, and together they made Carpathia the wealthiest country in Talbrinth. Then, about twenty years ago, the queen suddenly fell ill. For a vampire, that is unheard of, so we all knew it had to have been a curse. There were many who were jealous of her and the king, of her beauty, and the wealth of Carpathia. And to this day, we never found out who placed the curse on her.

"It slowly ate away at her mind, causing her to see things that weren't there, and wander at night. Trystan's father tried everything, called in every witch and mage and brought in physicians across the globe to see if they could fix her. But the curse seemed incurable against magic and potions, and it confounded everyone. It was something even vampirism couldn't fix. Once, she'd gone missing for three days. They couldn't find her because she'd taken off her amulet and left it on her pillow. A few guards finally found her on the far side of the island, standing on the edge of a rocky cliff."

Goddess above. "That must have been hard on Trystan."

"It was. There were nights she'd wander around the castle talking to herself. The king tried to hide her away, to keep her within the castle walls, to keep word of her illness away from the other royals. So, Trystan had this room set up for her so she'd have a place to come and be near him, and he could watch over her and make sure she was safe."

Hearing this made my heart grow even more for him. "What happened to her?"

Kylan inhaled deeply. "The curse was so strong, and the disease had gotten so bad, she begged a mage to take her life. Feeling sorry for her, the mage cast a powerful and dark spell that allowed her to go to sleep and never wake." Kylan looked back at the door and then at me.

"Did she die?"

Kylan nodded. "Whatever the mage did, siphoned the immortality from her. It was a devastating time for Trystan because he was very close to his mother. And his father … he had the mage beheaded and never spoke of his wife again. Maybe it's his way of coping. Who knows? But since her passing, he's changed. He's grown angry and hard and pushes his anger and most of his burdens on Trystan."

"I'm sorry to hear that. Trystan's father must be in a lot of pain. Especially if he loved her."

"He truly loved her in the beginning, but when she became ill, his heart became calloused, and he stayed away. I don't think he knew how to cope with her illness, feeling helpless to save her. So instead of being present for her, he buried himself in work and duty. We all know the queen felt his coldness, and I believe it was part of what drove her to seek out the mage."

That made me sad. To be sick and lose your love because of it.

"Is there someone we can ask about the spell Roehl cast on Trystan?"

Kylan nodded. "Brone found a mage last night, one who practices archaic sorcery. He said there is a loophole to every spell, but because Roehl created this spell, only he knows what that loophole is."

A loophole? Goddess, this was great news.

Except …

"There is no way in hell that asshole is going to tell anyone what the loophole is," I sighed. I was discouraged, but also encouraged to know there was a cure.

"What we need to focus on is your training. Roehl will be coming for you, and you need to be ready," Kylan said, walking back toward the door. "Nicolae, Kai, and Thalia have also agreed to aid in your training."

I nodded, hopeful that we were given even the tiniest spark of hope.

"I'll be ready in ten minutes."

"Good. One of us will be at your door, ready to escort you to the horses."

"Thank you, Kylan."

He bowed his head and slipped out of the room.

Gods. I needed to focus and get my head in the game. If there was a loophole, I had to find it. I had to save Trystan from Roehl's horrible Lethe potion and the curse he'd added to it. I had to find a way to free his mind. But I also knew how imperative it was to train. To learn everything I could about all my gifts, especially the gifts of earth and air, which had become my newest allies.

Thalia could teach me how to call upon earth, but I would have to figure out air on my own. Thinking back to last night when we were attacked, I remembered how Trystan used air to move and fight. The sight of him was beautifully terrifying.

Snapping my thoughts from Trystan, I quickly grabbed some black trousers, a crimson tunic, and my boots. After throwing them on, I quickly did my hair into two braids. My mother used to braid my hair and always did it in two braids down either side of my head. She would always say, "Two is better than one."

I smiled at the memory.

Placing my hand on my chest, I missed the amulet, but I also knew it was back with Trystan. It belonged to his mother, and hopefully, having it back would bring him some peace.

Before I left, I poured myself a large glass of ruby wine and gulped it down. The rush had me leaning against the nightstand for balance. Once it settled, I threw on my cape and headed out the door.

"Looking good, Calla," Andrés said, leaning against the opposite wall. "Are you ready to train?"

"I am."

Andrés smiled and offered me his arm. "Shall we?"

I linked my arm in his, and just as we started moving, I heard a door behind us snap shut. I became weak in the knees as the hallway filled with the most beautiful scent.

Andrés paused, and we both turned back to see Trystan, dressed in his royal finery. He was wearing all black, with a black cloak tied around his broad shoulders, and a simple gold crown circling his head.

Heavens above. He looked like … like a god. When those bright azure eyes met mine, I smiled. But I didn't get a smile in return, instead I saw him wince, his brow furrowing.

Tugging Andrés, I knew we had to go. I could clearly see that me being so close to him was causing him pain.

"We're headed to train," Andrés said to Trystan.

Trystan nodded, his eyes meeting mine. "You slept well?"

I swallowed the lump in my throat. "I did. Too well, until Kylan woke me up for training."

I thought I saw his lips slightly turn up, but I blinked, and his features went rock hard.

"Let's go," I whispered to Andrés. He nodded and led me forward.

Glancing back, I saw the pain in Trystan's eyes, and it was killing me inside. We had to find a way to make it stop. We had to find that gods damned loophole.

As Andrés led me down the hall, Feng, Kylan, and Brone were standing at the top of the stairs.

"Even at this hour, you look like you're ready to kick some ass," Brone said with a broad smile.

I grinned at him and snapped my fingers, flames danced across my fingertips. "Oh, I'm ready."

Feng laughed. "Don't play with fire, brother. You'll get burned."

Brone growled. "I've already been burned, and I don't want that to happen again."

He was talking about Incendia, when he was holding me back. I had called my power, and it sent him flying backward.

"I'm still sorry about that. I didn't know my own power." I made a fist and quenched the flames, then turned to Kylan. "We have to go. Trystan is behind us."

He gave a nod and started leading us down the stairs. "Let's get a move on boys. The sun doesn't pause for slackers."

Surrounded by Trystan's men, I never felt more secure.

As we came down the staircase, Nicolae, Kai, Markus, Sabine, and Thalia arrived.

I walked over to Sabine and shook my head. "Why did you come? You should have slept in." She looked exhausted with puffy eyes and hair quickly tied behind her neck.

Sabine, with a blanket draped over her shoulders, threw her arms on her hips and gave me her signature sassy glare. "Girl, I told you we are a team, even if I have to drag my tired ass out of bed and go to some uncomfortable training arena. Besides, Thalia is going, and I didn't want to miss out on anything."

I threw my arms around her neck. "You're the best."

I glanced at Markus. "So are you. Even though I knew you'd come."

He gave me a smirk. "I was ordered to protect you."

I gave him a warm smile. "I know. And I appreciate it."

"And what about me?" Kai asked, looking bright eyed, dressed in simple trousers and a tunic. His silvery hair was tied back at the nap of his neck.

"You know I appreciate you, highness," I said, bowing my head. Kai growled but didn't make any remark.

After greeting Nicolae and Thalia, I watched Markus's eyes snap up to the top of the stairs, and then, so did everyone else's. I knew Trystan was there.

"We have to leave," I said quietly, my back still turned to the staircase.

"I hope you all found your accommodations satisfying," Trystan said, his voice getting closer.

"More than satisfying," Sabine chimed, bowing her head. "Thank you."

"Yes, thank you," Nicolae, Thalia, and Markus replied, bowing their heads.

Sabine then turned to me and gave me a look. A look of... *damn, he is gorgeous*. And I knew the crown added to it. But I already knew how beautiful he was, and I knew if I turned around, I would get caught in his snare.

Kai glanced at me and knew I was torn. "Come, Calla. I'll take you outside." I nodded and began to follow him out. Kylan also followed right next to me.

"Kylan," Trystan called.

Kylan stopped and turned back to face him, hand over chest, head slightly bowed.

"Take a dozen of your most trusted guards and have them watch the arena. I don't want any unwanted guests popping in." Trystan's voice was even closer, too close.

"I will," Kylan replied.

Then, I saw movement on the side of Kylan and when I turned, my breath caught in my chest as my eyes met with Trystan's … again. Gods, he was so sinfully gorgeous in his royal garb, making so many emotions swirl through me. Sadness at the forefront, because I knew he was hurting. I could almost feel those demons torturing him from within at our closeness.

I bowed my head to him, breaking eye contact.

"What are your plans for this morning?" Nicolae asked him, breaking the thick silence.

"I have business to attend to. Princess Ivy of Northfall is arriving shortly," he answered.

I turned to Kylan and his brow furrowed. He gestured with his head for us to go, so I moved forward, toward the exit.

"Train well," Trystan said, his back turned toward us, walking in the opposite direction.

"We will," I replied.

As soon as we stepped outside, I inhaled the crisp, wintry air which smelled of morning dew and fresh pine. It was invigorating and brought my senses to life. The sky was still dark, with the moon and stars glittering above.

There was no snow in Carpathia yet, none that I had seen, even though winter was in full force. But I could tell the days were getting colder, and soon everything would be blanketed in white. I looked forward to that magical moment of watching the snow fall.

Out in the front, Kylan talked to one of the guards, who quickly ran off.

To the right of us, men brought horses for us, all saddled and ready to go.

But my eyes caught on one of the horses. A Friesian, with a sleek black coat, thick mane, and long tail, saddled with the crest of the royal Carpathian family—shield, dragon, and sword.

"Does he look familiar?" Kylan asked.

I gasped and faced him. "Is that my horse?"

When he smiled, I turned back, eyes burning with tears.

I knew Shadow had a small white patch on his right foot in the shape of a diamond.

I walked up to the familiar horse and ran a hand down his silky neck, then took a knee. Tears fell from my eyes as I spotted the white diamond patch on his right foot. Rising, I threw my arms around Shadow's neck and sobbed. I thought I'd never see him again.

Shadow had been one of my best friends growing up, a present given to me by my father on my tenth birthday. And now that he was here, I felt a bit of happiness return.

"Hey, boy. It's so good to see you" I said, placing my hand against his nose.

Shadow whinnied, then nudged me.

I threw my arms back around his strong neck again. He rested his head against my shoulder, just like he used to do.

"I missed you so much," I whispered, hugging him tight. "I was so worried about you."

When I turned around, everyone was standing still and somber, watching us. Sabine wiped a tear that had fallen from her eye, and I wiped my own eyes and turned to Kylan.

He strode over to me and took Shadow's reins in his hand.

"When Brynna first arrived," he started to explain, "Trystan had several conversations with her. She mentioned your horse, Shadow, and how much you loved the beast. Knowing the situation, Trystan sent some of his men on a ship to Sartha to pick him up."

"Of course, he did," I whispered. Just when I thought Trystan had done it all, I would find out he did something more.

Kylan held Shadow steady as I mounted him. The saddle was brand new, wrapped in black leather with silver trim. The seat was so comfortable, and the stirrups fit perfectly. Like everything else that had been provided by Trystan.

A cold breeze swept around, carrying a familiar scent. Glancing up, I saw a figure in one of the upper windows, but as soon as I looked, it moved back, out of view. I knew it was Trystan.

Everyone else mounted their horses, and we rode off, Kylan and Brone leading the way. I couldn't help but think Trystan was watching us the entire time, and it made my heart both swell and break.

CHAPTER FOURTEEN

The ride took about twenty minutes and was up a beautiful path lined with pine trees on either side. When we reached the arena, it wasn't what I'd expected. It looked like a colosseum, but was enclosed, with a dome shaped roof on the top.

Around the structure were tall columns that had dragons carved into them. Dragons that were similar to the ones carved into the columns on Trystan's veranda.

We dismounted our horses and tied them to a hitching rail before making our way inside. Kylan grabbed a torch on the wall and pivoted to me.

"Can I have a light?" he asked.

"Of course." I flicked a small flame from my fingertips to the torch.

"One down, fifty to go," he said, walking into the dark room. With my heightened eyesight, I could see the torches lined up against the walls.

"I guess this will be my warmup," I said, flexing my fingers.

Making my way out into the center of the arena, I called fire and threw my flame, one by one, lighting the torches until the entire arena was lit.

This training center was amazing, filled with everything a soldier or guard would need to train. Against one of the far walls was training equipment—wooden swords, shields, bows and arrows, axes, dummies made from hay, and lots more.

The center of the arena was manicured grass and along the outside was dirt.

"Oh, I see where I'm going," Sabine said, heading for a bunch of hay. She'd brought a blanket that was already wrapped tightly around her. "It's so cold in here."

Not far from her new bed of hay were stacks of wood.

I headed toward Markus and Brone, who were chatting. "Can we make a small fire for Sabine?" I asked. "She must be freezing."

Markus and Brone were on it. They easily picked up the wood and created a small fire pit directly in front of Sabine, but far enough away her haystack wouldn't catch fire. As soon as they were done, I lit it.

"You guys are the best," Sabine yawned, curling up on the hay. "I'll see you all later."

"Hey, I thought we were a team?" I teased.

"We are," she said, throwing her arm up in the air. "Go team!"

I laughed out loud. She was a good friend just for showing up.

"So, what are we doing first?" I questioned, returning to the center of the arena where everyone else stood.

"Are you able to manipulate more than one element at a time?" Nicolae asked, coming to stand next to me.

I shrugged. "I don't know. I haven't tried yet."

"How about we start slow," Kai said, standing on the opposite side of me. He had set out a few hay dummies about fifty yards away. "See that water barrel over there?" He pointed to the left about twenty feet away. "Send water daggers toward that hay man, aiming for the chest and head."

That sounded simple enough. Everyone stepped back behind me and stayed silent. I closed my eyes and concentrated on my water gift. Opening my eyes, I raised my left palm and water from the barrel came toward me. Doing what Kai had taught me, one by one, I formed daggers and sent them flying toward the dummy. After I counted ten, I stopped.

Kai ran over to the dummies and inspected them. A few moments later he hollered, "You hit everything *but* the head and chest."

Gods. "Are you serious?"

Kai let out a burst of laughter then jogged back and stood next to me. "Just relax," he said. "Take in a deep breath and call the water to you. But keep your eyes on your target." He stood behind me and grabbed my wrist, raising my left palm. "Feel the water coming to you. You don't need to watch it."

Concentrating, I kept my eyes on the target and called the water to me. "Feel it," Kai whispered. And I could. I could feel my palm vibrating. As the water got closer, the vibration became stronger.

"Now," Kai said, releasing my hand.

With eyes aimed at the head, I sent five water daggers, then looked to the chest and sent five more. Kai jogged back to the hay man, and I smiled.

He turned, with a disappointed look on his face.

"What?" I hollered.

A smile widened on his lips, and he gave me two thumbs up. "You nailed it! All ten, perfectly placed."

I turned to Nicolae who gave me a proud smile. "Good job," he said.

Next, Kai came to me with a shield, then called a water sword into his hand. Taking a fighting stance, he said, "Come on, Calla. Show me what you've got."

I called my own water sword and gave him a wicked grin. We circled around each other and then he swung. Back and forth our swords collided. They were strong, sounding almost like metal as they collided.

Everyone's gaze was fixedly on Kai and me as we practiced until my arms were tired and aching. Until I couldn't swing anymore, and my sword turned to water and dissolved into the earth.

Kylan strode up to me and held out a canteen.

"Time to power up?" I chuckled, unscrewing it, gulping it down, and handing the canteen back to him.

"Yes, we still have a few hours to go," he grinned. "We'll be on the opposite side of the arena training, so if you need us, just holler."

I nodded. "Thank you."

The cadre set up and began sparring one-on-one, and to see them in motion again … it was incredible. So fluid, so powerful, so fast. They even called Markus over, and it was amazing to see him in action too. He was just as agile and very powerful, fitting in with them perfectly.

"Are you ready? Thalia asked, stepping next to me to train me with her gift of earth.

Strengthened with the blood, I answered, "I am."

Thalia showed me how to call roots from the ground that could wrap around a body and pull it down. It was difficult at first, but soon, I was yanking hay dummies on their faces, until there were no more standing.

"Kai, run," I said, pointing toward the far end of the arena.

Those luminous blue eyes narrowed on me. "Why?"

Raising my palms I twiddled my fingers, a sinister grin rose on my lips. "Unless you want to be an easy target?"

"Oh, hell," he grumbled, then took off sprinting. I called vines and tried to wrap them around him, but he was fast, dodging them easily.

Dropping my arms, I sighed. Kai stopped and turned around, crossing his arms over his chest. "Is that all you've got, Sea Star?" he hollered, a smirk on his lips.

Thalia came and stood next to me. "Watch his pattern. Anticipate his next move and strike ahead of him. Also, don't aim for the waist, it's too high. Aim for his ankles."

I nodded, then grinned, and shot Kai a thumbs up. He was bouncing on his feet, ready for the next wave.

Kai took off and ran in a zig-zag pattern. Seeing where I thought he'd go next, I called a vine. He saw it and jumped, but I sent it wrapping around his ankle, yanking him to the ground. He hit with a thud and rolled over.

I glanced at Thalia who had a smile on her face. She held her hand up, and I smacked it. "You did it!"

"I did!" I released the vine and hollered to Kai, "Are you alright?"

He gave me a thumbs up, rolling over, and jumping to his feet. "Gods be damned. You got me."

Next, Thalia showed me how to call rocks and toss them. Not big rocks, though. I didn't want to destroy the arena.

"With your power, you can open the earth to swallow men whole, and then close it up again." Gods, that was a horrible way to die. But at least I had it as part of my arsenal. I wanted to learn everything, because I knew going against Roehl wasn't going to be easy.

Thalia didn't let me go easy. I realized why she helped command the guard in Incendia. After training with her, I was spent. But each time I called to my earth power, it became easier and easier.

Thalia said I was a natural, and they were all helping me fine tune my gifts. Teaching me things I never would have thought of and helping me expand my arsenal of power.

With not much time to spare, Nicolae was next. He taught me how to shape a bow and arrows with fire. I was in awe, watching a master do what he did best. His aim and posture, calling his fire bow and shooting fire arrows was nothing short of spectacular.

Everyone in the arena paused to watch him.

I felt my heart warm with pride as every arrow hit its mark.

This man was my grandfather but looked no older than my father. He was strong and agile and fit. I could see the muscles in his arms bulge as he stretched the fire bow.

And then, it was my turn. Shaping a fire bow wasn't as easy as he'd made it look. My first bow looked more like a harp, and my arrows fell way short. But I wasn't going to give up.

"You have already been through two rounds of training with water and earth and are not at your full capacity. Besides, I've had many more years of experience," Nicolae encouraged, coming up from behind me. He took my arms and positioned me like an archer. "Close your eyes," he said. "Imagine a bow, strong and taut, and shape it from the fire that burns within you."

I did as he said and through his touch could feel his power flowing through me. Opening my eyes, I was shocked. The bow I had created was perfectly shaped and strong.

"Now call an arrow, nock it, and mark your target."

Following his instructions, I eyed my target. A hay dummy Kai and Thalia had set up fifty yards in front of me.

"Fire is part of you. Do not fear it. Remember, you control it, Calla. It does not control you," Nicolae instructed. "Now pull back and send your arrow."

I nodded, sucking in a deep breath, pulling my arrow back and letting it go.

It flew fast, striking the dummy in the thigh, and Kai immediately sent water to put the fire out.

"That was good," Nicolae said. "Since this takes a lot of practice, let's try to use another one of your elements for help."

"What do you mean?"

"When you shoot your arrow, I want you to try to use air to guide it to its mark."

Air. The one element I had no trainer for.

"I'll try," I said, not feeling too confident.

Both Kai and Thalia cheered from the opposite side, standing off to the sides of the hay dummy.

"You've got this," Thalia yelled, pointing to the head of the dummy.

I nodded then sucked in a breath, while Nicolae stepped away from me.

Calling my bow, it was just as perfect as the last one. It felt strong and sturdy in my hands. Next, I called my arrow, aiming for the target, and sent it flying.

The arrow went a little too high, so I called air. A swift gust blew around us, sending the arrow way off target, heading straight for …

"Thalia!" I screamed.

Kai dove forward and pushed her to the ground, saving her just in time.

"Gods!" I cursed running toward them. "Thalia, are you okay?"

When I got there, she was still on her back, Kai still on top of her.

"Yes," she smiled, her cheeks flushed. "Kai saved me."

"I can see that," I said, relieved. Kai pushed himself off of her and stood, offering Thalia a hand. Her smile widened as he lifted her to her feet.

"Thank you," she said to him, her cheeks turning a darker shade of red.

"It was my pleasure," he said, bowing at the waist. Thalia was giddy. I could see it in her eyes, and it made me smile.

Nicolae came up from behind me and rested a hand on my shoulder. "Let's not use air with fire arrows just yet."

I nodded in agreement. "Yes, I would hate to impale anyone with a fire arrow first thing in the morning. Especially before breakfast."

The cadre ambled over with Markus, looking like they hadn't even worked out. No sweat, no gasping for air. That wasn't fair.

"You did good today, Calla," Feng said. "In no time you will be mastering all of the elements."

"Thanks. I think I have a good grasp on three of them," I said, and he nodded in agreement.

"We need to head back," Kylan said. "The sun will be rising soon."

After waking Sabine, we all mounted our horses and the dozen guards stationed around the arena were sent off by Kylan.

"Gods be damned," Thalia exhaled, her eyes on a hill above us. On a steed of black was the silhouette of a man, crown atop his head, cape blowing in the wind. He looked like a character taken directly out of one of my novels. The prince. The hero.

Brone let out a deep laugh. "Even with his damn memory erased and voices telling him to hate her, he still can't stay away."

"Well, to be fair, he had a strong pull to Calla before he even met her," Feng added.

My heart constricted, seeing Trystan's darkened silhouette up on the top of the hill. He looked like a dark knight. My dark knight. I wished I could ride up to him. To cast my own magic on him to release him from the spell, so the two of us could ride off into immortal bliss.

But that wasn't possible right now. I couldn't be near him, knowing it would cause him pain. Which was most likely why he was far away, watching us from a distance.

Andrés waved his hand in the air, but Trystan didn't wave back. Instead, he rode off, disappearing down the opposite side of the hill.

"Let's move," Kylan said, the sky already starting to brighten. We rode hard and fast back to the castle, my mind on one thing. Trystan.

Why was he on that hilltop?

Was it because he still felt a pull to me, like Brone had said?

Or was it for another reason?

CHAPTER FIFTEEN

Back at the castle, we made our way through the entrance, and I felt an empty coldness sweep around me. Glancing down one of the hallways leading to the back of the castle, four figures emerged. Brone and Kylan immediately stepped closer to me, just in front, almost shielding me from whoever was coming.

But I already knew who was coming, and my stomach twisted in knots.

The King of Carpathia walked toward us, escorting a beautiful young woman on his arm. She was around five-ten, her hair like silk, the color of ebony that fell down to her waist. Her skin was pale with lips a dark crimson red. She was wearing a long, black gown that hugged her tiny waist and showed a bit too much cleavage.

The king was exactly as I expected Trystan's father should look like. He was over six-foot tall and handsome with sharp features and hazel eyes. Raven hair fell to his shoulders, and he wore a full beard that was trimmed short. Under his royal garb, I could tell he was fit.

There was a definite resemblance between him and Trystan, but the king's presence felt cold and hard, mirroring the sternness in his eyes and the rigidness of his expression.

Behind the king and princess was another couple, wearing a set of matching silver crowns. The man was wearing a dark blue suit but was short and stout with a goatee. He had short brown hair, and dark brown eyes. The woman on his arm was nearly a foot taller than him. She was stick thin, her chocolate hair was tied up and wore a dark blue gown. She looked hard as nails, her nose turned up snidely.

Andrés and Feng stepped ahead of the group to greet them, while the others in our group stood behind me, Kylan and Brone.

The king walked over and stood in front of Feng and Andrés. They bowed low. Brone took a step closer to me as the king's eyes swept over the rest of the group.

"Who are your guests?" he asked.

Nicolae walked toward the king and bowed his head. "Your highness. I've been wanting to seek counsel with you. I am Nicolae Corvus," he said.

The king's scowl grew on his face. "Nicolae Corvus? The one who killed the prince of Morbeth?"

Nicolae stood tall and placed his hand to his chest. "I did not kill the prince. I was merely defending myself," he said calmly. "It was a misunderstanding."

The king's face twisted. "That's your word against Morbeth's, and I cannot harbor a wanted criminal here."

"He's not a criminal," I blurted, defending Nicolae. I knew the truth. I knew Roehl tried to kill him first.

Brone nudged me, but it was too late. The king's eyes snapped to mine, lips narrowed into a hard line. "Who are you?"

I swallowed hard, just about to speak when Kai interjected.

"She is with me," he said, stepping forward, standing so close behind me I could feel the heat of his body on my back. His right hand rested on my right shoulder.

"Kai?" the King addressed, his eyes softening a little. "It's been a while since I've seen you in Carpathia. How have you been?"

"Good, your highness," Kai replied, bowing his head. "Miss Caldwell was an honored guest in Aquaria when Trystan paid me a visit. Her grandfather is the one who saved my father's life."

"Is that right?" the king said, his cold eyes sweeping over me again.

"Yes," Kai replied. "She was there when Trystan invited me to come and stay a few days, to catch up on Princely duties. I asked if I could bring her along. She is a dear friend of mine."

"Who is she? Where is she from?" Princess Ivy bit, her eyes like sharp nails, raking down my face.

The tension in the room was now to the point of suffocation and I knew everyone in our group was feeling it.

Before I could reply, a voice called from behind. "Father."

The king's attention shifted, as did the princess. Her smug face quickly turned into a smile that was obviously fake and a little creepy.

Trystan made his way to them and bowed. "Father, these are my guests. I've invited them to stay. What Nicolae said is true. We've come to find that he is an innocent man. Roehl was the one who tried to take his life and is now wreaking havoc in Talbrinth."

"Trystan," the king exhaled sharply. "I forbid you to get involved," the king said, pointing his finger at him. "This is not a matter that concerns Carpathia."

"It does, father. Roehl kidnapped and tortured me as I was leaving Aquaria. It was Nicolae Corvus and Miss Caldwell who rescued me."

"What?" the king roared. The king and queen of Northfall gasped. The princess made a squeal that had Brone glance at me and close his eyes.

Trystan suddenly let out a moan, grabbing his head in between his hands.

"What's wrong?" the king asked. "Do I need to call a physician?"

"No," Trystan replied, straightening his back and shaking off the pain. "I'm fine.

Gods, he was paying a heavy price for going against what the voices inside his head were telling him.

Right now, Trystan didn't know who I was, so he couldn't have remembered me saving him. He was telling his father what he'd heard either from his men, or from Nicolae. And it seemed he was doing it to save us. Again.

"What is this about you being kidnapped?" The king snapped, stepping toward Trystan. "Why the hell wasn't I informed of this?

And why would Roehl do something so treacherous? He knows the laws."

Kylan stepped forward. "Highness, Roehl is not in his right mind. King Romulus banished him from Morbeth for placing a curse on him. Roehl had put a sickness spell on his father, so he could assume the throne. Trystan just happened to be a casualty of his madness. Roehl is jealous of Trystan. He has always been."

"Well, he shouldn't be. My son's priorities have been muddled as of late. He's been running all over Talbrinth, chasing some fantasy girl," he rumbled.

Princess Ivy's face twisted. As did the king and queen of Northfall.

I was frozen in place, my breath caught in my throat. The men around me stepped a little closer. But the king didn't seem to recognize me. He didn't know I was that fantasy girl his son had been chasing. Thank the goddess.

I wanted to fold into myself and slither out the door, but Trystan moved closer to his father and said, "I have promised our guests rooms for the time being. They are being trained by my men, to defend themselves against future attacks from Roehl."

The king's face was even more rigid, and I swear I could see rage smoldering in his eyes. "We will discuss this very soon, Trystan. As for now, take your fiancé and show her around the grounds. I have promised to take the king and queen of Northfall riding."

Trystan bowed, then held out his arm, and the princess quickly snatched it up, pushing herself as close as she could to him, squeezing her cleavage.

As Trystan led the princess out the door, Kylan grabbed my wrist and dragged me with him up the stairs. Brone and Andrés were right behind us. Feng stayed back with the others, leading them back up to their rooms.

At the top of the stairs, I glanced down, and the entire area was empty.

"That was close," Brone growled.

"Too close," Kylan exhaled, still tugging me down the hall.

"He didn't know who I was," I whispered, mostly to myself.

"Thank the gods for that," Andrés said. "If he found out who you were, you would probably be on your way to the dungeon."

"What?" I screeched. "He would actually throw me in a dungeon?" I'd been mortified, hiding from his father, and now I was terrified of being sent to the dungeon.

"No, he wouldn't," Kylan exasperated, throwing Andrés a narrowed glare. "But he wouldn't be happy you're here. Trystan's fondness for you has made it impossible for the king to gain control over him. We all know how deeply he feels for you, so much so, that he has forsaken his duties and his father's advice."

"Not anymore," I said sadly.

We came up to my door and Kylan stopped. "You're safe for now. Go soak in the tub and get some rest. I'll have one of the servants bring you lunch."

"In a wine bottle?" I chimed.

"Sure," he chuckled. "See you later, Calla."

"See you later," I said as he walked away. "And by the way, thank you, Kylan."

Kylan raised his arm and disappeared around the corner.

Slipping inside the room, I was relieved. But a wave of sadness crashed over me. Trystan was out there, arm in arm with his fiancé, showing her around his castle garden.

I would be lying if I didn't feel a tinge of jealousy, knowing he'd promised me a tour if I ever visited, before his memory was erased of me.

Walking over to my nightstand, I poured myself a glass of ruby wine and made my way out to the balcony. The sun had made its grand appearance, slowly nudging the town from its slumber. I stepped out and leaned against the railing, closing my eyes and letting my head fall back, allowing the sun to kiss my entire face. Even with the cold wintery breeze, the rays from the sun felt warm, and the light seemed to brighten my mood.

Blood was my fuel, aiding in healing, but the sun made me feel renewed and rejuvenated. It was like a gentle touch, comforting, soothing my tense nerves. Its warmth caressed my entire being, whispering softly in my ear that one day the anguish and misery would pass.

The sun was our life source, our power. It fueled us and gave us strength. I was beyond grateful I was able to bask in its glory, because inside these very walls were friends of mine who would die horrible deaths if the sun touched their skin. To them, the sun was death, and because of it, they had to live a life in the darkness.

Taking a long pull of my drink, I finally opened my eyes. The land was bright and so beautiful. Below, the citizens of Carpathia were beginning to wake and start a brand-new day.

Below, I watched the new shift of guards line up at the front entrance. To the right, two men led three horses up to where the future in-laws of Trystan—the royals of Northfall—were going on a horseback tour with the King of Carpathia.

Yet, here I was, stuck in a room, hiding my true identity.

I was sick of being in the shadows. I was meant to be in the light.

What if I was the one who could help Carpathia's prince be the greatest king who ever ruled in Talbrinth? Trystan was already more of a king than his father had ever been. And I knew he would surpass him. He would be a great ruler, because he truly cared about his people.

I gave the entire area a sweep and didn't see Trystan or Princess Ivy anywhere. The gardens must have been on the other side of the castle, which was a relief. I don't think my heart could handle seeing them together.

Finishing my drink, I headed back inside and after a long bath, noticed there were sleeping gowns folded next to the clothes brought in this morning. Throwing on a gown, I crawled back into bed. I didn't want to think about what Trystan and his fiancé were doing. I just wanted to sleep and shut off my brain. Thank the goddess I was exhausted from training.

In no time, I fell fast asleep.

"Calla?" A voice called, gently nudging my shoulder.

Blurry eyed, I saw the silhouette of someone familiar.

"Trystan?" I exhaled.

"Don't you wish," Kylan chuckled.

"Kylan, it better not be three in the morning," I groaned. "If it is, I'm staying in bed."

"It's noon, and I've come with your lunch … served in a wine bottle."

"Thank you." I pointed toward the nightstand, eyes still closed. "You can leave it there."

"Where'd you get this one?" Kylan asked, picking up the empty bottle and reading the note.

"The maid? But the handwriting looks like Trystan's." I tried to pry my eyes open, but they were dry.

"You aren't a morning person." It was a statement.

"I actually am, just not a three-in-the-morning person."

"Well, because you are a guest of Prince Trystan, you have been invited to dinner tonight. The king is throwing a dinner party in honor of Princess Ivy." His voice sounded irritated as he spoke her name.

"Can I decline?" I moaned, rolling over.

"It's not advised."

"I have nothing to wear."

"Yes, you do." Kylan pointed to a gown hanging in a small wardrobe.

Sitting up, I blinked at a gorgeous crimson and black gown.

"How?" Whoever snuck into my room was super stealthy.

Kylan shrugged. "Your friends have gowns as well. Also," he paused and sucked in a breath. "Brynna will be there."

My heart suddenly stopped.

"Drink some wine, it will be fine."

"That's what you think," I sighed. "I know she hates me."

"She doesn't hate you," he said, sitting on the edge of the bed. "I think once she sees you, things will be different. Right now, you've been gone. She's had nothing but sadness and anger to hold on to."

"I hope you're right," I whispered.

Kylan stood and gave me a narrowed glare. "Hey, if she doesn't, it's her loss."

"She's already lost everything."

"Which is why I know you'll find a way to work it out." Kylan made for the door. "One of us will collect you for dinner."

As the time for the dinner party drew near, two women came to my room with baskets in their arms, filled with things to help me get ready.

Both women seemed shy and weren't talkative, answering simple questions with one-word replies, but they were damn good at their jobs. In no time, my hair was curled, the sides pinned up to something they placed on top of my head. I wasn't even sure what I looked like because there was no mirror where I was sitting.

As soon as the women were done, they bowed and left the room.

About to walk into the washroom to view myself in the mirror, there was a knock at the door. Kylan had said that one of them was going to come and get me to escort me down to dinner, so I made my way over.

When I swung the door open, I froze, legs weak. The air became heavy, making it hard to breathe.

CHAPTER SIXTEEN

Trystan stood at the threshold, wearing an all-black suit with crimson trim and his golden crown circling his head. The sight of him began to unravel every part of me, making my insides bloom with warmth. He was so gods damned handsome, his thick dark hair combed back, a few unkempt strands falling askew.

Trystan didn't say a word, just stood there, hands tucked into his trousers, his eyes roaming over me from head to toe.

I suddenly felt naked under his stare, but his eyes didn't hold any emotion. I couldn't tell if he liked what he saw, or if he hated it.

And then it hit me. I looked down at my gown, realizing I was wearing the exact same colors he was.

Had someone planned this? Was this some evil plan to get the princess to hate me more?

If this dinner was for the Princess of Northfall, I surely didn't want to stand out. All I wanted was to be invisible here and stay that way until we made it out of Carpathia in one piece.

Maybe I was making a big deal out of this, and everyone was wearing the same colors. Maybe they had color coordinated all the guests.

I looked into Trystan's emotionless eyes. Eyes that were holding back pain I knew he was enduring being so close to me.

"Prince Trystan," I said, slightly bowing my head to him. It felt weird addressing him like a stranger.

"Calla," Kylan called from down the hall, concern filling his voice. I was glad for his interruption and felt I could breathe a bit more freely as Trystan took a few steps back.

"Trystan," Kylan said, "the Princess of Northfall is waiting at the bottom of the stairs."

His words made my stomach churn. Trystan gave him a nod, then his beautiful azure eyes met mine. Again, holding my gaze for what seemed like a moment too long.

I wished there was a way to break the curse. To have his memories come back. I wished he was here to escort me to dinner. That he would take my hand and introduce me to his father, we would eat, and then he would take my hand and lead me to the dance floor where we would remain the rest of the night, in each other's arms.

But the dream disintegrated in front of my eyes as Trystan walked away, hands still tucked into his pockets, and he never looked back.

As soon as he was out of view, Kylan raked his fingers through his hair, a little agitated. "Why was he at your door?"

I shook my head. "I was heading for the washroom and heard a knock. I thought it was you, but when I opened it, he was standing there."

"He just can't stay away," Kylan sighed, then laughed looking at me with a smirk in his turquoise eyes.

I held up my hands. "Believe me, I have tried to stay away. I know how much it hurts him, but I can't help it if he comes to me. I couldn't slam the door in his face."

"You're right. There is one thing about Trystan, when his mind is set on something, nothing in the world can steer his mind. He is stubborn. And it seems that even Roehl's power is no match for his thick headedness. Maybe he will be able to break the curse himself."

"Do you think it's possible?"

Kylan shook his head. "All I know is that he's fighting the curse, even now, on his own. But I'm afraid of what it will do to his mind if he keeps fighting. It could very well break him, like it did his mother." Kylan sucked in a deep breath. "The mage told Brone that if he keeps fighting it, the curse could get stronger. It could hurt or even—"

"Kill him?" I questioned in a shaky breath.

Kylan nodded.

Gods. I suddenly felt ill.

I couldn't … no, I *wouldn't* let that happen. I would tell Nicolae and the others tonight that we had to leave Carpathia as soon as possible. Trystan couldn't find out, but I would tell Kylan.

I had to get away from him. Far away. Until we found a cure. I wouldn't let him suffer because I was selfish and wanted to stay close to him. I would leave, because I didn't want him to be in pain. I would leave, even if it meant that I could lose him. But mostly, because I loved him.

"What are you thinking?" Kylan questioned, his eyes narrowing on me.

"I'll tell you later," I said, looping my arm in his. He looked handsome in an all-black uniform. "You have to wear a uniform to dinner?"

"I am a member of Trystan's cadre, and as such, we always don our uniforms," he said. "This is a more formal style. Why, is there something wrong with it?" He smoothed out the sides.

"No, I like the all-black. It suits you."

"Well, thank you," he said with a grin.

"You're welcome. Now, how about we get to dinner and get through it as quickly and painlessly as possible?" I held up my free hand, crossing my fingers.

"That sounds like a great plan."

As we came around the bend, Brone, Feng, and Andrés were waiting in the hallway. All dressed in their matching black uniforms.

"Don't you all look dashing," I said. When they turned, I gave them a little curtsey.

They all placed their fists to their chests and bowed their heads.

"Please, no bowing," I whispered loudly. "It's weird. And we don't want the king to know who I am."

"We won't bow in front of the king, but it shouldn't be weird," Feng said with a grin. "You are royalty, after all."

"And quite stunning," Andrés added. "Princess Calla, you should embrace who you are. If I was a royal, I would make everyone bow to me, like Princess Ivy does."

Brone flicked his cheek, making Andrés hiss. "What? I did nothing," Andrés blurted, in a stronger accent than usual.

Brone thumbed toward the stairs, where Trystan had just gone down to meet Ivy, and Andrés rolled his eyes. "Give Calla some time," Brone murmured. "It's only been several months since she found out she was a royal. She's not accustomed to being one. Most have been born into it or train their entire lives to marry into it."

I smiled at the big guy, and he returned a wink.

"Shall we?" Feng said, holding out his arm to me. I linked my arm in his and all four men surrounded me.

"I will be the envy of the dinner party tonight, with four of the best warriors on this planet as my escorts," I giggled, thankful for their company. I would need it, being the odd girl out.

"We have been ordered to keep an eye on you tonight," Andrés said with a wave of his brows.

"Why me?"

"Direct order, by you know who." Andrés made a gesture with his eyes toward the stairs. Trystan? But this was a dinner party. I highly doubted Roehl would attack, and Carpathia was heavily warded.

Andrés leaned closer to me and whispered, "Maybe it's because your friend Brynna will be there. And of course, Princess Ivy. We might have to block some of those claws." He swung his arms, like he was blocking an attack.

Brone flicked his ear this time. "I swear to the gods, Andrés," he growled. "You'd better keep your flappy mouth shut and behave at dinner."

Andrés shot Brone a smirk and me a wink.

At least I wouldn't be short of friends or fun this evening. But Andrés's words had my stomach in knots. Brynna would be there. And I had no idea what to expect.

CHAPTER SEVENTEEN

Slowly making our way down the stairs, I spotted the others in our group, except Nicolae. Sabine was wearing a flowing, forest green gown, and Thalia, a fitted gown of bronze. They both looked gorgeous, their hair and faces made up to perfection. But it also showed me that this ball was not color coordinated. I was still the only one dressed in the same colors as Trystan.

Markus and Kai were dashing in their all-black suits. Plain black, no crimson trim. We greeted each other before we moved down one of the hallways and into a large formal dining room.

"Where is Nicolae?" I asked Kai.

"He said he had to take care of some business and that he'd be back by morning."

"What kind of business?"

"He didn't say, but I'm sure he'll be fine."

I nodded, wondering why Nicolae would leave without letting me know. Maybe he didn't want me to worry. Maybe he'd left something back on his island he needed.

The dining room was huge, with a massive crystal chandelier hanging from the center of the ceiling. Expensive tapestries hung on the textured walls.

There was a small stage in one corner, with musicians setting up.

In the center of the room was one long table that could hold up to fifty guests, set beautifully, with gorgeous wintery themed arrangements and candles. Four of those places were set with dinnerware, for the non-vampires—Sabine, Thalia, Kai, and Brynna. The others were set with large, ornate chalices and glassware, to serve ruby wine and other drink.

The king was standing in the corner of the room having a conversation with the king and queen of Northfall when we entered.

There were other guests dressed in finery, who I assumed were the heads of Carpathia.

As soon as we entered, the room fell silent. I quickly scanned the area but didn't find Brynna, or Trystan and Princess Ivy. Maybe they'd taken a detour.

The king cleared his throat, and the room turned their attention to him.

"Everyone, please take a seat and I will introduce our special guest."

Everyone shifted and moved toward the long dining table

and took their seats. Kylan pulled back a chair and motioned for me to sit.

I was seated in between him and Brone. Sabine was directly across from me next to Markus. Kai and Thalia were next to them, while Feng and Andrés walked away from us to stand guard at one of the far walls.

"They aren't going to dine with us?" I whispered to Kylan.

He shook his head and leaned in. "We drew sticks. Two would accompany you and two would stand watch."

"Is that really necessary? I don't think there will be a great threat during dinner."

Kylan shrugged. "You never know. I've seen trouble in the least likely places these past months."

I sighed. "I can't argue with that."

He chuckled, but our conversation was cut short.

"Everyone, I would like to introduce you to the royals of Northfall—King Augustus, Queen Ravenna, and their beautiful daughter, Princess Ivy ... the future Queen of Carpathia."

Everyone began clapping, while Sabine gave me a pointed look from across the table.

From a side door, Trystan escorted Princess Ivy into the room.

Gods, the sight of him made my insides bloom with warmth. But as soon as my eyes caught her, that warmth immediately turned to acid. Ivy was wearing a navy-blue gown that didn't even match him at all. But I had to admit, she was beautiful. Her pale skin was flawless, her features pointy, and she was tall and lean. But there was something in her eyes that seemed … insincere. Maybe because I'd heard the horrible stories about her from Sabine, Kylan, and Kai.

Whispers erupted but I couldn't make out what anyone was saying. There were so many voices, that I had to place my hands to the sides of my head to quiet them.

Kylan nudged me. "You can tune them out. Focus on one person, direct your hearing to them, and the others will fade away."

I saw a couple across from me looking at the princess with hard faces, so I focused on the woman, whose mouth was barely moving. "If she becomes queen, Carpathia is doomed," she whispered. The man nodded slightly.

I decided I liked them.

As they neared the table, Trystan's eyes shifted over to where we were sitting. Princess Ivy caught it immediately and when she looked at me, it was as if she were throwing invisible daggers at me.

I smiled and clapped, like everyone else, even though I wished I was the one on his arm.

They were seated on the opposite side of the table as me, directly across from her parents, while Trystan's father was at the head of the table.

With a snap of his fingers, servants came through the doors carrying golden trays, each carrying fancy bottles of ruby wine. I'm not sure if that's what they called it here in

Carpathia, but I liked it much better than saying *blood*.

They poured the ruby wine into each of our chalices, while three servants came out with plates of food, and placed them in front of Kai, Sabine, and Thalia. Roasted chicken with vegetables and freshly baked rolls. I breathed in, the aroma immediately hitting my nose, making my mouth water.

"Where is Brynna?" I asked Kylan, trying to distract my senses.

He shook his head. "She couldn't make it. She said she was feeling ill."

I nodded, exhaling, knowing it was because she probably didn't want to see me, or wasn't ready to. I was fine with that. When she was ready, I would be waiting.

Music began to play softly behind us as we sipped on our dinner. I closed my eyes and imagined taking a bite of Sabine's juicy piece of chicken and dipping a roll in the gravy. Gods, it was torture sitting across from them. But I'd have to bear it. This was part of my new life. Part of the curse.

I felt a nudge from the side and opened my eyes.

"How about a dance?" Kylan asked, probably seeing my struggle. "And this time, I'll be dancing as myself." I smiled, thinking back to the Shadow Fest when we last danced.

"But no one else is dancing," I whispered, eyeing the empty floor.

He raised a brow.

"Isn't the princess supposed to start off the dance, since it's her party?"

Kylan sighed. "If they were getting married, yes. But this is a dinner party. Anyone can dance."

He pushed back his seat then stood, offering me his hand. Quickly glancing over to Trystan, his eyes were already on me.

"Calla," Kylan whispered, his hand still extended, so I slipped mine into his.

"Go, and have fun," Brone said in his deep voice. "Save a dance for me."

I gasped, throwing a hand to my heart. "You dance?"

He gave me a narrowed glare. "Of course, I dance."

I smiled at him. "Then I will definitely save a dance for you."

As Kylan escorted me out to the dance floor, I could feel the eyes of the room on our backs.

"Relax," Kylan said. "It's just a dance between friends. Besides, I sensed you were a little tense at the table and was hoping this would take off the edge.

Kylan faced me and bowed then offered me his hand. I took it, placing the other hand on his shoulder. He pulled me close, and we began to dance.

"Why are you really doing this?" I questioned, sensing those weren't the only reasons.

The corner of his lips curled upward. "I want Trystan to see that his most trusted friends are friends with you. That you aren't the enemy. But also, because I did see you were a bit tense."

"I was actually battling the food urges." My mouth turned downward. "I want chicken."

Kylan chuckled, then spun me around. "I forget you are still new at this."

The music picked up a little faster, and Kylan picked up our pace. I squealed, not prepared for such a fast spin. But like a gentleman, Kylan kept me steady, both of us laughing.

I noticed that everyone at the table had turned to watch us. Sabine and Thalia had wide smiles on their faces. Markus looked like the rest of the table, his face hard-set, watching me closely. Kai smiled, but he was more interested in the food on his plate.

When the song started to die, I spotted Feng standing nearby.

"It appears you have a dance card," Kylan said, escorting me over to him.

Feng bowed at the waist and offered me his hand, and Kylan handed me off, walking to where Feng had previously stood.

Feng was a bit taller and slightly thinner than Kylan, but still very toned. His hair was combed neatly and pulled back behind the nape of his neck. He was smooth and agile as he whisked me around the floor.

"Thanks for dancing with me," I said to him.

Feng smiled. "It's been a long time since we've had the opportunity to dance. I couldn't pass it up."

I giggled. "Well, I hope I'm a worthy partner. I haven't had as much experience as you."

"Just follow my lead and you'll be fine." He chuckled. "You're doing great. Not only with the dancing, but with the way you're handling the entire situation. I know it must be difficult."

"It is, but I am trying to stay hopeful."

"We are doing the same," he said. "But until then, let's

dance."

Feng and I danced around the floor, and I couldn't help but smile for a moment, free from the stress in the room.

As the next song ended, Feng twirled me in a circle and dipped me back. As he brought me back up, I saw Princess Ivy with daggers in her eyes leaning over to whisper to Trystan. I focused my hearing on her.

"Why is her dress color coordinated with you?" She gave him a pointed look.

Trystan shrugged. "Ask the servants. I had no say in what I wore tonight. It was hanging in my room when I arrived."

"She must have had something to do with it." Her expression soured. "She must be in bed with your entire cadre. Look at them. It's pathetic how they all hover around her."

I watched Trystan turn to her with a slight grin. "At least they're having fun."

"Who the hell is she? She's not even pretty."

Trystan ignored her, closing his eyes and taking a sip from his chalice. When they opened again, those gorgeous eyes met mine, and I immediately looked away, hoping he didn't know I was eavesdropping.

I could feel waves of anger rolling off of Princess Ivy. But why? I had done or said nothing to her since she'd arrived. I'd barely even looked at her.

"She's jealous," Feng whispered. "She's jealous of anyone our prince looks at or shows the slightest interest in. Would you like to return to the table?"

"No," I said, watching Andrés shrug at me. I gave him a nod, and he happily made his way over to us. "I guess I'm still on the dance clock."

"Keep an eye on that one," Feng said through narrowed eyes.

"I will," I giggled as Andrés came and took my hand. "Thank you, Feng."

Feng bowed his head and walked away.

I was lucky to have them to keep my mind occupied, and I was glad the musicians were playing happy, upbeat music that we could actually dance to.

Trystan's cadre were great dancers and even better company.

"So, Calla," Andrés began. "Tell me about that bird. The fiery one that went inside you and gave you wings."

I laughed at the way he presented his awkward question, especially with his accent.

"That would be Flint," I said. "He's a firebird who was created by Helia, the Fire Goddess. She gave him to me as a gift."

His eyes widened. "You met her? The Fire Goddess?"

"I did."

He paused for a moment, before picking right back up. "In my country of Almeria, we have a statue of the Fire Goddess. She is the bringer of light. With light, things grow and bloom and live." His smile widened. "I would be honored in my country if they knew I was friends with the one who has been chosen by the Fire Goddess."

"Aren't you already honored, being chosen as one of Trystan's cadre?"

He shook his head. "Not too many know about it. Just my immediate family and a few friends."

"Oh," I sighed. "Well, if we ever travel to Almeria, I will be sure to let everyone know I am your friend."

"Really?" he gasped. "You would do that?"

"Of course, I would."

Andrés spun me out, then back in, before dipping me backward. When he brought me back up, he gathered me in a bear hug that lifted me off the ground. "Thank you. You're the best," he said. He then grabbed my hand and led me off the floor.

He ambled back to the wall, but right before I returned to my seat, there was a tightness in my legs. Suddenly, I couldn't move, and started falling forward.

Throwing my arms out in front of me, I called air and a short burst of wind pushed me back up, steadying me on my feet.

I turned and looked at Princess Ivy who had a glare in her now darkened eyes and a smirk on her lips. It was her. She'd cast a freaking spell on me. Kylan told me she had powers like Roehl, only hers weren't as strong.

Well, the bitch didn't know who she was messing with.

I gained my composure and returned to my seat. Those who were sitting with their backs to me, didn't see, but Sabine, Markus, Kai, and Thalia saw.

Sabine tilted her head to the side and gave me a look. "Did you almost trip back there?" she giggled.

"Almost," I was debating telling her, but didn't want to make a scene. If I knew Sabine, she'd march up to Princess Ivy and tell her where to stick her powers.

"I saw that little burst of air power you used. Just enough to keep you on your feet. That was awesome. I'm impressed," Markus stated.

"So was I," Kai added. "I don't think anyone saw, besides us."

Brone nudged my side. "Did they serve you alcohol?"

"No, they did not. And I didn't trip. What happened was … complicated."

"I'm not used to walking in heels either," Thalia murmured, her thoughts turned elsewhere. "They aren't very comfortable."

I realized that none of them knew Ivy was the source of my near-falling tragedy. But if the princess tried to use her magic on me again — *Oh!* I hated bullies. They felt stronger picking on the weak, and for some reason she pegged me as being weak. But I wasn't. Not anymore.

Kylan had just returned from standing against the wall and stood behind me.

"Calla, can I speak to you?" I noticed concern etched in his turquoise eyes.

"Yes, of course."

He walked outside of the dining room, nearly to the exit of the castle before he stopped and faced me.

"I saw what happened," he said in a quieted tone. "She used her magic against you. It is forbidden to do so, maliciously, against another royal. Especially when they are guests of the royal family."

"She doesn't know I'm a royal," I noted. "She's also Trystan's fiancé and seems to hold sway over the king."

"It doesn't matter," he murmured, raking his fingers through his hair. "I just wanted you to know that I saw what she did and will be watching her closely."

I smiled, knowing I had at least one ally. "Thank you, Kylan. But I can handle myself against her."

"I am well aware of that," he said, lips turning upward. "I think I'm more afraid of what you could do to her. She is unaware of your powers, and I have a feeling she's not through with you yet. She's carefully watched Trystan glance at you one too many times, and she can't stand it." Kylan let out an exasperated breath and paced in front of me. "She finally managed to find a fiancé, someone she's sunken her claws into and she won't back down."

I sighed and shook my head. "I have to find that loophole. I love him, Kylan. And I won't back down either."

Kylan's eyes narrowed, his lips curled up at the sides. "I'm happy to hear that. I wish Trystan was here to hear those words. He deserves you, not that snake."

"He did hear them," I said, which made Kylan's brow furrow. "Right before Roehl forced the Lethe potion down his throat, I told him I loved him."

Kylan nodded, a smile blooming in his lips. "That's good. If we ever find the damned cure, he will remember the truth."

I sighed and nodded, wondering if that day would ever come.

"We better get back inside before they think something's wrong."

I followed Kylan back into the dining hall. Half of the people were dancing, including Sabine and Markus, and Kai and Thalia. They all looked happy together, dancing side by side, Sabine and Thalia laughing at something Sabine had said.

On the dance floor, right in the middle, was Trystan and Ivy. She had both arms wrapped around his neck, head resting on his chest, eyes closed, lips smiling. But Trystan looked … uncomfortable. He was rigid, his arms barely touching her sides and his eyes seemed distant.

My heart was breaking for him and there was nothing I could do about it.

CHAPTER EIGHTEEN

"Calla, are you ready to dance with me?" Brone's rich voice cut straight through my thoughts.

I turned to him, his big hand stretched out to me, so I placed mine in his. "Of course."

Brone led me to the edge of the dance floor and began to lead me in a dance. This tall, muscular, monster of a man, was smooth on his feet, and a surprisingly agile dancer.

"You doubted me," he stated, his eyes downward to meet mine.

"I had my doubts, but you are completely crushing them right now."

He grinned from ear to ear. This vampire who would normally terrify anyone with a glance, was laughing and dancing with me. Trystan's most trusted circle of friends were here to protect me, but they've become my friends as well. I felt comforted and safe with them around me.

As Brone and I danced, he made me laugh with his random banter. Glancing toward Trystan, I noticed his eyes were hollow, but now and then, they were fixed on me, causing all kinds of emotions to bubble inside.

I watched Ivy snuggle up to him. He wasn't just holding some girl. He was holding his fiancé. A woman who would never love him like I would.

As the music ended, the floor cleared, and a rogue tear slipped from my eye. I watched Trystan track it down my cheek before I quickly wiped it away.

Ivy had seen our interaction, her eyes moved to Trystan, who was still watching me. I swore I heard a growl when her eyes jerked back to mine. She leaned her head against Trystan's chest so he couldn't see her eyes. Eyes that had gone completely black, and the room suddenly became ice cold.

"I think we should leave," I whispered to Brone.

But it was too late. A magical coldness wrapped around my legs, slithering up my torso, to my chest and up around my throat, gripping so tight I couldn't breathe.

It was Princess Ivy. She was trying to kill me.

I struggled to gasp for air, but none came.

"Calla?" Brone's face showed serious concern as I clawed at my throat, trying to loosen the invisible rope strangling me. I couldn't breathe. Darkness hovering at the edges of my vision. "Calla, what's wrong?" Brone hollered, but I couldn't respond. I couldn't speak. Her magic had closed my airways.

Brone placed his palms on my shoulders and shook me. I collapsed to my knees, the magic tightening.

"Help!" I heard Brone's pleas, but his voice was dampened. The darkness now threatened to fill my eyes.

Markus was suddenly next to me, tugging me into his arms, "What's wrong, Calla? What can I do? Tell me how to help." But he couldn't help.

I shut my eyes, closing out the world around me. There were too many voices crying out. Too many hands trying to help, but powerless to do so. This was magic. And there was only one means to stop it.

I called to my magic and felt it writhing under my skin. I could feel its warmth, already soothing me. Calming my fears. I felt its immense power, readily answering my call. In a flash, I became the flame, my power searching out and incinerating Ivy's evil magic sent to harm me.

Suddenly, I could breathe again and move freely, and when I opened my eyes, those surrounding me backed up … except for my friends. I was still in Markus's arms. Brone was on his knees in front of me, his eyes wide with relief. Sabine, Thalia, and Kai were also there, right behind him.

"Calla," Sabine whispered. "Are you okay?"

But before I could answer, the king's voice roared behind them.

"What is the meaning of this?"

Markus and Brone helped me to my feet. I stood tall, my skin still heated.

"Someone was using magic against me, to harm me," I replied, my voice a bit hoarse.

Trystan dropped his hands from Ivy, his eyes moving to her. She blinked a few times, her black eyes returning to her natural hue.

"Who would use their power against you? And why would they have cause to do such a thing?" the king demanded.

Trystan's cadre lined up in front of me, but it was Kylan who stepped forward and bowed at the waist. "Your highness, it was Princess Ivy. This is the second time she's used magic against Calla tonight," he said.

Princess Ivy turned to the king and shook her head. "He's lying," she cried.

"Kylan, those are heavy accusations against a royal," the king warned. "And the future queen of Carpathia."

Those last six words cut straight through my core.

"I do understand the impacts of such an accusation," Kylan said, his head still bowed, "but I witnessed it with my own eyes."

The king turned a narrowed glare to me. "Who are you to come here and cause trouble?"

What the—? Was he seriously trying to turn this on me?

Every eye in the room was now on me, awaiting my response and I suddenly felt like I was on trial for committing a crime.

Hell, no. I didn't care if this man was Trystan's father.

"Answer me. Who are you?" he demanded.

I stood tall, hands clenched at my sides and looked at the king, my insides burning with rage.

I could feel my power scratching against my palms, begging to be set free. But I kept it at bay. Kept my wits and spoke calmly, in a way I knew my predecessors would be proud.

"I am the true heir of Incendia, Descendent of Princess Leora and King Romulus. And I have been chosen by the Fire Goddess, Helia."

Gasps and whispers erupted around the room. They didn't believe me. Didn't accept I was Incendian royalty. So, I would have to convince them. I would let a sample of my power out to play.

I let my fire magic encompass my body, then held up my palms encased in flame.

More gasps, mostly in awe, echoed around the room. The faces of the people in the room were confused.

The king blinked, then blinked again, his brow crumpled, mouth agape. As was everyone else in the room. Not to be overly flamboyant, I quelled my power.

The king turned his attention to Ivy. "Did you use magic against her?"

"No." Princess Ivy raised her eyes to Trystan and shook her head. "Aren't you going to help me?"

Trystan took a step away from her, his eyes found mine, but were serious, stern. "Are you certain Princess Ivy was the one who used magic against you?"

"Yes," I replied.

Trystan's expression turned bitter at Ivy, his hands tightened at his sides. "How could you use magic against another royal in Carpathia?"

"I didn't know she was a royal!" Ivy snapped before realizing what she'd said.

She'd just condemned herself.

Trystan raked his fingers through his hair. "It is forbidden to use magic against another royal, with no just cause."

Ivy grabbed Trystan's hand. "I did it because I know who she is," she bellowed, stomping her foot like a spoiled child. "She's the one you've been chasing all these months, isn't she?"

"Trystan, is this true?" the king's voice cut through the room, reverberating off the walls.

Trystan didn't answer. He couldn't because he didn't remember.

Instead, with his face still serious, he stole a glance at me, pivoted, tucked his hands into his pockets and walked out of the room.

"Trystan," the king roared.

"Trystan, wait," Ivy called out to him. "Trystan you can't leave!"

When Trystan didn't respond, Ivy's eyes snapped to me, twisted with even more bitterness. "You don't deserve him," she spat. "You are not a true princess. You have no kingdom or throne awaiting you. You are nobody."

Before any of my friends could answer and get into trouble, I spoke.

"I may not have a kingdom or a throne, but I know where my loyalties and true friends lie."

A deep guttural growl emanated from her chest, and I readied myself for an attack. But she stayed in place, knowing my power was greater than hers.

The king stepped toward me, his face rigid, eyes serious. "Are you the young woman my son has been chasing and disregarding his obligations for?"

My heart plunged, but I straightened my back. I wasn't going to be afraid of him.

"Your son has not been chasing me, your highness. He was trying to save me. And he has, more than once. I owe him my life." *I love him.* I wanted to say, but I kept those words to myself. I kept them hidden deep inside my heart, just for Trystan.

Holding my composure, I tried not to let my emotions get the best of me, but I was scarcely keeping it together.

The king directed a finger to Ivy, his eyes still affixed on me.

"He has a fiancé and will soon unite two countries. Trystan needs to get his priorities straight before I hand over this kingdom for him to rule," he said louder, his voice stern.

I sucked in a deep breath and blew out the negative energy bombarding me. "Your son is a great prince, and I have *no doubt* he will be an even greater king." I meant those words, deep down in my soul. Then, I turned my attention to Ivy. "You're right. I might not deserve Trystan, but from what I've seen tonight, you sure as hell don't deserve him either."

Ivy gasped, her eyes snapping to her parents. "Father, are you going to let her speak to me that way?" But her father remained hushed.

The king's face was hard as stone. "I know you are a guest of my son, but I will not tolerate trouble in my kingdom." He meant me. "I will give you until dawn." He then called to Kylan. "Be sure a ship is ready before dawn to take Miss Caldwell home."

I could hear Ivy snickering and turned to see her scowling.

I wanted to tell the king off, tell them all off, but I was a guest, and while here, I had to respect the fact that he was king. Even if he was a bastard.

I bowed my head. "I will be gone by morning."

"This dinner is over," the king declared. "Ivy, I would like to speak with you and your parents privately. Kylan, you and the rest of the cadre as well."

The looks on the king and queen of Northfall's faces were etched with cynicism. I wondered what they thought of their daughter's antics. They must have been immune because they didn't look embarrassed or even shaken by her tantrums.

"Come, Calla," Markus said gently, taking my hand. "Let's go." I nodded and let him lead me out. Sabine, Thalia, and Kai also surrounded me as we made our way out, and I was glad they were remaining silent.

"Calla," Sabine said when we were a safe distance out of the dining hall. "What the hell just happened?"

I smiled at her and shook my head, tears now pouring from my eyes. "It's nothing."

"Dammit, Calla. Don't lie to me. What did she do to you?"

"She tried to strangle her with her magic," Markus said.

"That bitch," Sabine seethed. "I'm —"

I grabbed hold of her hands and shook my head. "You're not going to do anything. Her magic was no match for mine. I stopped her, and I'm fine. Really."

"She's jealous of you," Thalia said, standing beside Sabine. "I could see it in her eyes, the first time she met you."

"That bitch is trouble." Sabine threw her arms over her chest. "Thank the goddess Calla is stronger than she is. And the king… he better not show her leniency," she huffed.

"I was afraid in there. Really afraid, because there was nothing I could do," Markus admitted. "I've been trained to take care of physical problems. But when the problem involves magic—" He shook his head frustratingly. "I was helpless to do anything to save you. I'm sorry, Calla."

I wiped the tears still flowing down my cheeks. "Markus, this wasn't your fault. But thank you for trying."

"Magic is something we aren't trained to combat," he added. "I'm glad you fought her, Princess, because tonight wouldn't have ended so … civil."

I smiled, knowing I had the best friends and companions any royal would be jealous of.

"I'm sorry you had to deal with that," Kai said sadly. "But you are all welcome to come back and stay in Aquaria."

I shook my head. "I will not put Aquaria in any danger."

Kai grabbed my shoulders. "Calla, there is nowhere to go where Roehl cannot find you."

"Exactly my point," I argued. "He will wreak havoc wherever I go. So, I will keep running, until I can't run anymore. Until I am certain I can win against him." I looked at my friends. "I know you will disapprove, but I want you all to go to Aquaria with Kai. You will be safe there."

"You are my duty, Princess. I will not leave your side," Markus said.

Sabine tilted her head to the side. "You know my answer.

I will not leave your ass alone either, especially when there are jealous royal bitches out there. You need me watching your back from now on."

I laughed and threw my arms around her. "I don't think there will be any more jealous *royals* where I'll be running. But it will be dangerous. Too dangerous for you."

Sabine huffed. "Yeah, yeah. I know I'm a mortal, but ever since I met you, my world has come alive. Live or die, these will be the best days of my life. And I will *not* miss them."

"You are so stubborn," I exhaled.

"I am." She turned to Markus. "Besides, he'll need company."

Thalia stepped toward me, a fist over her heart. "You are my kin, and the true Queen of Incendia," she spoke. "As long as there is breath in me, I will stand and fight beside you." Thalia bowed her head, but I grabbed her arm and yanked her in for a hug. Then, I grabbed Sabine's hand and pulled her in too, along with Markus and Kai.

"Well, then I'll have to come too," Kai said. "You still have a lot to learn, Sea Star, and will need guidance."

Tears flowed from my eyes. "You guys are the best friends a girl could ever want."

I felt the love and loyalty wrapping around me. And it was that, alone, that would give me the strength to leave.

"Oh, so you just dump me here and get a whole new set of friends?" A voice boomed from behind. My heart dropped. I knew that voice. And I knew it well.

CHAPTER NINETEEN

My friends unwrapped their arms from around me and stepped away, revealing a figure standing near the bottom of the stairs.

"Brynna," I breathed.

Her eyes were narrowed, brow furrowed, arms crossed over her chest. Her long blonde hair was down, curled on the ends, and she was wearing a fitted teal gown. She looked gorgeous but pissed.

"I think we should go," Sabine said, grabbing Thalia's hand and pulling her toward the stairwell. "We'll see you in the morning, Calla."

Kai patted me on the shoulder and whispered, "Good luck." Then quickly jogged up the stairs, followed by Markus. Neither of them made eye contact with Brynna as they passed her.

Cowards.

Brynna and I stood silent, staring at each other. So many unspoken words were said between us. So much pain and anguish and death.

I shook my head, my already fragile emotions tipped and spilled out of me. Deep sobs burst from my chest, tears burned and streamed down my face. I couldn't speak, because sorry just didn't seem like a strong enough word. Not for what she had to endure.

My best friend's parents were murdered in cold blood because of Roehl. She was kidnapped and spelled, held prisoner because he knew she was my friend.

Everyone around me, everyone I loved, was being beaten and broken or killed, because I was in their lives.

My heart was exhausted and couldn't bear to see any more pain.

"I'm so sorry, Brynna," I sobbed. "I realize what my friendship has cost you. I don't blame you for hating me."

Brynna's eyes were also filled with tears, but her face was still hard and upset. "So, what are you going to do, Calla? Are you going to run away and be alone? That's what you always do. You assume everyone around you will be better off without you." She paused, her words turning into sobs. "I have been here for weeks and have been worried sick about you. They said you were alive, but I knew they weren't sure because Melaina said you were in Morbeth with some wicked asshole. I thought I had not only lost my parents, but my best friend."

Tears were now falling in torrents down both of our faces.

"What happened to my parents was not your fault. I know that. And I was never mad. I was broken. My heart hardened, not knowing if I was going to hear that my best friend—my sister— was gone too."

My sobs turned to wails as we both ran to each other, colliding in each other's arms. We held each other and cried and cried and cried until we couldn't cry anymore, right in the middle of the castle foyer. I heard people shuffling around, but they steered clear of us.

"I'm so sorry, Brynna," I finally said, my face stained with tears. I knew whatever makeup the servants had put on it was now gone or smeared.

"I'm so glad you're alive."

"I'm so glad you're here, and I'm so relieved that we worked that out. I really thought you'd hate me for the rest of your life."

"I might have, if you didn't come and get me. And damn, Cal. What the hell happened to you?" Brynna sniffled, her eyes sweeping over me from head to toe. "You look amazing. You've changed so much," she said, wiping her eyes.

"You have no idea." I exhaled and laughed to myself.

Brynna grabbed hold of my hand. "They all told me what you did in Morbeth. How they came for you and you refused, telling them to take me to safety instead."

"You should know me by now. I would never leave you in danger."

"I do know you," she sobbed. "Your heart's too big for your chest, Cal."

We hugged again and cried, then she pulled away and wiped her eyes.

"Do you want to go to my room so we can talk privately?"

"I'd like that."

Brynna led me to her room, which was near Sabine and Thalia.

The room was beautiful, but it was a third the size of mine, and the bathroom was a normal size, like the one I had in Morbeth. But the furnishings, linens, and decorations were luxurious. Everything you would expect as a guest of the royal family.

Brynna dug out a sleeping gown and robes for both of us, and we got comfortable. We sat on her bed and talked for hours. I told her everything. From the time she had taken me back to my cottage in Sartha, after my eighteenth birthday, until the moment we met downstairs. I didn't hold back anything. Even the part where Trystan gave me his blood and had to take care of me because I was horny as hell.

By the end, Brynna was out of words.

"If I wasn't a guest in a vampire castle, I don't think I would believe you. Your story, what you've been through, in such a short time, it's hard for my human mind to wrap around. I've been sheltered here. They bring me my meals, and Melaina comes to visit me. But other than that, I'm usually alone. During that time, I realized how much I miss you."

"I don't know if you heard, but the king doesn't want me here."

"What? Why?"

"He thinks I'm a threat," I sighed. "When he found out I was the girl Trystan was chasing, he said I have to be gone by morning."

"That's bullshit," Brynna cursed. "Well, if you have to go, I'm going with you."

I grabbed her shoulders and shook her. "No, you are not. You have to stay here, where it's safe."

"What are you talking about? My best friend is a freaking elemental. You can protect me."

"No, I can't. Not against Roehl. I can barely keep myself out of his grasp."

"But you have," she said. "You're alive. Even though he's tried to kill you multiple times, you are still here."

"Brynna, it's dangerous out there, and I can't watch you get hurt or even die. If you do, I will never forgive myself."

"You wouldn't have to, because this isn't your choice. It's mine." Brynna grabbed my hands and looked into my eyes. "Cal, you are all I have left. I don't care if I'm human. I will manage, even if it means having one of your friends bite me."

"Don't you dare," I growled. "If you do, you won't be able to see the sun again. Or eat real food."

"But have you seen them? I mean, most of the vampire guys in this castle are freaking hot. Much hotter than any of the human boys I've dated." She giggled.

"And much more dangerous," I noted. "This world is not meant for mortals to see or interact with. Which is why they've remained hidden from everyone since the beginning. I'm terrified that I won't be able to protect you out there."

"Are you even listening to what I'm saying? I. Don't. Care. I've been here alone for too long. I am coming with you whether you like it or not."

"Fine," I said, knowing full well that Brynna would not relent. She was the kind of girl that would sit outside my door so I wouldn't sneak off without her.

"Go get some rest," she finally said. "By the way, where are we going?"

I shrugged. "I don't know yet. I'll have to wait until Nicolae gets back so I can talk to him."

She nodded then came and wrapped me in another warm hug. "Well, I'll see you in the morning, then."

"Yeah. Sleep well."

It was getting late, and I knew that in the morning, sometime before the sun rose, Kylan would be escorting us to the dock. I still hadn't figured out where I was going. And Nicolae still didn't know we were no longer welcomed here.

I wrapped the robe around me tightly as I made my way back down the hallway and then the stairwell. Thank the goddess the foyer was empty. I quickly ran across the large room and toward the stairwell that led up to my room, taking the stairs two at a time, reaching the top in record time.

Quietly, I made my way past the cadre's rooms and took a left down the hallway. The air in the hall was freezing cold, and there was a breeze.

How could there be a breeze?

Trystan's door was making a noise like the wind was pushing and pulling it against the frame.

Walking down the hallway, I heard a pained moan. I slowly moved to Trystan's door and placed my palm against it. It was cold.

"Trystan?" I said softly, hoping he was okay.

And then, a thought crossed my mind. What if Ivy was in there with him? Gods, maybe it wasn't a moan of pain, but of passion.

I stood there for a moment more, then decided to walk away. But as I did, I heard more sounds, and then I heard Trystan call my name.

"Calla," he moaned. "Don't do it."

Okay, if he was calling my name, Ivy must not have been in there. If she were, he'd probably get a magical ass whooping.

The wind was growing louder, pushing out from under the door.

He must have been asleep and was having a nightmare.

"Calla," he called again.

What the hell was I supposed to do?

I put my hand on the knob and twisted and a burst of wind blew the door right open.

Trystan's room was pitch black, but as my vampire eyes adjusted, I could see him on the bed. He was alone, wrapped in his sheets.

I quietly shut the door behind me and pressed my back against it, wondering if I should walk over and wake him up. Or walk back out and go to bed.

Trystan moaned again, tossing in his bed while strong bursts of wind tore through the room.

"No! No," he bellowed.

Gods what was he dreaming about? I hoped I wasn't killing him in his dream.

I decided to slowly and carefully walk over to his bedside, knowing it was probably the stupidest move I could ever make. Especially while he was asleep and possibly having a bad dream of me.

Who knew what the curse was feeding him in his dreams? I couldn't even begin to imagine the horrors and lies that were invading his mind. Making him hate me, even now.

Standing next to his bedside, I realized he was shirtless, his bottom half twisted in his crimson sheets. I could see pain riddling his beautiful face. Beads of sweat glistened on his forehead, his sharp jaw was tense, brows pressed together.

Then, he moved and the cords of muscles in his arms, chest, and abs went taut. Across his chest were tattoos, archaic symbols and swirls. Over his shoulder and down his right arm curled a long, barbed tail. A dragon's tail.

Heavens above, even in this state, he was perfect.

Trystan moaned again, and another frigid gust blew through the room, making me question my motive for coming here alone. I was here because it was him, this beautiful soul that had been cursed by my enemy. A soul cursed because of me.

"Trystan," I whispered softly. Possibly too soft, because I could barely hear the words over the wind rushing through the room.

"Calla," he exhaled. "Calla, I don't love—" He paused, moaning, his face twisted with pain.

Me? He didn't love … me? My heart was shredding to pieces.

He let out another pained cry.

Gods, what was going on inside his mind?

"Trystan," I whispered, gently touching his arm.

His eyes suddenly popped open, and the wind died.

The eyes looking at me weren't those beautiful azure eyes I'd grown to love. They were midnight black.

With a roar, Trystan grabbed my arm and yanked me onto the bed. He was suddenly on top of me, straddling my waist, his hands gripping my wrists, holding them above my head.

"What are you doing here," he growled.

"I—I heard you call my name. I'm sorry, I shouldn't have come."

"Why are you inside my room?" His voice was laced with malice. His face wasn't the face of the person I knew. This was a mask. A mask donned by the curse.

My body was trembling, pulse racing. But I knew Trystan was in there somewhere, and I knew he wouldn't hurt me. So, I spoke to Trystan. To the soul I still felt was tethered to mine.

"I came because I was concerned," I said truthfully. "Because you sounded like you were having a bad dream. You called out to me, so I came."

I tried to move away, to get away from him, but he held me in place.

"My mind," he rasped. "The pain in my mind is constant. The voices demanding that I hate you. They want me to hurt you. They want me to—" He grit his teeth together, and the agony in those eyes … it was heart wrenching.

"I know you Trystan. I know you would never hurt me. My heart aches, knowing you have to endure this pain and chaos in your mind alone."

Trystan's darkened eyes blinked and then blinked again. He brought his face down to the side of my neck and breathed in deeply, his body shuddering. "Your blood. The moment I caught the scent of it at the dock, I wanted nothing else. The thought of tasting it is driving me insane."

"You've already tasted it," I said softly. "You claimed me but gave me a choice. To run or drink your blood and seal the bond."

Trystan hesitated, then pushed off of me, putting a cold and calloused distance between us. "And you chose to run," he scoffed.

"I did," I confessed sadly. "I ran because I was terrified of the change happening to me. Of knowing there was someone hunting me for something I had no control over. Of sealing a bond with someone I knew nothing about." Trystan huffed and turned away. "*But* … if given the choice again," I breathed, sitting up, "knowing who you truly are, Trystan. Knowing how *deeply* I feel about you, I would have poured your blood down my throat and sealed our bond."

Narrowed eyes snapped back to mine, pausing for a moment. "How do I know you're not telling me lies?"

I carefully stood up from the bed and walked toward him, stopping about five feet away.

"There is no way I can prove it to you. Not after Roehl erased your memory and added a curse to make you hate me."

He paused, his onyx eyes softening, and with a blink were back to the familiar azure I loved. "How am I supposed to hate something I crave so desperately?"

"You can't, because we are meant to be together. We were always meant to be together."

Trystan suddenly cringed in pain, grabbing the sides of his head, his breath turned ragged, eyes becoming midnight once again.

"What's happening?" I asked, desperate to help him. "What are the voices telling you?"

I wanted to know but was deathly afraid of the answer.

"You have to leave. They want me to hurt you." With his eyes clenched tight, he dropped to a knee. I could see the muscles in his chest and arms tighten, like he was struggling against an invisible force.

"Trystan," I wailed, wanting to run to him, to throw my arms around him and help him, but I knew it would hurt him more.

"Leave," he ordered, fighting those demons in his head. *"Now!"*

I quickly scrambled for the door and pushed out into the hallway.

Knowing I couldn't leave him alone in that condition, I sprinted down the hall toward his cadre. I didn't know whose door I was knocking on, but I banged on the first door.

Feng answered, shirt off, eyes weary. When he saw me, his eyes widened. "Calla, what's wrong?"

"It's Trystan. He needs help," I sobbed.

Feng exited the room and banged on all three doors after him. Kylan, also shirtless, was the first to open.

"Calla?" His tired eyes focused on me.

"Help him, please," I sobbed.

Kylan's eyes closed knowing who I was talking about, so he grabbed a shirt, stepped out and closed the door behind him. "Where is he?"

"In his room."

Andrés and Brone opened their doors, also looking like they were waking from a dead sleep.

"Trystan needs us," Kylan stated, motioning down the hall toward his room. Kylan placed his hands on my shoulders. "Go back to your room, Calla. We'll take care of this."

I nodded as they hurried toward Trystan, my heart fractured, my head a whirlwind of emotion. I waited until I knew they were inside with him before I rounded the corner and slipped into my room.

I felt like I'd already cried enough for a lifetime but fell on my bed and cried some more. I cried for Trystan and the pain he had to endure. For my parents, for Brynna, for Sabine and Markus and Thalia and Nicolae. And the fact we had to leave in a few hours, and I had no idea where we were going.

The fabric of my existence seemed to be unraveling around me. Piece by piece, I was losing myself. My purpose. My hope. Everyone around me, everyone I loved, had died or was in danger because of *me*. And that realization was like a dagger being pushed straight through my chest.

I knew I couldn't leave them behind. I'd made a promise to let them know if I was ever going to leave. And I would keep that promise.

But the thought of leaving Trystan was the hardest. I knew it was for the best, because if I left the voices would hopefully be silenced.

CHAPTER TWENTY

I woke to a loud whooshing sound. A cold gust of wind whipped through gossamer curtains, making me realize I'd fallen asleep. My eyes were still puffy as I swept them across the room, finding it empty. It must have been near midnight because through the curtains I could still see the night sky speckled with stars.

My head and heart were throbbing as I stood from the bed and poured myself a glass of ruby wine. I figured a glass would calm my nerves, but what I wished even more was that it could heal my broken heart.

I wondered what happened with Trystan and what he had told his cadre. Did the pain leave when I left?

My heart palpitated as I rewound the moment he pulled me onto the bed and straddled me. I could see the anguish in his darkened eyes, but also saw the tenseness in his jaw and neck and arms as he internally fought back. Fought the voices that were telling him to hurt me.

He could have bitten me, sucked me dry right then and there, but he didn't. Instead, he pulled away and demanded I leave.

Too many things were bombarding my mind and I couldn't make them stop. I wondered where Nicolae had gone and when he would return. I had to tell him that we were no longer guests in Carpathia, and that we would be leaving with one extra mortal. A mortal who was even more feisty than Sabine. Goddess above, I hoped they would get along.

Nicolae had said he'd traveled from place to place all his life. Maybe we could do the same until I was ready … until *we* were ready for Roehl.

A wave of sadness hit me again, knowing Trystan's cadre would have to stay here to protect the castle. Who knew what Roehl had planned, knowing he'd let Trystan free.

Peace. I just wanted a moment's peace. From my own thoughts and mind.

Topping off my glass and wrapping a robe around me, I strode past the gossamer curtains and made my way across the marbled veranda.

I looked out over the railing at the mortal city beyond. A city oblivious to the vampires who lived right above them, ruling them from afar. An entire vampire kingdom, veiled in magic.

I took a sip of the ruby wine and closed my eyes. A gentle breeze wrapped around me carrying … *his scent.*

"Calla," a voice from a corner of the veranda called.

I gasped, dropping my glass. It shattered, blood coating the marbled floor. Out of instinct, I reached down to pick it up and — "Shit," I hissed as a sharp edge of the glass sliced my finger, drawing blood.

"Don't move," Trystan said, stepping out of the shadows.

His eyes were black, teeth elongated, brow drawn together. He clearly wasn't himself. Thank the goddess I'd been sipping on blood, because my finger had already healed.

"Trystan, you shouldn't be here," I said softly, carefully, my body trembling, heart hammering against my chest.

But I couldn't deny the charge in the air, the suffocating heaviness that came when he was near. The distance between us, the hollow void, was cold and unnerving. I craved his closeness, his touch, his kiss.

I could still taste his blood on my lips, feel his fingers trailing over my bare skin before satisfying my burning needs.

He stood still, the moonlight gilding the lines of his handsome face, riddled with torment. His bare, muscled chest rose and fell with deep heavy breaths.

"Don't move," he said again, as if moving was going to trigger a spontaneous reaction. "Don't speak."

I nodded and froze in place, hoping to keep those voices at bay.

His eyes were weary, dark circles encompassed them—repercussions of the gods damned curse. It was bearing on my already battered soul because I was helpless to do anything to help him as it slowly siphoned life from him.

"I'm sorry for what my fiancé did tonight. She was out of line and will not go unpunished."

I nodded, my heart shredding a bit more hearing him refer to her as *fiancé*. "Kylan also told me what my father said," he continued, a harsher tone to his voice. His hands fisted and flexed at his sides. "I made a promise, and I will uphold my word." His eyes shut for a good ten seconds and when they opened, they were azure again. My Trystan was back.

"I'm trying to sort things out in my mind, what is truth and what is lies. I know for a fact my men would not lie to me. They have sworn their lives to me, and I trust them wholeheartedly. Which is why, I've—"

He moaned, his face twisting in pain.

I waited. Stayed in place. Stayed quiet, just as he said, so as not to make matters worse.

His weary eyes opened again, shredding my already lacerated heart a little more. How much more could we endure? I knew I had to stay away, to leave him so his mind could rest, but the thought of never seeing him again was like a constant stabbing pain in my heart.

A tear trickled down my cheek and his eyes followed it. He blinked, a sliver of emotion in those exquisite eyes.

"Hold up your palms and face them to me," he instructed calmly, carefully, his voice just above a whisper. "But stay still. Don't move."

I did as he said, holding up my hands, palms outward, facing him, wondering what this was about. Was this a last-minute training? Was he going to show me how to summon a tornado, or move like the wind?

Trystan didn't move, and time seemed to ebb and flow between us. Then, I watched him take in a deep breath, straighten his back, and quickly moved toward me, placing his hands against mine.

Startled at this unexpected move, I flinched, but then fixed my eyes on his.

Power hummed between us, through us, a current of it flowing through my palms, wrists, arms, tingling throughout the rest of my body. Gasping, I watched the veins in my arms glow a bright blue.

Trystan stepped back, pulling his palms away from mine. Then, he stepped back further and further until his back was pressed up against the far wall, putting a bitter and sorrowful distance between us.

Glancing down at my palms, which were glowing bright blue, realization hit me at what he'd done. What he'd risked.

I'd felt that same power before—with Kai and Nicolae. But with Trystan, it was different. Somehow stronger, more intense. My palms were still tingling, my body inebriated from his touch and his closeness.

Trystan had connected us. Connected our elements.

But what if it came with a great price? What if it made the demons stronger and drove him to madness?

"Trystan," I breathed, but he held up a hand, silencing me.

"I don't know who you are, aside from what I've seen and what my men tell me," he breathed, his eyes fastened to mine. "There is darkness in my mind that haunts me. It is with me every waking moment and follows me into sleep.

"My dreams have become nothing more than tormented nightmares. Nightmares of death and destruction all around me—of my kingdom and my people. But there is always a tiny speck glittering in that darkness, in that withering chaos. A speck of light that catches my eye. And the more I focus on it, I see … *you*." Those azure eyes met mine, softer, sweeter, almost as if a glint of memory were there. "And for a moment, I feel a bit of happiness, before the darkness gobbles you up, telling me that *you* will ultimately be the source of my destruction." He shook his head, eyes clenched, jaw tensed. "I have to go."

Without saying another word, he pushed through the gossamer curtain and disappeared inside. Seconds later, I heard the door open and then shut before I let out the breath I'd been holding.

Every cell in my body demanded I run after him, to run into his arms and tell him that I wasn't the enemy. That I was his friend. His soulmate. And *he* was the one who held every piece of my broken and battered heart. He was the reason I was still alive and breathing. He was my life, my glimmering light, my hope for a future.

But now that he didn't remember me, I was falling apart, my foundation crumbling into sand, slowly eroding the once sturdy ground I stood on.

Turning my palms over, I realized what he had done. His mind was completely erased of me. The curse telling him I was his enemy and would bring him and his kingdom ruin. And yet… yet—

He connected us.

I stayed frozen for a few moments, trying to fully understand his motive. But I couldn't. I had no clue what was going on in Trystan's mind, and I didn't think anyone else did either.

I placed my still tingling fingers o n t he r ailing, t rying to sturdy my trembling nerves.

Morning would come soon, too soon, and it was the first time I had no desire to welcome it. Because in the morning, we would be leaving Carpathia. And Trystan.

I still needed to talk to Nicolae and had no idea where our next destination would be. All I knew was our safety would mostly rely on Nicolae glamouring us and warding the places we would stay. I was terrified for the lives of my friends and allies. Markus, Kai, Thalia, Sabine, and now Brynna. Terrified that Roehl could show up at any given moment with an army and take any one of them from me.

Even though I felt like every part of me was falling apart, I had to be strong. Weakness wasn't an option. Especially with a death threat following me wherever I went.

I now had a glimpse of what a ruler might endure. Kings and Queens of their kingdoms fought to keep their land and people safe. I didn't have a kingdom, or a throne, or a crown. But I had a group of people around me who I loved and wanted to keep safe. Their lives were now my priority. And I would fight for them.

CHAPTER TWENTY-ONE

Sadness filled my soul, and it wasn't going away anytime soon.

As I shuffled through the gossamer curtains, I noticed the room was clean and a large satchel was sitting on one of the dressers. Ambling over to it, I pulled back the flap and spotted all the clothes I'd been given, neatly folded inside. I sniffed the air for any out-of-place scents, but there were none. Then, I hurried to the bathroom to find it was empty.

I swore there was some phantom maid who tended my room.

After a hot, relaxing bath, I changed into a matching black and crimson tunic and pants, slipped on my boots, and threw the cape Sabine had given me over my shoulders.

Trystan's men would be here soon, and I wanted to be ready.

Pacing the room, thoughts of Trystan barraged my mind. We were connected now, and I wondered if we could communicate through our new bond. I felt the connection, the buzz still lingered in my veins and tingled in my palms. I held up my hands and studied my tattoos. Simple lines and curves and symbols that held so much power.

I wasn't going to be the one to initiate that conversation. If he wanted to connect with me, I'd let him be the first to reach out. The last thing I wanted was for those voices to kick in and hurt him or drive him mad.

Walking over to the bottle on my nightstand, I emptied the contents into my glass and took a seat on one of the chairs by the fireplace, wondering if Trystan's mother had done the same. I couldn't imagine what she must have been feeling. To be immortal, yet have a curse placed over you that wrecked your mind so badly, it had you begging someone to end your life.

A soft rapping on the door had me gulping down the rest of the ruby wine.

"Come in," I hollered.

The door swung open and Nicolae, along with Kylan, strode in.

Nicolae's brow was crumpled as he walked over and wrapped me in a hug. "I heard what happened at dinner. I'm sorry I wasn't there."

"Don't be," I said. "It was nothing I couldn't handle."

"Still, you are royalty and shouldn't have been made to feel less than that."

I shrugged it off, knowing this royalty thing was just a title. No one knew who I was, and I had yet to prove myself as a true royal.

"Where did you go?" I asked, shifting the conversation.

"I had to gather a few things. After what happened at the

dock, I don't want to be vulnerable again."

"We have to leave soon," Kylan said, standing near the door. "The sun will be rising in a few hours and I'm sure Markus won't enjoy seeing it. Neither will any of us."

"No, I guess not," I laughed.

Kylan threw my newly packed satchel over his shoulder. "We'll be traveling on the outskirt of the city below. There is a ship waiting at the port that will take you wherever you decide."

My eyes shifted back to Nicolae. "Where are we going?"

"What do you think about returning to Sartha?" he asked. "It's the last place Roehl might think you'd go back to, and I have a small home near the shore."

"I would like that."

But going back to Sartha, knowing my parents weren't going to be there, was going to hurt like hell. And if I was feeling this way, I couldn't imagine what Brynna was going to feel.

Nicolae held out his hand to me and I took it. Before we left, I glanced around the room one more time, taking it all in. It was such a beautiful room, and I felt we were leaving much too soon.

We met up with the rest of Trystan's men in the hallway and made our way down the long, marbled staircase. As soon as we stepped outside, the crisp, icy air greeted us, and the clear sky had turned a dark gray.

Nicolae and the cadre excused themselves before striding off to talk to the guards.

"Calla," Brynna called, waving a hand at me.

She was dressed in winter clothes, wrapped in a warm cloak, bright eyed, with a smile on her lips. Markus, Kai, Sabine, and

Thalia were standing around her, and my heart felt happy to see them all.

"Are you all ready for our next adventure?" I asked, throwing my arms to the sides.

"Girl, no one can prepare for your adventures," Sabine joked. "We are just swept up in them and have to hold on until the ride is done. Then, if we're still breathing, we have to build up enough strength and courage for the next one."

I laughed, because Sabine had been with me from the start. She knew what it took for us to have gotten this far. What we had endured and survived. Yes, she was mortal, but she was tough, and I loved her for it.

"Hey, Sea Star," Kai beamed. "Your friend Brynna was telling us about how you were *before* you became—" his hand swept up and down, "the new you."

"Oooh," I sang. "You mean the boring introvert who craved her books and isolation over boys and parties?"

"Yes," Brynna chirped. "I still haven't seen this new you they've been gushing about. The royal who can wield the elements." She twiddled her fingers in front of her.

"Ah, that's nothing." I waved it off, shaking my head. "I'm still me. Just, a little stronger."

"Stronger is an understatement," Thalia blurted. "You are likely the most powerful royal to walk the earth."

A cold breeze blew around us, making Brynna and Sabine hug their cloaks tightly to their chests. They were shivering.

Kylan called Markus and Kai over, probably discussing the details of our trip.

I could sense a shift in the weather, so I walked out onto a grassy area nearby. Tilting my head back and gazing into the gray sky, I saw it. A glistening flake of white, gently floating down to earth. Then hundreds more followed.

"Goddess above!" I exclaimed, turning to the girls. "The first snowfall!"

But none of them looked thrilled about it. "What if it's not the first snowfall?" Sabine questioned.

I smiled widely. "It is for me!"

"You can have the snow," Brynna shivered. "I want a fire and a warm blanket."

"I second that," Sabine said. "I'm freezing my ass off."

"I really don't care for the cold either," Thalia added.

I narrowed my eyes at the three of them. "Are you kidding me? All three of you? It's the first snowfall. *This is magical.*"

"Calla, you *are* the same," Brynna said, shaking her head. "Simple things like snow falling make you giddy."

I laughed, throwing my head back and my arms out to my sides and twirled around and around, letting the cold flakes melt against my face.

"It's very magical," a voice spoke next to me.

I dropped my arms and whipped my head around to see who had spoken to me. But I was the only one out on the lawn. Brynna, Sabine, and Thalia were still at the front of the castle chatting away and waiting on the carriage making its way up the cobbled path.

Snowflakes started to swirl around me, and then I caught an enticing scent. A scent that made my entire body tingle and my knees go weak.

Glancing upward, I saw a dark figure standing on a balcony.

Trystan. It was *his* voice I'd heard through the bond.

"You're leaving soon," he said.

"Yes." I didn't know how else to respond. Could I talk to him without that damn curse making his head hurt?

He stepped away from the railing and it made me wonder if maybe I shouldn't have answered.

"As long as I don't make eye contact with you, or am close to you, the voices are subdued."

"How are you feeling right now?"

"Now that I can't see you, the voices are quiet."

"So, as long as we are apart, we can speak freely through the bond?"

"It appears so."

Gods, this was a game changer. I knew Roehl hadn't expected Trystan to connect our elements, so maybe his curse wasn't specific enough. Maybe it was only strong when we were close, or like he'd said, when he could see me.

"Calla, the carriage is here," Brynna called, waving me over.

Sabine, Thalia, Kai, and Markus were already inside, and Brynna was halfway up.

"I have to go but I wanted to thank you. For everything."

"Where will you be heading?"

"I think we're going to Sartha. Nicolae has a place we can stay for a while."

"Safe travels to you and your friends."

"Be happy and well, Trystan."

He didn't respond after that, and I didn't mind. In his mind, I was still an enemy, even though he was slowly fighting through it.

As I neared the carriage, Trystan's cadre came riding up on horseback. Kylan was holding the reins to a horse saddled next to him.

Shadow.

Holding the reins out to me, he grinned. "I thought you'd like to ride him down to the port."

Tears immediately pooled in my eyes. "I wouldn't have it any other way."

I took the reins from Kylan and hugged my horse around the neck, giving him a kiss on his nose before I mounted him. It was comforting, knowing my hooved friend for the past eight years was here, ready to escort me to my next grand adventure.

We rode in silence through the darkened road. Snow was still falling, and the sounds of the horse's hooves clomping against cobbled stone were calming.

We took a route on the outskirts of the city that led straight to the port. Kylan led us down the dock to a large ship. It was about as big as Sebastian's, but this one was much more modern. The sails were black with Trystan's family crest in the center.

I could already hear Sabine and Brynna approving of our new ride. The sounds of them getting along made my heart happy. I had been so worried that they'd hate each other, because they were both headstrong with even stronger personalities.

So far, so good.

We stopped on the dock and dismounted the horses. The guards that rode in with us started carrying our things on board, while Trystan's men lined up to bid us farewell.

I hugged each one of them.

"Don't get into too much trouble, Princess," Brone said with a sinister grin. He wrapped me in a bear hug and lifted me off my feet.

"You as well," I said. "And please don't hit Andrés in the head. You'll damage his sensitive brain."

"Too late," Feng laughed. I hugged him next, and he whispered in my ear. "Have faith, Calla. And don't fear the dark days coming. Remember, you are light. And light easily snuffs out the darkness."

"Thank you, Feng," I said, my eyes burning, threatening to fill with tears.

Kylan was last, and he wrapped me in a warm hug. "This is not goodbye. We will see each other again," he said.

I nodded, those damn tears now rolling down my cheeks. He reached in his pocket and pulled out a small box. "Trystan wanted you to have this." He placed the box in my hand.

Slowly lifting the small lid, a deep sob ripped from my chest.

It was the amulet. Trystan's mother's amulet.

"Why?" I asked. I knew those wicked voices had demanded he take it back and give it to his fiancé.

Kylan gave me a sad smile. "This amulet was spelled so his father could find his mother. Trystan could also tap into the amulet but only slightly, because they share DNA. But a few nights ago, Trystan called in a mage to break his father's spell.

Then, he used his blood to create a new one. If you are ever in trouble, Calla, he will easily be able to find you, as long as you are wearing this."

I shook my head, overwhelmed with emotion. I held the amulet in my palm and folded my fingers around it.

Closing my eyes, I spoke through our bond. *"Thank you so much for this priceless gift. It will be worn over my heart."*

"You're welcome."

I wiped my tear-stained face and placed the amulet around my neck, tucking it into my tunic so it lay flat against my heart.

The guards began to mount their horses.

"What about Shadow?" I asked, looking at Shadow.

Kylan crossed his arms over his chest. "Shadow is royalty in the stables now, and we will make sure he stays happy until you are both reunited."

"Thank you," I breathed.

At least I didn't have to worry about my hooved friend. I had no doubt he was in the best hands.

After all the goodbyes, we boarded the ship and Brynna came over and slipped her hand into mine.

"Are you going to be okay?" she breathed. "I know how much you hate being on ships."

I smiled at my best friends, then wrapped her in a hug. "It's so good to have you back."

"Well, it took you long enough to come and get me," she huffed, her lips curling up. "I missed you."

"I missed you too."

The captain of the ship was a middle-aged man with clean cut salt and pepper hair. He was trusted by Trystan and his cadre, so I knew we were in good hands.

We each got our own room, and thank the heavens, they were nothing like the room we had on Sebastian's ship. These rooms were spotless, the floors were clean and there was a small bed and side table in each one.

There were two shared washrooms outside that had a toilet, sink, and a stand-up shower. One for the men and one for the women.

As we disembarked from the port, we stood on the deck and waved goodbye to Trystan's cadre. The snow was still falling, heavier now. The sky was still a dark gray, so Markus was able to stay with us on the deck.

"Will we be safe out at sea?" I asked Nicolae who had come up to stand next to me.

"I've glamoured the ship. Roehl won't be able to track it, unless he has some very powerful spell."

"The Wanderer's can, can't they?" I remembered the time Erro broke through Melaina's glamour.

"Let's hope not," he said, holding a bunch of small onyx stones in his hand. "These are what I left Carpathia for. They have been spelled by a powerful mage. When used precisely, these stones enhance whatever spell you use. I've secured some to the four corners of this ship. Most living beings I know of, won't be able to break through my glamour."

I smiled at him. "Thank you for finding me."

"Finding you wasn't an option," he said, placing his arm around my shoulder. "I've always wondered what it would be like to have a family of my own, and never thought it was possible. I thought I'd live out the rest of my days wandering alone. But all this time I wasn't alone. I had a son. And now, I have you, and a greater purpose in life. My son is dead, but I will do what I can to make sure you live a long and happy life."

"Thank you," I said, as he wrapped me in another warm hug before walking away.

I stood on the deck, and slowly watched Carpathia disappear, and a sudden gust of wind blew around the ship, and then I caught his scent. My heart warmed inside, knowing Trystan was responsible.

Footsteps shuffled behind me.

"Things will work out," Sabine said, leaning on the railing next to me.

"They will," Brynna added, grabbing my hand and resting her head on my shoulder. "Because while I was in Carpathia, Trystan came to visit me a couple of times. And I knew, the moment he left, how deeply connected he was to you. He wanted to know everything about you and sat there while I told him countless stories of us growing up.

I've never seen a man so invested or interested in someone else." She let out a sigh. "He truly loves you, Cal. And I am so incredibly jealous."

"We all are," Thalia added with a giggle. She was on the other side of Sabine.

I laughed and squeezed Brynna's hand. "I'm shocked you didn't find someone while you were there."

"Believe me, there were at least a dozen guards I wanted to throw myself at. But I was a guest of Trystan and representing you. I didn't want to embarrass either of you."

"Well, I'm glad you stayed celibate," I said, nudging her.

"Hopefully, not for much longer," she said, wagging her brow. "Now let's get our asses inside before we freeze to death."

CHAPTER TWENTY-TWO

With a firm wind at our back, we reached Sartha in four days' time. We had no complications, and I'd slept like a baby, thanks to a remedy Nicolae gave me. A concoction of herbs and whatever else he'd mixed together. The taste wasn't bad, but it packed a punch and had me sleeping most of the trip, which I didn't mind.

I hadn't heard anything from Trystan during our voyage, and it made me wonder if he was regretting our bond. I also could have been overthinking it, and he was busy running his kingdom. He had mentioned a lot of duties to attend to, and I was hoping one of those wasn't the Princess of Northfall.

Above, the sky was covered in dark clouds while we disembarked the ship. We climbed into a rowboat and two of the crew members took us to the shore. Then, we headed toward a small cottage on that secluded shore. Snow still hadn't fallen in Sartha, but I knew it would be coming soon.

My eyes swept the entire area, and I realized the only way you could get to this property would be from the sea, because behind it was a steep and dangerous rock face.

The cabin was about the size of the one I had, and it was a bit tight for the seven of us. But we'd manage because we had to.

"Hey, Sea Star," Kai said, pulling me to the side. "I've already talked to Nicolae and Markus, but I have to leave for a few days. I left Aquaria in a rush and felt I should at least return and check in. You know, since I'm a prince and all."

"Of course," I said. "Thank you, Kai. For everything. If you need anything, just holler," I said, raising my palm.

He gave a sinister grin. "Like you'll answer."

"I will. I promise. That other situation was just … complicated."

"Okay, fine," he said. "It shouldn't be more than a few days. I'll let you know when I'm on my way back."

"And let us know when you arrive. We want to know if you made it safely."

"Ah," he smiled. "So, she does care."

"Of course, I care. It's just—"

He held up his hands. "You don't have to say it. I already know."

I grabbed his wrist and dragged him out the door, just so the others couldn't hear. "Thalia really likes you," I said.

Those luminous blue eyes narrowed on mine. "I know she does, and I like her too. I just want to take things slow, because right now there are greater priorities than finding love."

"Are there?" I cocked a brow.

"Yeah, like keeping you alive."

"You are not responsible for my life. Besides, you've already saved me once. I'm the one who owes you now."

A grin rose on his handsome face. "How about a kiss?"

I laughed and shook my head, then rose on my toes and kissed his cheek.

"Not the kind of kiss I was looking for, but it'll do," he said, nudging me.

"I love you, Kai," I said.

"I know. As a friend."

I nodded and reiterated. "As a friend."

"I'm coming to terms with that. And you know what, I'm okay with being your friend. You'll always be close to my heart, Calla."

"As are you to mine," I said, smiling.

"My parents and kingdom will be broken hearted, though. They really thought you'd be the next Queen of Aquaria."

"Well, if things work out between you and—" I nudged my head inside the cabin. "We'll still be connected. She is my cousin."

Kai shrugged, a glimmer in those ice-blue eyes. "I'll see you soon, Sea Star."

"Be safe."

Kai jogged into the frigid sea water but didn't flinch, then dove under and was gone.

Walking back inside, all eyes were on me.

"Where's Kai?" Thalia asked.

"He had to go back to Aquaria, but he'll be back in a few days."

Her face soured, and it made me smile.

I knew Nicolae and Markus heard our conversation because their faces were solemn. They must have felt for Kai. But Sabine, Thalia, and Brynna seemed like they were oblivious. Which was good.

Nicolae had placed wood in the furnace and with a snap of his fingers, it roared to life, making Brynna and Sabine, who were bundled up on a couch, clap and cheer.

"How long are we going to be here?" Brynna questioned.

"I don't know," Nicolae replied, adding another log to the fire. "I have to go into town to gather some supplies."

"Can I come with you?" I piped. I needed to get out and clear my head. Besides, I'd spent the past few days sleeping on the way here. "I promise to be on my best behavior. You will also have an extra set of hands to carry supplies."

Nicolae hesitated, then let out a deep sigh. "Fine, but you will not leave my sight."

I threw a hand over my heart. "I promise."

Markus gave me a narrowed glare, and I knew he was torn. He was supposed to protect me, but he was also the only male left who could protect my mortal friends. I'm sure Thalia could manage, but not alone. And not against Roehl.

"How are you going to get to the town?" Brynna asked. "There is no way up that steep rock-face."

"Nicolae has a way," I informed with a wide grin. "Kind of like teleporting."

"Is it like how you described with the Wanderer?" Sabine asked.

"Sort of. Erro's was like being carried through the wind. While Nicolae's is more like a step in the darkness."

Sabine's face crumpled. "Just be safe. I'm going to stay right here next to this fire."

"If you happen to go near the bakery, I'd love something chocolate," Brynna said sweetly, hands pressed together.

"We'll, see," I said.

Nicolae didn't look too thrilled about the request, but he kept quiet. I knew this wasn't a sight-seeing trip. It was a get out, get what we needed, and get back quickly and safely kind of trip.

And I was all for that. But I owed Brynna.

After giving Markus some instruction, Nicolae and I walked outside to the back of the cabin.

"Do you think we could stop by my cabin?" I asked. "I want to pick up some skrag so I can help."

"I have enough skrag for what we need," he said. He finally looked at me and his eyes softened. "Fine. Where is this cabin of yours?"

After giving him directions, Nicolae grabbed my hand, and we were instantly enveloped in darkness. After a few moments, the darkness subsided, and we were standing in front of my parent's house.

I wasn't ready for the emotions that slammed into me, causing my entire body to tremble and travail. It hit me hard, the realization that my parents were gone. They hadn't gone on a trip to Trader's Port to barter and sell, and they weren't going to be back in a few weeks' time. Because they were dead. Murdered in cold blood by a wicked asshole.

I would never see them again. Knees buckling, I fell to the cold earth and wept. Nicolae came over and kneeled next to me, wrapping his arms around me to try to comfort me. I missed them so much it made my bones ache.

"They are together," Nicolae said softly. "And they are watching over you."

I knew that was the truth, and those spoken words were what got me to my feet and moving again. They were together. And they were happy. That's all that mattered to me.

I led Nicolae to my cottage and as soon as I opened the door, I knew someone had been here. It was ransacked. Books and dishes and bedding and clothes … everything was thrown on the ground, like they were looking for something.

But I didn't keep my skrag in the cottage.

My father knew that having wealth in Sartha, with still so many poor, came with a price. Many thieves robbed and even killed over a few gold skrag. So, my father created places to hide our skrag. He hid it in the woods, inside hidden compartments within some of the trees.

I walked out onto my back porch and headed for the small forest, with Nicolae close behind. I counted five trees, then stopped and felt for the hidden knob in its bark and yanked on it. A small door opened up, and inside, a little compartment that held my skrag. Pulling out the bags, I handed them to Nicolae.

"How much do you have here?"

"Enough to last us a while," I said. This was only one stash. "There is more, but we can come back later."

Nicolae gaped at me.

"My father owned a few mines. He was a very wealthy man."

I walked back inside and grabbed a bag, throwing warmer clothes and socks in it for Brynna and Sabine.

"We shouldn't stay too long," Nicolae said. "We need to get to the town and back to the others."

I agreed and as soon as we stepped outside, a voice called. "Calla."

Grant Willbrow, the boy who taught me self-defense for a full year after I'd turned ten, was standing on my parent's lawn. He was still as handsome as I remembered, tall and tanned, wearing his military uniform. His eyes widened, mouth agape, like he wasn't expecting to see me.

"Grant? What are you doing here?" I questioned.

"Your father's ship. I-I heard—we all heard about the accident," he stuttered. "They said your mother's body was on the ship, along with the others onboard, but they said they never found your father's body. They said you had disappeared. So, I came to check on things, and see if maybe your father, or you, had returned."

I shook my head, tears pooling in my eyes. "My father is dead."

His expression saddened, brow tightened. "I'm so sorry, Calla. I can't imagine what you're feeling."

"It has been. Very hard."

Grant's eyes moved to Nicolae.

"This is my —"

"Uncle," Nicolae answered. "Nicolae Corvus," he said walking toward Grant with his hand out. Grant shook it and nodded. "I came from Northfall as soon as I heard about my brother and his wife."

"Will you be staying here?" Grant asked, his eyes back on mine.

"No," I replied. "Not for long. I'll be staying with my uncle for a while. Until everything gets sorted out."

"I understand," he said sadly.

"It's good to see you, Calla. You've grown up since the last time I saw you." His chestnut eyes glimmered. He'd never looked at me like that before, like he admired what he saw. But I guess that would have been creepy. I was ten years old the last time he saw me, and he was nine years my senior.

"We have to leave. We have to head into town for some supplies," Nicolae said.

Grant smiled and nodded. "Then I won't keep you waiting."

"It is good to see you, Grant," I said, waving goodbye.

"Maybe I'll see you again sometime?"

"Maybe," I smiled then followed after Nicolae.

Gods that was awkward.

"Slow down, Uncle Nic," I teased.

"I didn't think he'd believe us if we told him I was your grandfather."

"No, he wouldn't. So, thank you for jumping in."

"Who is that young man?" Nicolae asked in a protective tone.

"His name is Grant Willbrow. His father was a miner who was employed by my father, and because Grant knew about war and weaponry, my father hired him to come and teach me self-defense. He wanted me to be able to defend myself."

"The boy was infatuated with you." He wasn't asking, he was telling me.

"No, he wasn't," I puffed.

Nicolae gave me a narrowed, side-eyed glance. "You are an immortal, Calla. Mortal men cannot help but be infatuated with you."

"Well, when I was younger, I did have a crush on him."

Actually, I'd had a major crush on Grant Willbrow from the day I'd met him, all the way up until my eighteenth birthday. I'd dreamed of him falling in love with me, and one day marrying me. Brynna knew my one-sided infatuation and she tried to get me to date other boys. I was stubborn and knew what I wanted. And that was Grant.

Until I met Trystan.

Now, after all those years of dreaming of what it would be like with Grant, and seeing him again… I felt nothing. There wasn't even a spark.

My heart was no longer mine. It belonged to Trystan.

CHAPTER TWENTY-THREE

When we were far enough away from Grant, Nicolae took my hand and transported us, through his magical darkness, to a secluded area right outside of the town.

"Remember, Calla, don't go anywhere I can't see you. Roehl has eyes and ears everywhere, especially with his magic. I've glamoured the both of us, but here," he tucked a few of the black stones he had on the ship, into my pocket. "Just a little added protection."

"How are we glamoured? I can still see you."

"I've glamoured our powers and also our looks. We both look the same to each other, but everyone else sees us differently." He pointed at a shop window, and I gasped at my reflection. Literally gasped.

I looked nothing like myself. Actually, I wasn't even a girl. I was a tall, teenaged, red-headed boy with freckles.

Goddess above. This was crazy. But I could rock it.

We first went into a small apothecary shop, and Nicolae strode over and conversed with the woman behind a table. I knew her. She and my mother were close friends, and she would have recognized me instantly. But being glamoured, she just smiled at me and ignored me after that.

Nicolae asked her for specific herbs and tonics and a few other supplies, and I wondered who had taught him about these things, and how to use them. In reality, I truly didn't know how old Nicolae was. He could have been over one hundred years old when he had my father. That was something I'd have to ask him the next time we were alone.

After the woman collected what he needed, they exchanged goods for skrag, and we were on our way.

"What is all that stuff for?" I asked him.

"Added protection." His brow furrowed. "You said you were bound with the same type of spelled ropes and cuffs as I was at the dock in Carpathia?"

"I was." I hated thinking back to that time, when Roehl had the upper hand, suppressing my power. "But the spell on the ones bound around you was much stronger."

"That's because he's testing us," Nicolae said quietly. "He's checking to see how much stronger he needs to be."

"That's terrifying," I sighed.

"Let's not worry about that right now," he said, with a broad smile. "Do you know where we might find food for your friends?"

He was trying to steer my attention, but what he'd said had my stomach knotting. Roehl was gathering strength and was preparing to fulfill his last words to me.

"I will come for you Calla. And next time, you won't survive."

I knew now, I couldn't do this on my own. If I was to survive, if any of us was to survive, we had to do this together.

"I do," I replied to his earlier question. "There is a small shop right down the road. Follow me."

As we ambled down the cobbled streets of Sartha, I'd forgotten how much I loved this town. I was born in Sartha, grew up here, and knew a lot of the people who lived here.

After we picked up some food from the shop, I dragged Nicolae to the small bakery on the corner. He reluctantly agreed and waited outside as I went in and bought assorted pastries. Brynna loved the lemon tarts, so I made sure there were a few.

"Why are you in the town?" A voice boomed in my head, making me jump. Trystan.

"Are you okay?" The baker asked through narrowed eyes.

"Yes. Sorry, I—I thought I saw a spider."

The baker's brow crumpled, and eyes narrowed, so I quickly paid for the pastries and walked out.

"I'm with Nicolae gathering supplies."

"I have one more shop I need to visit," Nicolae said, heading toward a small shop across the street that sold alcohol. Nicolae walked up to the woman and whispered something to her.

"You shouldn't be in the town. There are too many people. It's too risky."

"Nicolae glamoured us. I'm a red-headed boy."

"What?"

"Nothing. We're leaving now and heading back to the others. How do you know I'm in the town?"

"The amulet shows me where you are."

The woman went into the back room and brought out four dark bottles and handed them to Nicolae. While they chatted, I stayed in the corner.

"You can see me?"

"No. I have a map that has been connected to the amulet. It tracks your movements."

"Can anyone else see my location on the map?"

"It was spelled with my blood, so no one, but me, can see what the map reveals."

That was a relief. The thought of Roehl getting his hands on a magical map that showed my exact location was terrifying.

"How are the voices right now?"

"Gone, for now."

"That's good." I was happy he finally had some relief, even though I was thousands of miles away from him.

"What were you thinking when you first saw me? You said it was in Sartha on your birthday?"

His question threw me, but I would gladly answer. Maybe if he relived the memories, without his mind being bombarded, there would be some kind of recollection. A spark.

"Yes, Brynna had thrown me a party for my eighteenth birthday. I was standing outside near her pool when you first walked in. When your eyes met mine, I thought I was dreaming. They were the most beautiful color, and I thought you were the most handsome man I had ever seen. You had worn a black button-down shirt, and black slacks, and no one knew who you were. But when you came and stood a few feet in front of me,

I couldn't breathe. It was like all the air around me had been siphoned away. I was completely mesmerized by you. And then you wished me a happy birthday, and kissed me on the cheek, and my entire body tingled with warmth.

"Then, you grabbed hold of my hand and asked if you could speak with me. You led me upstairs to one of Brynna's guest rooms. You told me there was a connection between us. That's why you were there. You had asked me if I wanted you and were adamant about getting an answer. And after I told you to come, you kissed me. While I had some common sense left, I pulled away, asking who you were, and you replied, 'A dark knight come to protect you. A knight who can pleasure you beyond anything you've ever imagined.'

"You kissed me again, passionately, and then, you bit me. I didn't know what had happened at the time, that you had claimed me in an attempt to save me from Roehl. But I went home and spent the next three days in agony. But I am pretty sure you were there, helping me through it. When I finally woke, changed from mortal to immortal, you were gone, but left me a note and flask of your blood. You said I had a choice. To either run or to seal the blood bond."

I wondered what he was thinking. The silence on the other end was unnerving, and then he spoke.

"I have to go."

And that was that.

I felt hopeful, even though he hadn't said much. He was searching for answers, probably heavily weighing the words I'd just spoken to him. But the fact was, he contacted me first because he saw I was in the town. It showed he was concerned for my safety, and that made my heart swell with warmth.

"Let's go," Nicolae said, walking past me, the bottles tucked into his satchel.

We walked out into the woods, where no mortal eyes could see us. And then, I felt a stirring in the air, and a gust of wind.

"Calla!" a voice called from behind us.

Nicolae turned, his hands up and ready to use his magic, but as the figure with wild red hair and jade green eyes stepped out of the trees, I pushed his arm down.

"Melaina?" I exhaled. "What are you doing here?"

I ran over and threw my arms around her, and she hugged me back.

"Erro brought me," she said, but there were no signs of him. He must have left as quickly as he brought her. "He told me that your glamours and stones don't work on Wanderers." I glanced at Nicolae and his brow crumpled.

"Trystan wanted me to come," Melaina added. "His cadre told me everything that happened, about the Lethe potion, his memory being erased, and that Brynna had left with you."

I nodded, and her eyes shifted to Nicolae, widening just a bit.

"Melaina, this is my grandfather, Nicolae Corvus."

"I know," she said with a grin. "I remember his face from my session in the cave. The gold eyes are also a dead giveaway."

I twisted back to him. "Nicolae, this is Melaina," I introduced. "She's the witch who would have saved me in Morbeth, but I made her take Brynna instead. She's a trustworthy friend."

"It's nice to meet you, Melaina," Nicolae said, bowing his

head.

"Why did Trystan send you?" I asked.

"He wants me to help find the cure, or loophole, to reverse whatever Roehl did."

"He told you that?" I said, breathless.

She shrugged her shoulders. "In so many words. Whatever Roehl did is hurting him."

"I know," I replied, my heart heavy. "I'm glad you're here. Hopefully we can find a way to help him."

"We really need to get back," Nicolae urged, walking up to us.

I nodded, taking hold of his and Melaina's hands, and instantly we were enveloped in darkness and magically carried to the cabin on the shore.

Melaina's eyes widened, like she was thoroughly impressed. "Will I be able to do that?" I asked Nicolae, as the darkness dissolved.

"Yes," he replied. "It took me years to master, but I think with coaching and a lot of practice, you could learn to travel much faster."

"How far can the magic take you?"

He tapped a finger to the side of his head and gave a crooked smile. "As far as your mind will allow."

"I wish I could travel like that," Melaina said. "That would be so convenient."

Nicolae made his way to the cabin, but Melaina grabbed my wrist. "Can I talk to you privately for a moment?"

"Sure," I said, watching Nicolae turn back to us with that

protective look. "We'll be right in. I promise."

Melaina led me down closer to the shore then paused and pivoted to face me. "I'm concerned for Brynna," she said, brow furrowed.

"What do you mean? About her safety?"

"No, it's not that," she exhaled. "When we returned from Morbeth, I had to break the spell Roehl had placed on her. But there seems to be a residual stain on her being. A lingering darkness I can't put my finger on."

"Is it life threatening?" That's all I wanted to know. After hearing about the curse on Trystan's mom, I was worried.

"No, I don't think so," she said, shaking her head. "Brynna is healthy, Carpathia's physicians confirmed it, and she also shows no signs of illness. But whenever I'm with her, I feel like there is something … off. It could be that she is a mortal, and her fragile body is having a hard time releasing whatever Roehl did to her, leaving that residual taint."

My heart hammered heavily against my chest, and my breath quickened. "At the Shadow Fest, Roehl put a spell on her so she wouldn't remember me. Do you think he gave her the Lethe potion?"

"I don't know," Melaina sighed. "I mean, it could be nothing, but I feel it is a residual similar to Trystan's. And a bit of uneasiness when I'm around her. How do you feel when she is around you?"

I didn't feel anything when I was with her, but when we met in Carpathia, I had so many emotions rushing through me I could barely think. I was just happy to see her and thrilled she didn't hate me.

"I'm not sure," I said honestly, "because I was already expecting our meeting to be an awkward one. But after seeing and talking to her, she seems like the same old Brynna I've known all my life."

Melaina blew out a loud breath. "Good, then. Just be aware from now on. Let me know if you sense anything out of the usual."

"I will," I agreed. "Should this be something I share with Nicolae?"

"Not yet. I don't want anyone to be suspicious of her, if there is nothing to be suspicious of."

"I understand."

"Well, we should head inside, because this witch is freaking freezing."

I laughed and grabbed hold of her hand. "I'm glad you're back, Melaina."

"I am too," she said. "I was so worried about you."

"Yeah, my life has been a crazy shambles, but I'm still breathing."

"That's a good thing," she laughed.

"I guess it is."

"I have dessert!" I said as I walked into the door holding up the box of pastries. "And a guest!"

Brynna's eyes widened as I stepped away from the door.

"Melaina? What are you doing here?"

She hopped off the sofa and ran over, throwing her arms around the witch. Melaina wrapped her in a warm hug.

I could tell they'd gotten close. Especially since Melaina was her only friend in Carpathia.

"You left and didn't say goodbye," Melaina growled.

"The situation was complicated," Brynna said. "The king pretty much kicked Calla out of the castle, and I begged her to take me, since I felt I'd also worn out my welcome. So here, I am." Brynna smiled sweetly at Melaina, in a way I wasn't expecting. "And so are you."

Brynna then turned to me and snagged the box of pastries out of my hand.

"You're the best, Cal," she chimed, carrying the box to the others who could actually eat them. Thalia grabbed a chocolate donut, and Sabine a berry muffin. Brynna held out the box to Melaina and glanced at the space next to her.

"Go ahead. I'll be with a napkin in the corner, wiping the drool from my mouth," I laughed.

Melaina giggled, then sat next to Brynna, taking a strawberry scone. Brynna raised her lemon tart and exclaimed "Cheers!"

All four girls tapped their pastries together and took a bite. All moaning like it was the best thing they'd ever tasted. And yes, I was freaking jealous.

CHAPTER TWENTY-FOUR

We'd spent the next week in the cabin. It snowed heavily outside, so the girls played a lot of card games. Markus stepped outside to get some fresh air nearly every hour, if there was cloud cover, and I didn't blame him. The cabin was too warm and stuffy. But the mortals were happy, and that's all that mattered.

I hadn't heard from Trystan, but I knew he was busy with his duties. I also hadn't told anyone that Trystan had connected our elements, because I wasn't sure if he wanted anyone to know. Right now, it felt like it was something special between the two of us. A secret bond shared between us alone, that not even Roehl knew about.

Kai let me know he wouldn't be back for a few more days. He also had duties to attend to and a few meetings he couldn't miss.

I also found out that the bottles Nicolae had bought from the alcohol shop were actually filled with blood. I guess there were a few people who knew there were immortals amongst them and capitalized on it. But the supply was getting low, and he would have to make another trip soon.

I felt claustrophobic in the cabin, having all this energy and power inside of me that needed to be put to the test and I had nowhere to test it. I needed to use it so it could grow stronger.

"I need to get more wood," Nicolae whispered, putting another log on the fire. There were only five logs left.

It was morning, and everyone was sound asleep. The sun was shining this morning, so even Markus stayed in bed.

"I'll go with you," I whispered back. "I need to get out of this cabin and let out some of my power. I feel like I'm going to combust."

Nicolae nodded and grinned, then waved for me to follow him outside.

"We'll stay right at the edge of Whisper Woods." White puffs of smoke exited his mouth as he spoke. "Do you think you can pull a few trees down? We'll look for the dead ones first. They should be the easiest."

"Of course. That shouldn't be a problem." I'd learned that a lot of my power came from my mind. The stronger my mind was, the easier it was to call the gift. Doubting in the power made it weak and when suppressed, harder to break through.

I knew Nicolae was wary of leaving the cottage area which was heavily warded, but we had to get supplies and food. Our fire gifts could only do so much. The snow was now nearly two feet deep, and the temperature had dropped to around ten degrees. The fire had to be constant, keeping the cabin warm for my friends, so we needed the extra wood.

I was excited to use my power. It had been a while since I'd done something significant. The past week I'd only lit candles and heated things up for them … food, drinks, cold bathwater, etc. But that was easy.

I couldn't beat Roehl using simple power. I needed everything I had, because I knew he was out there, gathering potions and magic, no matter how dark or evil, to kill me.

Taking Nicolae's outstretched hand, he transported us right outside the Whisper Woods. It was quiet, and serene. The freshly flocked trees glistened in the morning light, and the ground sparkled like a million diamonds. I stood in awe of it all.

"Come, Calla," Nicolae said, walking into the woods. The edge of the woods was bright and open, but as you got farther back, the trees were denser.

"Here's one," Nicolae said, pointing at an old spruce that had died and was leaning against another. "You got it?"

I nodded then positioned myself in front of the tree. Holding my arms out, I called to my earth power. Roots from surrounding trees began to crawl up the dead tree, wrapping tightly around it. I slowly pulled my hands back, and the roots moved with me, yanking the tree to the ground.

Relaxing my hands, the roots withdrew back into the frozen ground and disappeared.

Nicolae shook his head with a broad smile on his lips. "I couldn't have done it better myself."

"Thank you, I said, a beaming smile on my own face.

Pulling that tree down took no effort at all. It was simple, and

I was ready for more.

Most of the trees in the area were still alive, so Nicolae carefully maneuvered a little further into the forest. "Stay close to me," he said, and I did.

About twenty yards in, there were a few more dead trees.

"Can you do it from here?" he asked.

"I guess we'll see," I said with a grin. I stood in place and held my hands out in front of me, again calling to my power, and was thrilled when I saw those roots burst out of the ground and wrap around — Oh shit. It was wrapping around the wrong tree.

I quickly dropped my hands, but the roots followed my movement, pulling a massive tree that was still alive down.

No, no, no, no, no!

Pushing my hands back in front of me, the roots stopped pulling and started pushing the tree back upright, until it was back in its place. I fisted my hands, letting the surrounding roots disappear back into the ground, and then willed the healthy tree to dig its roots back in. And it did.

"Do you know what happened?" Nicolae asked. He was testing me. In a good way.

"I think it was because I couldn't see the dead tree clearly, and because it was so close to the other tree, I might have lost focus."

"Good," he said. "Now try again."

Wanting to get a little closer, I began to trudge through the snow, into the thicker part of the forest. When I was about ten yards away and could see the dead tree more clearly, I raised my hands and called to my earth power.

This time the roots twisted and coiled around the dead tree and as I pulled my arms back, the tree came crashing down.

I turned around to get an approval from Nicolae, but he was gone.

"Nicolae?" I called, but there was no answer.

Something was wrong.

Nicolae wouldn't have left me alone.

My heart started hammering inside my chest. I pressed myself against a large tree and listened for any sign of Nicolae.

"Trystan," I called down our bond.

"Calla?"

"I don't know where Nicolae is. He was here, and now he's gone."

"Where are you?"

"In the Whisper Woods."

"Why are you there?"

"We are gathering wood for the fire."

"Calla!" It was Nicolae. And it was the first time he'd ever spoken though our connection.

"Where are you?" I asked.

"I don't know, but we're not alone. Stay hidden and stay put. I'll find you," he said.

"Trystan, Nicolae is in the Whisper Woods, but I don't know where. He said we're not alone."

"Wait there, Nyx is nearby."

I heard a familiar caw above us and knew Flint must have been near too. Where was that crazy bird?

Not far away I heard snow crunching and a few branches

breaking.

"Someone is coming," I told Trystan.

"There are eight men headed your way. You're going to have to fight."

Fight? Goddess above.

I closed my eyes and took in a deep breath, trying to steady my fraying nerves. Where the hell was Flint?

Eight men. I could take on eight men.

"They're heading toward you. Four from the front, and four coming in from behind. They know you're there." Trystan was watching, through Nyx's eyes.

I slid down the tree and kept low, then slowly peeked my head out to see where they were.

I saw one of the men, crouched low, with a sword in his hand.

Pushing my hands down through the snow, my heated palms melted the frozen earth, letting me sink my fingers into the soil. I felt closer to the earth this way, connected to it. I could feel the earth's life force, radiating through my palms. Digging my fingers deeper into the soil, I felt an even deeper connection. Closing my eyes, I focused on the earth. I could feel where each man stood in the forest, feel the vibrations of their movements in the earth.

I could feel the earth in my fingertips, alive and breathing. I could feel it pulsing, ready to do my bidding.

With my eyes open and focused on the first man, I spoke to the earth, calling it forth. The trees came to life, creaking and cracking around me, answering my call.

From the ground, huge roots shot upward and then aimed at the unsuspecting guard. Like a javelin, a massive root sailed right through the man's chest, impaling him. The guard let out a blood-curdling scream as the huge root picked him up and slammed him to the ground. More roots surrounded him, making a cage around him, and then they began pressing, forcing his body beneath the frozen ground. The sound of bones snapping, and screams filled the air, then finally, the forest went silent, and the only thing that remained was blood-stained snow.

My mind was at war with itself. That man had died by my hand.

"He was going to kill you," the earth seemed to reply. That was true. I couldn't let my feelings get in the way. This wasn't practice. This was war. This was life or death.

I leaned out even further, readjusting my fingers in the soil, watching the three other men who had witnessed the macabre assault. They weren't moving. Not yet.

A caw in front of me, broke my attention. Sitting on a branch, two trees away, was Nyx. I knew it was her, because Flint had fiery eyes.

"Flint, where are you," I whispered.

I felt a calmness in the air and a vibration in my soul, and I knew it was him. Flint was out there, nearby and ready. But he knew I was strong enough to do this on my own. That's why he hadn't come yet.

"On your left," Trystan urged through the bond. I glanced at Nyx and gave her a nod. Gave Trystan a nod.

Pivoting on my knees, I saw them. Four men spread out,

trying to surround me. They had no idea what wrath was coming.

I dug my fingers deeper and pushed my power and will into the soil. The ground shook violently, throwing the men off balance. Suddenly there was a loud rumble followed by a deafening crack. The ground beneath the men fractured, opening up, swallowing them. I could hear their screams as I pulled my fingers from the soil, letting the earth close back over them, devouring the men whole.

I stood to my feet and faced the last three men. Calling to my fire, my entire body engulfed in flame. The men glanced at each other, then back at me. I raised my palms, and large flames danced within them. All fear had melted away, and all that was left was survival.

Tilting my head slightly to the side, I glared at the men. A wicked grin rose on my lips.

"Come and play with me … if you want to die."

"Fuck that, I'm out of here." The guard who was closest to the man who'd been impaled by the roots, turned and sprinted away.

My smile rose, the flames in my palms danced higher, brighter. "He's smart."

The other two looked at each other, then dropped their swords and slowly backed away. As soon as they broke through the forest, they took off running.

"Nicolae," I gasped, my thoughts kicking back into reality.

I stood there, body now trembling, palms still warm. I glanced over to the blood-soaked earth and snow, where the man had been impaled and pushed underground. In pieces.

A deep sob ripped from my chest, realizing what I'd done. My body shuddered, and I dropped to my knees.

I killed them.

Yes, those men deserved to die, but —

I killed them.

My eyes blurred with tears. I glanced down to my palms, to the tattoos. So much power within these hands. Too much. The power of life and death.

"You did what you had to do. It wasn't your fault." Trystan spoke, as if he knew what I was thinking and feeling. *"They would not have hesitated to hurt or kill you."*

Nyx flapped her wings, flying up above the forest. In a few moments, I heard Trystan's voice.

"Nicolae is safe. It looks like he had a battle of his own, but he's making his way back to you." His voice was softer, kinder.

"Thank you." I quickly wiped my tears and pulled myself back up, not wanting Nicolae to see me in this condition.

"Where is Kai?" Trystan asked, probably wanting to change the subject.

"He left for Aquaria as soon as we arrived. He also had duties he needed to attend to."

"Why did you call me, and not him?"

That was a good question. Calling Kai through the bond hadn't even entered my mind. When I called down that bond it was Trystan my mind and heart wanted.

"I honestly didn't even have to think about it," I answered truthfully. *"When I was alone and afraid, I called out to the one person I knew would be there. The one person who had always*

been there for me in the past. Thank you for answering, Trystan. I wouldn't have been able to do it without you."

There was a slight hesitation.

"You could have, but you're welcome. You did well."

"Calla!" Nicolae called, his voice much closer. "Calla, where are you?"

"I'm here," I said, running toward his voice.

As soon as he saw me, Nicolae ran over and wrapped me in his arms, squeezing tightly.

"I'm sorry you were left alone. A Wanderer took me, but as soon as I felt that power, I fought back, and was suddenly in a different part of the forest. There were two men who came after me, but they're gone now." He unwrapped his arms from around me and gazed into my eyes. "Are you okay?"

"I am," I said, then told him everything that had happened. "I'm starting to believe in myself."

"I'm glad," Nicolae said, a broad smile rising on his lips.

"How did they find us?" I asked. "We were glamoured."

"We were, but it was the Wanderer who found me."

"Will they be able to find us, regardless of the strength of your glamour?"

"It seems that right now, they can. But I will find a way around it. There has to be a way."

"You managed to stay alive and hidden all these years," I said, nudging him.

"Yes, but Roehl had never targeted me. Not until that night they came to kill me. And until then, there were no Wanderers seeing me out."

"Goddess," I moaned. "Will we ever have a moment to breathe?"

"Not as long as Roehl is alive, I'm afraid." Nicolae gave me a sad smile. "Let's gather some wood and head back to the cabin. I don't think more men will be back anytime soon, but we'll have to move from this place. They know we're here."

I nodded as Nicolae used magic to slice through the wood. He unfolded a blanket he'd had in his satchel and laid it on the ground, then piled the wood on top of it. Touching a piece of the blanket, and taking my hand, he transported us right in front of the cabin.

Gathering pieces of wood in his arms, he turned back to me. "We don't have to tell the girls what happened. I don't want to spook them, but I will talk to Markus as soon as I get a chance."

"Good idea," I said. Brynna wouldn't be able to process what had happened to me, anyway. Sabine might have, and Thalia definitely would have, but it was better to just let them know we would have to move. They knew it would happen, just not so soon.

CHAPTER TWENTY-FIVE

Nicolae told the group about our next move. We would be heading northeast to Baelfast. I wasn't too thrilled about that move, because Baelfast was close, not only to the Morose Mountains, but Morbeth as well. Two places I wanted to stay far away from.

Brynna was fine with it because she loved to travel, and Sabine was giddy to just be experiencing the world outside of Morbeth. Thalia was so relaxed about everything.

Nicolae and Melaina worked together to try to put together a stronger spell to keep the Wanderer's blinded by a glamour. Was it even possible? Between the two of them, I was hopeful they would find a way.

The entire next day, we packed and prepared to leave the cabin.

"How are we all going to get there? Baelfast is inland, we can't take a ship," Brynna said.

"I will be transporting you two at a time," Nicolae said.

"Calla and Thalia will go irst, and Markus will be the last."

That was a smart move, because if anything should happen, Thalia and I would be able to fight together.

Nicolae had already set up a suite directly in the middle of the city. It was a place that he'd already warded. Hopefully, the bustling city would be a deterrent for those trying to kill us. We just had to be on our guard. At all times.

Two by two, Nicolae transported us through his magical darkness to Baelfast. First, it was me and Thalia, then Sabine and Brynna, and lastly, Markus and Melaina.

The suite was a lot larger than the cottage. It was an entire upper floor, with three bedrooms and two washrooms. The center of the room was large and open, with a sitting area and a small kitchen. I made sure all the curtains were drawn, so Markus wouldn't get a fatal sunburn.

"Now this place, I like," Brynna chimed as soon as they arrived.

"Me too," Sabine added, peeling off her cloak. "It's a lot warmer here."

When Markus and Melaina arrived, Markus excused himself and picked a room, shutting the door. He was probably grumpy because he hadn't fed, but Baelfast was bustling with people, and I was sure he'd make an exit as soon as the sun set.

Ambling into one of the rooms, I fisted my hands.

"I just wanted you to know we're in Baelfast," I said to Trystan.

"I know. I'm sending Brone and Feng there for extra protection."

"You don't have to do that. I know your kingdom depends on your cadre."

"They do, but we aren't the ones who are on the verge of war. Nor is someone actively hunting us down to kill us."

"You've given me so much already. I will never be able to repay you."

"I don't expect anything in return. Like I said before, I made a promise, and I am keeping that promise."

Of course, he was.

My heart ached a bit knowing he wasn't doing it because he'd felt something for me.

I had to find that damn loophole. I had to talk to Melaina. She was sent to help me figure it out.

The past few nights, I'd woken up sobbing, my sheets partially incinerated, the rest wet with tears and sweat. I'd dreamed of those men I'd killed. It wasn't a quick and easy wave that had washed over them, like I'd done in Incendia. Those men, I didn't know if they'd died or survived because I wasn't there to see the repercussions.

But this was different. I'd tasted the fear of those men. I saw the pain that wracked that one guard's face as the roots crushed his bones, and the grotesque sound of his limbs being pulled apart as the roots dragged him beneath the ground. I heard the tortured screams of the men who had fallen into the crevices in the earth—that I created. And then, the dead silence as the earth closed in on them. Those screams echoed in my mind and reverberated through my soul.

I knew it wasn't over either. There would be more encounters, and more death. I just had to ind a way to deal with it.

Brone and Feng arrived three days later, after having to take a ship and ride on horseback to get to Baelfast. And when they arrived, it was a welcome sight.

"Princess," Brone said as his huge frame stepped inside the suite. He picked me up in a hug and set me back down carefully on my feet.

"It's good to see you, big guy," I laughed.
His eyes shifted to Melaina sitting at the dining table. He leaned in close to my ear. "The witch is here?"

I nodded and whispered back. "Trystan sent her."

"He did? I didn't know."

I nodded, and he shrugged his broad shoulders.

That struck me. Trystan had done another thing to help me without his cadre knowing.

Feng stepped in and greeted me with a smile and a bow of his head. "How have you been, Calla?"

"I'm okay," I said. But Feng tilted his head to the side.

"Are you sure?"

"Did Trystan tell you about what happened in the Whisper Woods?" I said softly.

He nodded. "He did. And he said he was … impressed."

"I'm still trying to deal with it all," I sighed. "With what this power can actually do."

Feng placed a hand on my shoulder. "Sometimes, you have to do things against what your heart and mind agree with. But you are alive because of it," he said with a sad smile.

"When your heart is soft, it is never easy. For you, I don't think it will ever be, but you must do what you have to in order to survive."

I nodded. Trystan must have told them about my breakdown. These men were warriors. They had seen countless men die, and many of them by their own hands.

Did it ever get easier? Did they have nightmares of the men they killed?

As night fell, Markus disappeared into the town to feed. While Brynna, Sabine, and Thalia played cards, I called a meeting with Nicolae, Melaina, Brone, and Feng.

We all sat around the table, because I didn't want my friends to think we were hiding anything from them. They would still be able to hear, but they were having fun.

I started. "I'm sure everyone here knows what happened to Trystan. Roehl gave him the Lethe potion, and with it, a curse that won't allow him to be around me. But Brone said a mage told him that with every spell, there is a loophole."

"Yes, there always is," Melaina agreed. "Sometimes those loopholes are difficult and involve more than one thing. But other times, it could be very simple. What do we know about this spell?" Melaina asked.

Nicolae leaned his elbows on the table. "We know the Lethe potion completely erased his memory of Calla."

"Yes," I agreed. "There are also voices inside his head, telling him that I am his enemy and will destroy him and his kingdom. I also know they are much stronger when he is near me, or when he can see me, but—" I hesitated, knowing I had to tell them.

If we were going to find a cure, they would have to know everything. "The night before we left Carpathia, Trystan came to me and connected our elements."

"He did what?" Feng questioned, his eyes narrowing. "Was this after the encounter you had in his bedroom?"

"What encounter? What happened in his bedroom?" Nicolae boomed, his eyes narrowing, brows crumpling.

"Girl, you know you're going to have to spill details later," Sabine giggled from the couch. Brynna nodded, pointing a finger at me.

Thalia shook her head at them. "Brynna, it's your turn." She then turned to me with her cards in hand and winked.

I definitely wasn't g oing t o g ive d etails r ight now, but Nicolae needed to know. As well as Melaina.

"Trystan was having a bad dream, probably of me killing him or ruining his kingdom. I heard him call my name and went to make sure he was okay. I'd startled him, and he demanded to know why I was in his room. Maybe he thought I was going to actually kill him. But the voices in his head were telling him to hurt me, so he told me to leave."

"I want to know more about him connecting his element to yours," Feng said, tenting his fingers. "How did it happen?"

"I—I decided to have a drink out on the veranda, and when I stepped outside, Trystan was already there. It was after our encounter. After you and the others must have left him," I said. "Trystan told me not to move, but to hold my palms up, facing him. I did as he said, and he came and placed his palms against mine. I immediately felt our elements connect."

"And what does that mean? When your elements connect?" Melaina asked. She wasn't around when Kai had explained it.

"It allows me to make contact with him. We can speak directly to each other through the connection, but that's it. We can't see each other, like we did with the partial blood bond." My eyes shifted to Brone, Feng, and Nicolae. "He said that through the connection, the voices are quiet. It's like the curse doesn't know, maybe because I'm not close and he can't see me. I was hoping it could have been the loophole, but it's not. It didn't cure him. But it is a way we can talk freely without the curse hurting him."

"And have you been speaking through the connection?" Melaina asked, cocking a brow.

"Not a lot. But when Nicolae and I were in the Whisper Woods, I called him through the bond. Nyx and Flint were nearby so Trystan used her to help me find the enemy. He helped me defeat them."

Feng smiled. "It confounds me. Even after a curse was placed on Trystan to eliminate you from his mind and life, you both still found a way around it." His eyes went distant for a while. "I don't think Roehl had time to create a complicated loophole to the spell."

"I don't either," Nicolae agreed.

"Then the loophole should be simple," Melaina said.

"Maybe it's true love's kiss." Sabine stood and dramatically threw her hands over her chest, batting her eyes, swooning.

"It could be," Melaina said. "If Roehl used the Lethe potion to have him forget you and put a spell on him, that anytime you are near, it causes him pain. The last thing he thinks is that he would touch you, let alone kiss you, when he is supposed to hate you. That's probably why the curse is blind to the connection of your elements."

"She's got a point," Nicolae said.

Sabine chimed back in. "Roehl didn't know how strong of a connection Trystan and Calla actually had. He thought it was superficial, but we all know it went much deeper."

Everyone agreed.

"I can attest to the fact that Trystan cannot stay away from Calla," Feng said. "Despite our advice against getting close, to keep those voices at bay, he always seems to be nearby, still watching over her. And now, we find out he has connected their elements? If that doesn't confirm he still feels a connection with her—"

"Oh, it definitely confirms it," Sabine said. "Trystan felt something even before he met Calla. I know something like that cannot be taken away so easily. Even with a potion or a curse."

I sighed, my mind spinning. Could it be that easy? Could it be as simple as a kiss?

Melaina suddenly moaned, her fingers grasping the table, her body trembling.

"Melaina, what's wrong?" Brynna hollered, running over from across the room.

At the same time, I heard Trystan through the bond.

"There is trouble."

Melaina blinked, and her eyes went white.

"Brone, Feng, are you there?" Trystan's voice spoke through Melaina.

"Yes," Brone replied.

"Whoa, that is some crazy shit," Sabine murmured to Brynna.

Markus had just returned, and even he paused, his eyes wide with horror.

Brynna stood to the side, mouth agape. She looked afraid, and I knew it was the first time she'd witnessed a channeling. Even I had freaked out the first time Melaina channeled Trystan.

"What is it?" Feng asked.

"Are you able to speak in private?"

Feng glanced at me, and I shook my head. *"I am not leaving,"* I mouthed to him.

"We are in a large space, but it is open," Feng replied, not lying.

"Is Nicolae and Calla nearby?"

"Yes, they are here."

"We just received word that King Romulus died. Roehl has assumed control of the throne until he is given the title king."

I felt as if the earth opened up under my feet and swallowed me whole. Markus cursed and walked away. He was the Captain of the King's guard. He was very close to Romulus, so I knew he was going to hurt.

"Roehl killed him," I wailed, dropping to my knees. "The bastard murdered his own father."

CHAPTER TWENTY-SIX

My body was trembling, tears falling. So much death. So much agony. My heart still hadn't healed from the death of my father. It would never heal until Roehl was dead.

But what hurt most, was that Nicolae would never get to meet him.

"Are you sure Romulus is dead?" Nicolae questioned.

"Yes. Our spies in Morbeth have confirmed it."

"How?" I sobbed. "How did he die?" Did I want to know?

There was a slight pause and during that time, I couldn't breathe.

"He was beheaded."

"No," I wailed, doubling over. I couldn't breathe.

Nicolae came and wrapped his arms around me while I cried.

"Brone. Feng," Trystan spoke through Melaina. "Keep them safe. Make sure they don't leave. Kylan, Andrés and I are on our way."

I felt claustrophobic with everyone gathering around, trying to help and comfort me. I couldn't breathe. My mind and heart were throbbing. I needed to process and grieve what had just happened. No, I wasn't going to run, but I felt smothered.

"I need a moment alone," I said, walking toward one of the bedrooms.

"Don't you even think of leaving," Sabine warned.

"I won't. I made a promise, and I'm staying. I just need some space."

"Cal, are you sure you don't need a friend?" Brynna asked.

"Thanks, Bryn. Maybe later, but not right now."

"Okay," she said, with a knowing look.

Inside the room, I closed the door and pressed my back against it, sliding to the ground, my emotions poured out. I cried for King Romulus, and for those loyal to him. I cried for Nicolae and that he hadn't gotten the chance to meet him. I cried for every one of my friends in the other room, and those coming to help me. Because I knew we would be going to war and our lives would change.

Roehl now had his army. With his father dead, he had the entire Morbeth army to command. I knew that beheading his father in front of everyone in the kingdom sent a solid message. Follow him. Obey him. Adore him ... or you die.

That's how he ruled. He didn't give a shit if anyone loved him. As long as they feared him and obeyed, they would live.

But he'd gone too far this time. He showed the rulers of Talbrinth how sick and twisted he truly was. Would any of them join us against him and Morbeth's army? Or would they remain neutral?

"Calla, where are you?" It was Kai.

"Did you hear about Romulus?" I sobbed.

"I did. I'm so sorry, Calla. Are you okay? Are you safe?"

"Yes, I'm with Nicolae and the others. Trystan sent Brone and Feng and he is on his way with Kylan and Andrés."

"That's good to hear. When we received word, I told my father about what Roehl did to you. And he wants you to know that you have the full support of Aquaria and our army."

"Kai," I sobbed. I couldn't help but feel overwhelmed.

"I told you before, your grandfather was a hero in our kingdom. We vowed to protect his heirs. It isn't only an honor, Calla. It's our duty."

"Kai—"

"You are not alone, Calla. Remember that," he said. He wasn't the only one to say that. I just had to allow them to help me, knowing they could get hurt or killed. *"My father is calling meetings with the royalty of Northfall, Aquaria, Sartha, Baelfast, and Hale."*

"Don't count on Northfall. Not while their princess is engaged to Trystan."

"My father is a very persuasive man, and I'm going to stay here and help him. I'll keep you posted."

"I don't know what to say."

"Say you love me."

"I do love you, Kai—"

"Don't say anything else to ruin it. I'll take those words for whatever their worth."

I closed my eyes and smiled. Kai was an amazing man.

One of the most amazing men I had ever met. He was handsome, charming, and magical. He had the full package — everything a girl could ever want. But he wasn't Trystan. And that sealed it for me.

"Please tell your father that I am so grateful."

"He already knows. I have to go, but I'll be in touch soon."

"Be safe," I said.

"You be safe," he replied.

That night, Nicolae and Melaina did whatever they could to make sure the wards on the suite were at maximum strength. Everyone, including Markus, slept out in the living area. They said it was because they wanted to be ready in case anything did get through the wards and glamour. But I had a feeling they were also watching me. Making sure I stayed put and didn't run.

It was after midnight when everyone finally fell asleep. But I couldn't turn my mind off. It was a whirlwind of thoughts, calculations, and outcomes. Then, I felt a charge in the air and a burst of wind.

In the corner of the room, standing in the shadows, was a dark figure. Not breathing, I gently touched Feng's leg, and he immediately woke up, his eyes following mine. He jumped up, crouching, with his staff pointed at the figure. "Who are you?"

Everyone else woke. Markus, Brone, and Nicolae were on their feet in seconds and Melaina was already starting a spell.

The figure stepped out of the shadows with his hands up.

"Erro," I exhaled. "I thought someone had broken through and was going to kill us."

"I would never hurt you," he said. "But you are in danger."

"We heard about Roehl," I said.

Erro shook his head, his eyes saddened. "Yes, but there is more. Roehl demanded all Wanderers to find you. But I ordered them to tell Roehl that we cannot break through the magical barriers you have recently put up. We told him that you have powerful magic from the Fire Goddess. And he believed it. I want you to know that my Wanderers will not come to you."

"*Your* Wanderers?" I questioned.

Erro nodded and smiled. "I am their ruler, Calla. Not many know the Wanderers have a ruler, because we like to keep it that way."

I was in awe of this man with great magic. I thought he was just a kind Wanderer, but he was their ruler. "I didn't know," I said, feeling bad I hadn't regarded him as such.

"Erro, my friend," Nicolae interjected. "I know there is more to your visit."

Erro sighed. "You know me well, friend. I hate to be the bearer of bad news, but Roehl has given the Wanderers twenty days to find you or get word to you. If you and Calla do not return to Morbeth by the twentieth day, he will burn all of Romulus's witches alive, and hang all of his loyal guards."

Nicolae stepped toward him. "Erro, you have done so much to help us already. You risk too much."

"We are simple people who keep to ourselves. When Roehl first demanded we come or he would slaughter our families, we had to obey.

"I have come to realize, we cannot let the wicked rule our lives, especially when it is out of fear or malicious intent. Even if threatened, we cannot be fearful to stand up for what we believe is right. I will not bow down to a haughty prince who cares nothing for the lives of others, discarding bodies like they were trash. No, I have chosen to do what is right. I have chosen to stand with you, Nicolae and Calla. As will my men."

I didn't know what to say. My head was still throbbing, and heart pounding, hearing about what Roehl was going to do to the witches and guards. Was Spring's grandmother, Aurelia, one of the witches he was going to burn? She was one of Romulus's witches and was the very one who broke the spell Roehl had cast over him. She was also one of the few to help me escape the dungeon in Morbeth.

Twenty days. We had twenty days.

Gods and Goddesses, please help us.

Thalia grabbed my hand and squeezed. Brynna grabbed hold of my other hand, and Sabine placed her palms on my shoulders.

"We've got you," Sabine breathed. "We won't let you do this alone."

"No, we won't," Brynna said. "I may not have powers, but I have a mouth that can be a great distraction."

"I love you guys."

Sabine nudged me. "Yeah, we know."

"You get me a bow, and I'll kick some ass next to you," Thalia added.

"But you can manipulate the earth." Sabine said. "Why would you need a bow?"

"Because I am much more comfortable with a bow in my hands."

"Then maybe you need to show Calla a thing or two. Especially after she nearly impaled you with one of her fire arrows."

"I can show you," Thalia agreed, but I shook my head.

"I don't think twenty days is long enough." I sighed.

"Where will you go?" Nicolae asked Erro.

"I will return to Morbeth and play my part. Roehl needs to believe that we cannot break through your ward. If I were you, I wouldn't stay in one place for more than three days," Erro suggested.

"What about the witches and guards?" I questioned. "We cannot forget about them."

Melaina turned to me, her eyes welled with tears. "Sometimes sacrifices must be made for the greater good."

I shook my head, knowing this was right in some instances. But not this.

"Those men and women are going to die horrible, painful deaths because of me and Nicolae. Right now, every one of them is putting their trust in one thing … that we will come, so they can live."

Nicolae strode over and stood in front of me. "We have twenty days to figure this out. And we will. We just have a lot of work to do."

I hoped we would find a way. We had to. There was no other option than to try to save all of those innocent lives that had dedicated their lives to protect my great-grandfather.

CHAPTER TWENTY-SEVEN

"Don't run, Calla," Trystan said through our connection. There was no way he could have known unless Melaina had informed him. *"I have been told that you run away to keep those you love safe. But you cannot win this war alone. You need help and I have already given my word to do so. Promise me you'll wait until we get there."*

He was right. I couldn't do this alone. Not this time.

"I promise," I replied.

"We will be there before the sun rises."

Nicolae was already making arrangements to leave the suite as soon as Trystan arrived. We would be heading north to an abandoned mine in Morose Mountains, far away from where Roehl's crooked kingdom dwelled.

I spoke to Nicolae about hiding Brynna and Sabine somewhere else to keep them protected, but Melaina heard and dragged me to the side. "I'm still not sure of the feeling I get around Brynna. If you leave her alone, Roehl might easily find her. He knows how much she means to you, so he would not hesitate to use her as bait, again."

Melaina had a point, and even though I didn't feel anything unusual with Brynna, she did. I wasn't going to risk it. They would have to stick with us.

Before the sun rose on the next day, Trystan arrived with Kylan and Andrés. I had fallen asleep in one of the rooms with Sabine, Brynna, and Thalia, realizing the demons would be back with me and Trystan in close proximity. I could hear his faint voice on the other side of the door and my heart began to race. I heard him talking to Nicolae and also heard Melaina's voice.

Melaina came in about an hour afterward and explained that Nicolae would be taking everyone up to the mine, two by two. Trystan and Kylan had already left to make sure the mine was secure when we arrived. Brynna and Sabine were next, then me and Thalia.

When it was my turn, I noticed that Nicolae had looked fatigued. We all did, but he looked extra depleted.

"When was the last time you fed?" I asked him.

"Yesterday," he answered, taking Thalia's hand. "Don't worry about me. I'll be fine. Once I get everybody over, I will have my fill."

"Good. Because I need you to survive. You and Thalia are the only family I have left."

Nicolae smiled affectionately and held out his hand to me. "We will survive together."

"Together," I reiterated, before we were whisked away.

We landed in a darkened tunnel where the air smelled stale and felt like it was below zero.

Down the passageway, a light gleamed against the damp mine walls.

"Follow the light," Nicolae said. "It will take you to the others." Before I could answer, he disappeared.

Anxious butterflies flitted in my stomach knowing Trystan would be there, but I felt I should let him know we had arrived, so he could prepare.

"Thalia and I are coming. If you need me to remain hidden, I will."

"Tell Thalia to come. The others are waiting for her, but I would like to speak to you only."

I wasn't sure if that was a good idea, but, *"Okay."*

"Thalia, Brynna and Sabine are waiting for you. I'll be right there."

Thalia gave me an eye. "You shouldn't be alone."

"Trystan wants to talk to me. I'll be fine."

She finally conceded and gradually moved toward the light, so I pressed my back against the icy wall to wait for him.

As soon as she departed, I detected his scent in the air. Gasping, Trystan was suddenly standing in front of me, against the opposite wall.

"The witch told me about the possible loophole," he declared through our connection.

I couldn't breathe. All the coldness in the air seemed to disappear.

"Do you think it would work? A kiss?"

I shook my head. *"I don't know. And I would never force*

you to—"

Before I could finish, Trystan moved forward wrapping one arm around my back, his other hand grasping the back of my neck.

His lips gently pressed against mine. His kiss was slow and affectionate, instantly making my mind numb and sent a hum of heat and electricity through my entire body.

I stayed in place but melted into his arms. His tongue swept across my lips seeking entrance, so I opened and let him deepen the kiss. Tongues, teeth, lips … my dark knight had come and swept me to a place far, far away.

Trystan's mouth ravaged mine. His kiss was so deep, so passionate, that I felt it had to break the curse. But suddenly, he pulled away, leaving me breathless and dazed. I stumbled backward and found the ice-cold wall again to brace my trembling body.

Trystan had also moved backward, his back pressed against the opposite wall.

Did it work? Had the curse been broken?

Suddenly, Trystan let out a pained cry and dropped to his knees, cradling his head between his hands.

"Kylan!" I screamed. "Kylan!"

I kneeled in front of Trystan, wanting to touch him but knowing I couldn't. "How can I help you?" I wept. Seeing him suffering and in so much pain was shredding my soul to fragments.

"Go away," Trystan spoke, his breath ragged.

This damn curse was going to kill him.

Kylan arrived moments later, and with one look at Trystan,

he closed his eyes and combed a hand through his thick, dark hair. Before he could ask what happened, I answered.

"He kissed me."

Then I spun and rushed down the tunnel, heart bursting, praying the demons would leave him alone.

"Calla, what's wrong?" Sabine asked as soon as I entered the space they were gathered in.

"Love's kiss didn't break the curse. It made it worse," I sobbed, tears now streaming down my face.

"Oh, girl, come here." She wrapped me in a tender hug while I let out another wave of sobs.

Brynna and Thalia made me a bed in a far corner of the area, where I settled down and tried to rest. I hadn't had a proper night's sleep in days, and it was catching up to me. I was an emotional wreck.

All the ladies huddled around me, trying to support me, while Trystan stayed at the opposite side of the area, circled by his cadre.

"If it wasn't love's kiss, then what could it be?" Thalia questioned.

"Maybe Trystan has to claim Calla again," Sabine replied. "Think about it. He claimed her once, but now his mind is erased of her. Who in their right mind, especially a prince, would claim someone they know nothing about?"

"Trystan," Melaina replied. "He first claimed Calla, knowing nothing about her."

Sabine shrugged. "Does Roehl know that?"

"He probably doesn't." Melaina sighed, shrugging her shoulders. "That wicked prick."

"Don't tell Trystan what you're thinking," I told all of them. "After seeing what the kiss did to him, claiming me might actually kill him. I won't risk it."

"Too late," Melaina whispered, pointing across the place to where Trystan and his cadre were staring at us.

My cheeks instantly flushed with warmth.

"Don't mind the girl chatter," Sabine blurted.

Andrés opened his mouth to respond, but Brone smacked him on the arm. I grinned at the powerful brute, pleased he had listened and hadn't smacked him in the head.

My eyes drifted to Trystan, who looked fatigued. I settled back down, breaking eye contact, hoping the voices would remain silent. *"I'm sorry you were in pain and there was nothing I could do to help."*

I wasn't expecting him to answer.

"I'm sorry I ordered you to leave. I didn't mean to upset you. And just so you know, the kiss ... it was worth it. The feel and taste of your lips was worth every bit of the pain."

My heart warmed and broke at the same time. I ran my fingers over my lips, still feeling the tingle of his lips against mine. I knew I would have no problem kissing him forever.

On the third day, after mostly sleeping the entire time, we were packing to travel to the next location. I was thankful I didn't wake with terrible nightmares or dreams of Trystan. With everyone in one area, that would have been awkward.

We would be going to a place I had been to before. After long discussions, it was decided that we would be staying in the cave where I had first met Trystan's cadre—in the midst of Whisper Woods.

The cavern was wide and at least familiar, and there was ample space to keep the voices in Trystan's head quiet.

Packing our things, Trystan spoke through our connection.

"There are a few questions I want to ask you."

I picked up my blanket to fold it. *"You can ask me anything."*

"Do you truly love me?"

I paused, his question taking me aback. I spun and found his eyes already on me.

Dropping my blanket, tears instantly pooled in my eyes.

Looking at him was always like I was taking in a breath of fresh air. The warmth in his eyes always seemed to scrape against my soul.

"I never knew what true love was until you came into my life. You have been the one constant that has kept me alive and kept me moving forward. And through every trial we have been through, I can honestly say, yes. Yes, Trystan. Every single part of me is completely in love with every part of you."

His eyes broke away from mine. He shifted, facing the opposite direction, so I was unaware of his expression.

"Is there something else you needed to ask?"

"No."

Gods, I hope he saw the sincerity and knew that everything I spoke was nothing but the truth. I loved Trystan. From the beginning, it had always been him.

"Hey, are you feeling okay?" Brynna asked, coming up beside me. Her baby-blue eyes seemed to have dulled in the past days, and it concerned me, especially after what Melaina had said. But it also could have been a product of being on the run. Not to mention the uncomfortable nights sleeping on the cold ground.

"I'm fine. How about you?" I nudged her arm. "Are you still up for running with me?"

Brynna gave a weak smile. "I might be having second thoughts," she replied, then snorted. "I have to run with you because there is no other place for me to run to."

"I'm so sorry, Brynna." I wrapped my arms around her, and she wrapped hers around me. "I wish I could make this all go away."

Her eyes met mine. "We'll make it through this, won't we?"

"Of course, we will."

"Do you think they can defeat him?"

Even though I wasn't sure how this would play out, I smiled at her and nodded. "I do. We have a lot of allies now. Powerful ones."

"Good," she said. "Nicolae said we will be leaving soon."

Brynna turned to walk away, but I grabbed her arm. "You will always have me, Bryn. I am your family now."

"I know," she breathed. "And you have me."

I still wasn't sure what Melaina was talking about, in regards to Brynna. She seemed like the same girl I'd grown up with. Maybe Roehl's spell did leave a blemish on her mortal soul, but I didn't see or feel anything differently.

Our circumstances weren't typical, so I didn't expect anyone in our group to act normal.

"Calla." Nicolae called me over. "I'm going to take Trystan and Kylan first. Then you and Melaina."

"Okay, I'm ready," I said, but noticed he looked even more drained. The dark circles under his eyes were even more prominent. "How are you feeling?"

"I'm fine," he murmured. "I've been pushing my magic, taking it to the limits by transporting everyone. All I need is to feed and rest."

"Please take care of yourself," I said. "I need you now, more than ever."

Nicolae smiled and enveloped me in his arms, pressing a kiss on the top of my head.

"Roehl's just jealous because you both got the better genes, and he's upset he won't be invited to future family reunions," Sabine said, making everyone around us laugh. Nicolae included. It was good to see a smile back on his weary face.

CHAPTER TWENTY-EIGHT

We had seventeen days left. Seventeen days until Roehl would be executing the witches and guards in Morbeth. Seventeen days until an inescapable war, because I would not let those innocents die. I didn't care what the others thought, they already knew how I felt. They now had to determine whether they wanted to fight alongside me or stand back and watch.

As soon as Nicolae transported us, I felt his power falter. His grasp on my hand suddenly slipped, and he passed out, his body collapsing to the ground.

"Nicolae," I screamed.

"Calla, where are we?" Thalia asked, her voice stressed.

The darkness diminished and fear gripped every part of me, realizing we were somewhere in the midst of the Whisper Woods, without wards or protection. Talia immediately closed her eyes, palms outward, and I watched a dense, briar patch form around us.

"Trystan! Nicolae passed out," I shouted down our connection.

"Thalia and I are lost somewhere in the Whisper Woods without a glamour."

"Are you wearing the amulet?"

"Yes."

"Stay put. Kylan and I will be right there."

"Okay. Please hurry."

"Trystan and Kylan are on their way," I told Thalia.

"How will they locate us? We could be anywhere in the woods."

I drew the amulet out from my tunic and held it in my fingers. It was warm and started to glow brilliantly. "Trystan had this spelled. He can find me anywhere as long as I have it on."

Thalia smiled. "He truly is your match."

Nicolae groaned and moved, his jaw tense.

"Nicolae." I grabbed his arm and shook him, but he didn't respond. His powers must have exhausted him.

"Maybe he needs to feed," Thalia noted.

I knew he did. He was functioning on whatever rations we had left, while running on minimal sleep, and it had consumed his strength.

I drew a small blade from my boot. "Thalia, you're going to have to help me open his mouth."

She kneeled beside Nicolae and inclined his head back, tugging his jaw open. Running the blade across my wrist, I held it over Nicolae's mouth. At first, there was no response, but as the blood rushed down his throat, he clutched my wrist and held it to his mouth.

I let him take what he needed from me, feeding until his eyes snapped open and were clear.

He sat up and pushed my wrist away, realizing he'd just fed from me.

"What happened?" he exhaled, running the back of his hand across his lips.

"You passed out," Thalia said. "We're somewhere in the Whisper Woods."

Nicolae immediately pushed up to his feet but faltered a bit.

"You're still weak," I said. "Trystan is on his way and ordered us to stay put."

Nicolae shook his head, taking in a deep breath. "I can transport us to the cave."

"Calla, maybe we should go," Thalia urged. "Roehl could be on his way. It's not safe out here."

A furious wind rushed around us, shredding the briar hedge piece by piece. Thinking it was Trystan, I rushed to meet him. But the figure standing outside wasn't him.

It was a lanky man, around six-five, with blond hair and pale green eyes.

"Calla!" Thalia screamed as the man raised his hands.

Still baffled by the sight of him, the man thrust his power toward us. Before I could lift my palms, the wind punched me in the gut, slamming the air out of my lungs. All three of us flew backward. My body twisted sidewards, and I struck a tree, hearing a loud snap.

I suddenly couldn't breathe. I couldn't draw in air without agonizing pain.

"Trystan, an air elemental is here. He attacked us," I wailed

through the connection. *"Be careful."*

"Are you hurt?"

"My ribs are broken."

I thought I heard him curse before he went mute.

The air grew even colder around us, and the sky blackened. Thunder boomed and a bolt of lightning cracked from above, striking the elemental in front of us. His body was propelled backward, but he drove his hands behind him, and a rush of air caught his fall.

The elemental's green eyes locked on mine, a grin lifted on a corner of his lips like he realized he'd discovered his target.

"Calla!" Nicolae hollered, his voice faint. "Fight back."

I could scarcely breathe, let alone lift an arm without shooting pain. I heard a weak moan behind me and knew it was Thalia.

Trying to raise a palm to defend myself, a burst of air curled around me. Within it, I detected that perfect blend of earth and wind and spice. When it died, Trystan was standing in front of me, his eyes completely black, hands fisted at his sides.

After taking in my brokenness, he crouched, his eyes snapped back to the elemental, and a terrifying growl burst from his chest.

The elemental saw Trystan and instantly shoved his arms forward sending a spiraling blast of air toward us. Trystan sprinted forward, raising his palms, and I gasped at the unmitigated power radiating from him. My eyes witnessed that great power as it shot from him like an arrow, slicing straight through the elemental's attack. Without hesitation, Trystan moved like the wind, only stopping when he was inches in front of the elemental. Before the man could fight back, I watched with absolute admiration and dread, as Trystan grabbed his head and twisted, snapping his neck. His lifeless body collapsed to the ground with a thump.

Goddess. The sight of him caused my entire body to shudder.

Another strong gust of wind brought Trystan back to me. He stood about ten feet away, his eyes fixed on mine, his face grim. When he blinked, his face relaxed, and his eyes went from black to that beautiful azure.

He kneeled in front of me, leaning closer, but keeping his distance.

"Kylan is on his way to help you," he spoke through the connection, not letting the demons know.

I shook my head. *"You already have."*

Trystan stood then twisted the other way, raking his fingers through his hair. *"When you said you were attacked by an elemental and he had broken your ribs, I first felt rage, like I wanted to tear his heart out. Then, I felt fear.*

"I didn't recognize it at first, but now I understand what it was. I was terrified of losing you. Afraid that you would disappear, and I would never find you. That was something real, something I felt deep inside. That struck my heart, making me realize it was real. It has to be for me to have such deep affections."

I nodded, my own emotions overflowing from my eyes and falling down my face. When he turned back to me, I saw the seriousness in his eyes and it lifted the pain away, for a brief moment.

"Do you love me, Calla?" he challenged. And no matter how many times he would ask, I would answer.

"With my entire being," I responded.

Trystan's eyes pooled with tears. Without pause, he stalked toward me, and I gasped as his arms wrapped securely around me, pressing me tightly against his muscular frame. His gorgeous eyes met mine for a brief moment, before he sunk his teeth into my shoulder.

I moaned, arching into him, knowing the intention behind his bite. This life altering bite that had once set my life on this spiraling journey. A journey that had brought me down this long and deadly path, directly to him.

Trystan suddenly drew away, my blood still wet on his lips.

I searched his face, wondering if it had worked? Had it broken the curse?

Stumbling back, Trystan's face suddenly paled, his eyes tormented, and his features wracked with pain. He let out an intense, anguished moan.

No, no, no.

This can't be right. The curse should have been broken.

"Trystan!" I wailed as he collapsed to the ground, his body writhing in pain.

He was dying. The curse was killing him.

"Help!" I cried.

He couldn't die. There was no way I would be capable of dealing with his death.

And then, in the chaos, I heard a small voice in the recesses of my mind. A familiar voice that had always brought me solace.

Leora.

"You must also claim him, Calla." She spoke calmly yet urgently. *"Claim him and seal your bond to break the curse."*

Was that it? What if I claimed him and it didn't break the curse? What if I claimed him and he died?

But Leora was never wrong, and I knew she would never steer me down a misguided path.

The only question left was …

Was I ready to seal the bond with Trystan?

The answer was a resounding yes. Yes, I was ready to seal the bond with him. I wouldn't let my fears get in the way this time. This was my choice. The only choice I was certain of.

I had been through hell and back, and my affection for him had only grown deeper, stronger. Trystan had stolen my heart from the moment he strolled into my life. His love for me had never wavered, not even once. Even with the curse, he still chose me, continuing to save and protect me.

Those azure eyes, now bloodshot, met mine. I grabbed hold of his hand and drew his wrist up to my lips while he observed me cautiously, still fighting the curse within.

"I love you, Trystan," I declared to him. "And I also claim you."

I sunk my teeth into the smooth flesh of his wrist and as soon as his blood entered my mouth, I felt a crack of power between us and that bond sealing us together. It was deep and intense, causing me to unlatch. Breathless, I felt Trystan's blood dripping down my lips.

Trystan smiled. His eyes rolled back, and he slumped forward into my arms.

Holy shit. I killed him.

"Trystan!" I wailed, laying him on his back. "Help me!

Somebody help!"

Nicolae was the first to us. Seeing Trystan on the ground, he dropped to a knee next to him, then closed his eyes, running a hand over his chest.

"He's alive," he finally replied.

I was suddenly frightened that the damn curse was still there, and now we had sealed our bond. Trystan was mine, and I was his … for life.

Nicolae gathered Trystan's body in his arms and told me to hold on to him as he whisked us into the cave. He walked over and settled him on a blanket I quickly laid out.

"Stay with him," he said. "I'm going to get Thalia and Kylan."

"Are you strong enough?"

"I am, thanks to you," he replied with a loving smile.

When he left, I grabbed Trystan's hand and held onto it. The pain in my ribs was still there, but after biting Trystan, it had subsided a bit.

I couldn't help but admire him, how truly beautiful this man was, inside and out.

My friend.

My love.

My mate.

As soon as Nicolae returned, Kylan ran over to us, eyes narrowed, brows knitted together. "What happened?"

His turquoise eyes were on Trystan but shifted to mine. Then, they fell to my lips, where Trystan's blood still remained.

"Did you two?" he murmured, his finger aiming back and forth between the two of us.

I nodded, powerless to hold back the flood of tears. "He claimed me, Kylan. And I sealed the bond."

"Gods," Kylan exhaled. "Is the curse—?"

"I don't know. He passed out right after I bit him."

Kylan laughed out loud, shaking his head. "I don't blame him. Since the beginning, we all knew that's what Trystan wanted. We just never expected it would happen while he was under the curse."

As the others showed up, Kylan explained what transpired and kept them away from our tiny corner of the cave.

I settled next to Trystan, our hearts now sealed, connected with an immortal bond that could never be broken.

I wondered why I hadn't felt the overpowering passion and impulse to want to jump on him like I had the last time. Maybe it was because this bite was different. This bite wasn't to heal or feed. This bite was done with the intention to seal a blood bond.

Noticing I was in pain, Melaina came over and performed a spell that snapped my ribs back into place. It hurt like hell, but I could finally breathe without pain.

Kylan gave me some blood, and even after it coursed through my body, I still felt drained. I needed to sleep, so I curled up next to Trystan and fell fast asleep.

"Calla?" a voice whispered, nudging me from my slumber.

Opening my eyes, a figure moved into focus.

"Trystan?" I breathed.

"I'm here."

His finger traced the line of my jaw, a tender smile playing on his lips.

He was close. Too close.

I examined his face and peered deep into those eyes, searching for pain or torment, and found none.

My heart began thrumming loudly inside my chest. I had to know.

"Is the curse still there?" I questioned. "Do you remember anything?"

Trystan hesitated, his lips angled down, and my heart plummeted. Dread started to fill my veins.

But his smile grew, and those azure eyes brightened.

Trystan slid a hand under my head, then pressed a slow and intimate kiss on my lips. The kiss of a soulmate. The kiss of a lover.

When he drew back, his eyes fastened to mine.

"I remember *everything*."

NOTE FROM THE AUTHOR

Hi, friends,

Thank you for making it this far. I really hope you enjoyed this story, and Calla's continuing journey. Again, I am so sorry for leaving you on another cliffhanger, but I will be hard at work getting you the FINAL book in the series, which you can pre-order on Amazon now!

OF KINGDOMS AND CROWNS
Heir of Blood and Fire Series
Book Four

If you loved this story, please feel free to leave a review. They are warmly and greatly appreciated. Thank you again for reading my stories. It really means the world to me.

XOXO,

ACKNOWLEDGEMENTS

I have to give a shoutout to my girls.

Kimberly Belden who edited this book and sent me hundreds of notes and comments. No joke. She knows this story better than I do. Ha!

Ali Winters, who made all the words look beautiful with her amazing formatting.

And my betas, who always kick-ass and keep me on my toes. I am so blessed to have you all on my team. Thanks for finding all the little details, plot holes, wrong words, and giving great advice. I seriously have the best team of ladies supporting me.

I couldn't have done it without you all.

You know I love you!

Halee Harris

Jaci Chaney

Cheree Castellanos

Karla Mathis Bostic

Emily Piland

Ewelina Rutyna

Amber Garcia

And as always, my husband Vance, who has been my greatest fan.

I love you, always.

ABOUT THE AUTHOR

USA Today Bestselling author, Cameo Renae, was born in San Francisco, raised in Maui, Hawaii, and now resides with her husband in Las Vegas. She's a daydreamer and a caffeine and peppermint addict who loves to laugh and loves to read to escape reality.

One of her greatest joys is creating fantasy worlds filled with adventure and romance and sharing it with others. It is the love of her family and amazing support of her readers that keeps her going. One day she hopes to find her own magic wardrobe and ride away on a magical unicorn. Until then...she'll keep writing!

www.cameorenae.com